SECRET AGENT "X"

THE MAN OF A THOUSAND FACES

Volume Two

Airship 27 Productions

TM

SECRET AGENT X: VOLUME TWO
An Airship 27 Production

"Secret Agent "X" and the Masterpiece of Vengeance" © 2008 Sean Ellis
"Secret Agent "X" and Betty Dale: Gun Moll" © 2008 Kevin Noel Olson
"Secret Agent "X" and The Plague Doctor " © 2008 G.L. Gick
"Secret Agent "X" and The Gateway Machine © 2008 B.C. Bell

Cover by Rob Davis and Chris Carney
All original artwork in this book is © copyright 2008 Rob Davis
Production and design by Rob Davis

Second Edition

ISBN: 978-1-969285-00-4

Printed in the United States of America

10 9 8 7 6 5 4 3 2 1

SECRET AGENT "X"
Volume Two
CONTENTS

SECRET AGENT "X" *and the* MASTERPIECE *of* VENGEANCE

An old foe from the past resurfaces and only X can foil his plans for death and destruction. By Sean Ellis **05**

SECRET AGENT "X" *in* BETTY DALE: GUN MOLL

The Agent's most loyal ally has suddenly gone gun-crazy and he must stop her before she kills! By Kevin Noel Olson **58**

SECRET AGENT "X" *and the* PLAGUE DOCTOR

An entire town is quarantined by a diabolical madman. Secret Agent must find an antidote before it is too late. By G.L. Gick **81**

SECRET AGENT "X" *and the* GATEWAY MACHINE

Terror looms over all mankind as Agent "X" races to find and destroy a man-made portal into a nightmarish dimension. By B.C. Bell **112**

Afterword by **RON FORTIER** **149**

Prologue

No one saw the figure in black lingering in the North Gallery, despite the fact that he made no special attempt to conceal his presence. He had situated himself in a corner of the great hall, out of the way to be sure, but in plain view of anyone who might have happened to glance in his direction. Of course, no one did; people came to the Metropolitan Museum of Art to look at renowned works of paint and sculpture, not to peer into musty vacant corners. Even fewer eyes strayed to the corners where the wall met the ceiling, some sixteen feet overhead, which was, in fact, where the dark-clad man waited, secured by a rig of ropes and hooks screwed into the plaster, biding his time until the museum closed for the night.

The North Gallery was busy that day, as it had been for two weeks already, owing primarily to the exhibition of Rembrandt originals on loan from the Rijksmuseum in Amsterdam, but the crowds thinned out with the onset of afternoon and before the last rays of the summer sun dimmed into twilight, the Museum was all but deserted. The man in black however, did not stir. Only when the lights were turned down and the watchman completed his first sentry round did he leave the perch he had occupied since the early dawn hours before the first visitors began touring the museum.

He moved with an economy of motion, dropping spider-like from his fixed line, and crept stealthily toward the one painting he had been watching throughout the day: The Night Watch. He did not pause to admire or appraise the arrangement of oil on canvas; it was merely an object, which he wished to possess. He was far more interested in what lay behind the image.

The display frame, he knew from careful planning and hard bought intelligence, was part of the museum's protective system. It was no mere construct of wood, but rather was connected to an elaborate network of electronic detection measures. Any attempt to lift the frame from its mount would immediately sound an alarm. Likewise, if a burglar were to try breaking the frame apart in order to remove the canvas itself, the result would be an immediate clamor. Even the swiftest thief could not hope to gain the exit with his prize before the uniformed security guards swept in like a flash flood. Success in this venture hinged upon defeating the alarm system, which was why the thief had spared no expense in learning the intricacies of the device. And because forewarned is forearmed, he had brought exactly the right tools to complement the knowledge he had acquired.

With deft precision, he exposed the electrical filaments embedded in the segments of the frame, splicing in extra lengths of wire to bridge the connection and maintain the circuit. Only when he was satisfied with his handiwork did he began separating the ornately carved pieces of the frame.

The last bit required extreme care. A pressure sensitive switch behind the

"...where the wall met the ceiling was where the dark-clad man waited..."

painting itself was keyed to sound the claxons if the canvas was lifted away, but the burglar knew exactly how to fool the system. He took a long strip of metal, thinner than the blade of a surgeon's scalpel, from his tool satchel and insinuated it into the imperceptible gap between the canvas and the wall. His sensitive fingers felt the slightest resistance as the shim slid across the pressure switch and a faint smile crossed his lips.

Success!

Still cautious, he lifted the bottom of the painting, sliding his fingers along the metal strip to maintain the illusion of normalcy for the sensors beneath, until the wall was completely exposed. Laying the portrait aside, he crossed the shim with a thick piece of adhesive tape to secure it in place, and with that final touch, was done. The painting was as good as his.

No one saw the black clad man lingering in the corner of the North Gallery, and no one saw him leave. The theft was not discovered until more than hour after he crept through the 53rd street exit with his prize wrapped in a piece of dark velvet, and despite the best efforts of the museum staff to hide the deed, news of the daring escapade made the front page of the late edition of The Herald. The scandal was the talk of the town for more than forty-eight hours as frustrated policemen and insurance investigators chased endless leads to fruitless conclusions. It seemed destined to become a crime for the ages.

Then the unimaginable happened. Following up on a vague telephone call from an anonymous tipster, a beat cop discovered the canvas, still wrapped in a swatch of black fabric, in a public restroom in Central Park, less than ten blocks from the museum's main entrance.

"The rascal was feeling the heat," Police Commissioner Foster explained to reporters. "The moment he tried to fence the goods, we would have had him, and he knew it. Giving the painting back was the only thing he could do."

The affair of the stolen masterpiece quickly slipped from headline to footnote, and although the thief was never apprehended, interest in bringing him to heel soon waned in the face of more immediate crimes and misdemeanors. As far as everyone was concerned, the story was over.

Of course, the real story had only just begun.

❌❌❌

Chapter One
THE ART EXPERT

Betty Dale sat primly in the hard wooden chair, her petite form seemingly immune to its intentionally uncomfortable planes and angles, and regarded the man across the desktop with a curious expression. Without breaking eye contact, she slid a hand into the deep recesses of her purse and, by touch alone, found a pack of Beeman's gum. Her nimble fingers unwrapped the foil and with a minimum of effort, brought forth the slim white stick of candy. Her ruby lips parted in a wry smile as she popped the gum in her mouth and began chewing.

The man on the opposite side of the tableau, the one man for whom the museum theft was not old news—Detective Malvern—watched the performance as if hypnotized, and for a moment completely forgot what it was that the slim blonde reporter had just asked him.

"Ah, no," he finally managed, shaking his head in an effort to bring himself back to reality "Nothing new on the case, but I'll be dam... er, pardon my language, Miss Dale... but I'll be danged if I give up on this one. That scoundrel made a mockery of the museum's security. He might not have gotten away with it this time, but there's nothing to stop him from doing the same thing to a bank vault or a jewelry collection. I'll warrant he'd have a much easier go of fencing the Hope diamond than he would have that painting."

"If he was such a smart fellow, why didn't he realize that from the start? There's something fishy about the whole thing, Jim."

"You're telling me, Betts."

Betty popped her gum thoughtfully. She was no stranger to the crime beat, and the time she had spent following and chronicling the exploits of some of the city's most diabolical villains had given her unique insights into the criminal mind. Out of the corner of her eye, she glimpsed a well-dressed man entering the precinct station house. The newcomer, almost youthful with a shock of tousled blonde hair and a pair of wire rimmed glasses looked out of place in the dreary environs of the police station. Betty watched him gaze around the open area until their eyes met, then snapped her attention back to the detective.

"How do we know he didn't swap it for a fake?"

Malvern smiled confidently. "Give us a little credit. That was the first thing we thought of. The museum is putting together a panel of art experts to go over that canvas inch by inch."

"Ah, excuse me..."

Malvern looked up to the source of the soft interruption; the sandy-haired newcomer now stood a few steps to Betty's left. "Be with you in a moment, pal."

"Yes, quite." The man's tone was affable, but he did not retreat. "I do have an appointment, detective."

Although he had spoken only a few words, Betty did not fail to peg his British accent, and was immediately intrigued. Her keen instincts told her that this fellow was not here to report a petty crime.

Malvern's eyebrows came together in a crease. "Oh, you must be the fellow from Lloyds."

"Indeed. Well met, sir." A pleasant grin cracked the blonde man's countenance as he proffered a business card. "Jonathan Rhys-Reynolds at your service."

Malvern stood, took the card and politely extended a hand, which Rhys-Reynolds grasped and shook in a quick business-like manner.

"Hiya!" Betty chirped, interposing herself between the men. She scrutinized his face, memorizing every detail right down to the mole below his left eye, and seized his hand as soon as Malvern let go. "Betty Dale from The Herald."

Rhys-Reynolds' smile did not falter. "Charmed," he answered, inclining his head. "The Herald, you say? Then you are a journalist?"

"Betty covers the city crime beat," Malvern intoned, and then enunciating clearly so that there would be no mistaking his meaning, added: "She was just leaving."

"Not on my account, I hope." The Englishman gave a light chuckle. "There's no reason to conduct this business under a veil of secrecy, detective. Miss Dale's readers might find the business of art appraisal less than sensational, but I see no reason to keep her in the dark."

"Great! It's settled then." Betty threw a triumphant glance at Malvern then looked back to the newcomer. "So, you're the guy who's going to authenticate the painting?"

"Oh, good heavens no. I wouldn't know a real Rembrandt from a cigar box lid. No, I am simply a representative from the insurance company, here to observe the panel of experts."

"One of our early theories," explained detective, "was that the thief might have been in cahoots with one of these experts. Switch the original with a fake, and then have an expert authenticate the phony. Mr. Reynolds is here to make sure that no shenanigans of that sort are in the works."

Betty raised an eyebrow. "Do you really think that's possible? An art expert turning into an art thief?"

Rhys-Reynolds waved airily. "Oh, probably not. Doesn't hurt to check though."

Malvern shuffled some papers on his desk and then passed over a small bundle held together with a paper clip. "Here's the list. Everyone seems to be above suspicion; all native citizens in good standing… except for the last one, Professor Richard. He's actually a Belgian immigrant. Still, nothing out of the ordinary there."

The Englishman flipped through the papers quickly—too quickly for more than a cursory examination. "Jolly good, detective. You seem to have everything well in hand."

"So you're not going to check up on these guys?" Betty challenged, chewing her gum with an unconscious intensity.

"Oh, I'll probably do a little investigating on my own, especially this Richards fellow, but I see no reason to interfere with the appraisal." Rhys-Reynolds tucked the sheaf of paper into a small leather portfolio, then again extended his hand to Malvern. "Thank you for your cooperation, detective."

"No problem."

Betty's instincts were buzzing. "Mind if I tag along?"

The Englishman's mouth parted in an expression that lay somewhere in the middle ground between amusement and dismay. "I'm not certain that it would be proper…"

"Ah, come on, pal. This is America and I'm a big girl. Why don't you buy me a cup of coffee, and we'll call it a date?"

Rhys-Reynolds seemed about to choke and Betty expected his cheeks to flush with embarrassment, but strangely his pale complexion remained unchanged. He shook his head in apparent consternation, and then offered his arm to her.

As Detective Malvern watched them leave a low whistle escaped his lips. "That Betty Dale is a spitfire," he said to no one in particular. "No doubt about it."

✪✪✪

Ever the perfect gentleman, Rhys-Reynolds opened the passenger door of the sedan and offered a helping hand as Betty slid into the seat. The pretty journalist was a bit surprised to find that the visitor from across the Atlantic had his own automobile, even one as bland as the brown 1935 Ford Tourer, and said as much once he was seated behind the wheel.

"A hired car," he explained. "And please, if this is to be a date, then I must insist you call me Jonathan."

Betty laughed. "Don't get the wrong idea, chum… Jonathan. You're sweet and all, but I'm here for the story."

Rhys-Reynolds started the engine and decisively pulled out into traffic. "I wouldn't have it any other way."

Although she made small talk during the drive, Betty observed that her foreign companion navigated the city streets with the surety of an inveterate taxicab driver. He never once consulted a map or appeared to scrutinize street signs as he traveled main thoroughfares and side streets, some familiar and others totally alien to the city girl beside him. She filed the inconsistency away for future consideration and silently congratulated herself for having made this play; there was a lot more to Jonathan Rhys-Reynolds than met the eye.

In short order, they found their way to Fifth Avenue, and it wasn't long before the grand Beaux-arts façade of the Metropolitan Museum of Art hove into view. Betty had spent more than a few afternoons admiring the exhaustive collection of artwork on display, but since the theft, she had spent an inordinate amount of time in the vaulted halls of the Met. Nevertheless, she had a feeling that the man driving the sedan knew far more about the inner workings of the fifty-odd-year old institution than she did.

"The Rembrandt is under constant guard in a private viewing room," he explained as they left the car, and made the short hike down the sidewalk and up the chiseled marble steps to the entrance. "The appraisal will be closely supervised and each one of the judges will be permitted only fifteen minutes with the painting. The museum director personally chose this panel of experts, so I don't anticipate any problems."

"What happens if they discover it's a forgery?"

"Oh, I think that quite unlikely. You see, this is a mere formality. The director has already conducted a cursory examination of the painting and declared it authentic."

"Uh, huh. Okay, so what happens if they discover it's a forgery?"

Rhys-Reynolds chuckled. "Why then, Miss Dale, you'll have a front page exclusive."

✪✪✪

There was little time to admire the architecture of the vast museum complex, much less its priceless collection of art both contemporary and antique. The Englishman briskly led Betty past the grand galleries to a section of the Met she had never before seen. The corridors they traveled were less elegant than the public area, but retained a bit of its old world charm and featured assorted pieces of art and ancient relics, though there was a sense that these works were of inferior value and purely decorative. At one point, she chanced to catch a glimpse of the interior of one adjoining room and saw what appeared to be a small classroom, but Rhys-Reynolds whisked her along before she could get a better look.

"It's right up here," he explained, directing her attention to another nondescript doorway. The only difference this time was that two uniformed guards, with large holstered pistols on their hips, stood to either side of the portal. The guards admitted them, a terse nod the only form of communication that was exchanged. The insurance representative escorted her into a chamber that was nothing like the modest classroom she had spied moments before.

The anteroom had been richly appointed with velvet wall treatments, extravagant cherry-wood tables and several divans upholstered in dark leather. Betty felt her heels catching in the nap of the rug and looked down to find the elaborate designs of an honest-to-goodness Persian carpet. Yet, despite the trappings, she detected a hastiness about the décor; it was as if this room had been slapped together on the spur of the moment. Betty made a mental note of this bit of theater, adding it to her already deep suspicion that something was up.

There was a second door leading out of the sitting room, and two more guards posted there, but aside from that pair and Betty and her guide, the room was empty. The Englishman gestured to one of the sofas positioned at the back of the room, facing a large courtyard window, and took a seat beside her. Not long thereafter, the first door opened and an older man with the demeanor of a college professor entered the room. Rhys-Reynolds stood and greeted the fellow as if they were old friends, then introduced him to Betty as the museum director.

The older man sat with them, and over the course of the next few minutes, several more people entered the room. Each time, the director supplied a name, which prompted the Englishman to consult the documents in his portfolio. One by one, the art experts arrived and took their turn in the second guarded room. Without exception, each man emerged from the viewing chamber with a confident smile and a nod to the director.

"Well, that's that," the older man said. "Not that I had any doubts."

Rhys-Reynolds smiled, then as an afterthought, consulted his papers. "Wasn't there supposed to be one more...? Ah, yes. Professor Richard?"

A nerve in the director's cheek twitched. "Professor Auguste Richard," he said with a sigh, correcting the Englishman and pronouncing it *Ree-shard*, "is a very private man; a bit of a recluse. I didn't have much hope that he'd actually put in an appearance, but he's the absolute authority on the Dutch masters so I had to extend the invitation."

Rhys-Reynolds shrugged. "No matter. We have five perfectly qualified experts who all say yea; I think the case has been made adequately." He got to his feet and offered Betty a hand up. "It seems all of this was much ado about nothing."

The director grimaced. "If nothing else, we were found wanting in our security precautions. The police are still at a loss for how this devil got in and out without attracting notice..."

The older man's voice trailed off as the guards opened the door admitting two more people. Betty's gaze snapped to the second of the pair, a young woman dressed to the nines. A spark of innate jealousy caused the reporter's shoulders to tense up as she watched the other woman stride confidently into the anteroom; this lady was a Grade A knockout. Not a strand of her stylishly cut auburn hair was out of place beneath the spiffy green trilby, which perfectly matched the lady's handbag and shoes and nicely accented her dark red suit. She tore her gaze from the woman and glanced at the Englishman, expecting him to be likewise entranced, but to her surprise, Rhys-Reynolds was staring transfixed at the other newcomer. The intensity of his scrutiny prompted her to then give the lady's companion a closer look and as she did, she heard the director's muted exclamation:

"My goodness, it's him!"

Like the young woman beside him, the man was immaculately dressed, though his perfectly tailored charcoal gray suit was a good deal more subdued than hers, appropriately enough since he was old enough to be her father.

"Professor Richard, I presume?" the Englishman asked, quietly.

The director nodded, still breathless in amazement. "I didn't dare to hope... The young lady must be his daughter Amelia. I've not seen her since she was a child."

Professor Richard inclined his head toward the director, giving Betty her first real look at the elusive art expert. His erect posture, along with a mane of silver hair and a slightly darker Van Dyck beard lent an air of regal majesty to his countenance.

Betty cleared her throat impulsively. "I thought this guy was a hermit."

Richard did not loiter, but moved immediately toward the viewing room doors, while his daughter took a station near the window, casually assuming a pose to rival a department store mannequin.

The director shook his head. "Perhaps I misled you. Professor Richard stays out of the public eye, but he is a man of means to be sure. He has donated several of the pieces that are now in our permanent collection, but those are a drop in the bucket compared to the private collection he keeps at his estate in the Hamptons."

Betty glanced at the Englishman again. "A wealthy reclusive art collector and he's keen on Rembrandts? Sounds like the sort of guy who might want The Night Watch for himself."

Rhys-Reynolds continued to watch the door of the viewing room, oblivious to her comment, but the director came quickly to Richard's defense. "Miss Dale, I'd think twice if I were you, before making such a libelous accusation in your newspaper. Professor Richard is a man of the highest character."

The Englishman nodded absently but said nothing, and an uncomfortable silence ensued, until after what seemed an eternity, the viewing room door opened and Richard emerged, his magisterial face now wearing a mask of reverential awe. He caught the director's eye and nodded.

"There you go," exclaimed the museum official. "Six of six."

Abruptly, Rhys-Reynolds took a step forward. "I say, Professor, might I have a word in private?"

Betty gasped at the sudden turn of events, and was almost speechless when the Englishman turned to her apologetically. "Forgive me, Miss Dale, this won't take a moment."

Betty's eyes flashed from the now confused countenance of the art expert back to her own companion. "No trouble at all," she said, with a wan smile. "In fact, I should probably be running along anyway. Gotta scoop The Clarion with the big news that the painting ain't a fake… not that it's really news." She was rambling and she knew it.

"But I promised you a cup of coffee…"

Betty grinned and raised her hands. "Rain check. Gotta make the evening edition."

She hastened from the room, stealing a look over her shoulder as the sandy-haired Englishman and museum director moved off to stand next to Richard. The latter's daughter remained where she was and with placid indifference, took a cigarette from a silver case, lit it, and pressed it to her painted lips. But as Betty opened the exit door, she paused and affected a dizzy expression. "Whoops! Forgot my pocketbook."

She turned back inside, but now her strides were as stealthy as a stalking panther. No one in the anteroom paid her heed or even seemed to notice as she returned to the divan and knelt as if to search for something lost. She lingered there a moment, out of direct view of the others, then crept forward until she could hear their voices.

The director was making introductions. "Professor, this is Mr. Jonathan Rhys-Reynolds of Lloyds—"

"Your faithful servant," the Englishman exclaimed quickly. "Forgive me, but what I have to say is for Professor Richard's ears only."

"Ah, I see." The director was clearly disappointed at the dismissal, but regained his composure. "Professor, it was good to see you again. We must arrange for a future rendezvous."

"It would be my pleasure," answered a third voice, a rich baritone, faintly accented, that could only belong to Richard.

Betty crawled closer, straining to hear the voices that now dropped to barely a whisper, and what she heard made her fingertips tingle in anticipation. She hastily fetched her notepad and pen and began scribbling furiously.

"Professor Richard," began the Englishman. "I apologize for deceiving both your honored self and the director, but I am not from Lloyds of London, and my name is not Jonathan Rhys-Reynolds ..."

✪✪✪

Andre LeMartre stood in the grand central lobby of the museum, nervously fingering what looked to all appearances like a large crucifix depending from a silver chain around his neck. Aside from the religious icon, his attire was plain; he seemed no different that the hundreds of other tourists wandering the vast repository of aesthetic treasure. But LeMartre's dark eyes did not seek out works of art on display; his gaze was fixed on another man, similarly dressed to blend in, and somewhat less conspicuously, also wearing a large silver crucifix. Though nearly a hundred yards separated them, the two men were deep in conversation.

"This is the man we seek," the second man observed, confirming their suspicions.

LeMartre nodded, then replied: "Do nothing. I will attend to this."

The other man's face was a mask of concern. "This place is too public..."

LeMartre looked away, effectively silencing the protest. Had anyone in the museum cared to observe the men, they would have noticed no strange behavior, and certainly nothing they would have understood as communication. The entire exchange of had occurred without the use of spoken words—their common tongue was a language of signs and gestures, which to the untrained eye seemed like little more than the tics of a nervous man fidgeting anxiously. It was just one of the skills that made LeMartre and his comrades into one of the most effective infiltration and espionage forces on the planet.

There was no need for the young man to explain himself; though he was only a second tier apprentice, he was still senior to the other operatives spread throughout the museum, and more importantly, he had been given complete oversight of the mission. His success would guarantee his ascension to the first tier—perhaps even a leap forward to knighthood; he wasn't about to let anything prevent or delay the accomplishment of his sworn task. And there were other reasons why he longed to see this mission finished as quickly as possible.

Gripping the upright length of the crucifix in his left hand, he strode from the lobby and hastened through the maze of exhibits and dioramas to the section reserved for offices and classrooms.

The guards spied him from a long ways off, but failed to see the obvious warning signs in his determined stride and the intensity of his gaze. It was only when it became plainly obvious that he was heading for the very door they protected that one of them stepped forward to block him. It was an error in judgment he would never get the opportunity to repeat.

LeMartre closed with the guard and tugged at his crucifix with his right hand. The seemingly solid piece of silver came apart—the long vertical shaft of the cross still depended from a chain about his neck, but the cross piece and upright came away in his hand, along with a deadly revelation. He swiped the metal across the guard's throat, and then pirouetted on his left foot like a ballet dancer, spinning completely around and slashing the second watchman before the first one even realized he was dead. A sharp tang of iron filled the air as the stricken men sank to their knees, struggling in vain to staunch the pulsing flow of crimson. Le Martre lingered long enough only to unlimber a holstered revolver from one of the slain men, and then burst through the door.

He surveyed the sitting room in an instant, his eyes alighting on the target of his quest, but not remaining fixed there; there would be time enough to savor that blow. He dismissed the young woman near the window and the young blonde-haired man as posing little threat, but a second pair of guards demanded his full attention. Like their ill-fated counterparts in the corridor, the two men were slow to recognize the danger they were in, but one of them spied the revolver in LeMartre's hand and instinctively reached for his own sidearm. The killer however, had the element of surprise on his side and used it decisively,

The stout little police model revolver thundered twice in the confines of the anteroom, and two well-placed rounds punched the watchmen back against the wall. The young woman at the window let out a shriek of alarm, but the sound was lost in the ringing echo and miasma of cordite.

A triumphant grin broke across LeMarte's face as he strode boldly forward to confront the silver-haired man. He exchanged the gun in his right hand for the bloodstained cruciform object in his left and looked the man squarely in the eye. "For Mont Sacre!" he cried, and then struck with all his might.

Chapter Two
THE LONG RUN

"**M**y name is Alec Devine, and I'm an agent of Interpol—the International Police agency."

Professor Richard's eyes narrowed defensively at this strange admission. "Interpol? Am I some sort of trouble?"

"You may well be, sir. Have you ever heard of an organization called The Fraternis Maltae–"

That was all the sandy-haired Englishman got out before the door burst open and hell exploded into the room. Richard stood still as a statue, seemingly paralyzed with fear as the dark-eyed killer dispatched the two guards then hastened toward him. In a moment frozen in time, he saw rays of sunlight streaming through the window—where his daughter stood likewise transfixed in terror—and glinting on the red-tinged metal blade in the assassin's right hand. He barely heard the man's exclamation as the dancing reflection began to move. But the blade never reached his throat.

Faster than lightning, the man who had identified himself as both Alec Devine and Jonathan Rhys-Reynolds—and yet was neither—thrust his hand out to arrest the deadly arc. An iron grip stopped LeMartre's slash mere inches from its intended victim, and before the killer's dark eyes could confront the source of the interference, an open-handed blow struck him in the sternum. The assassin staggered backward, falling over the back of a couch and momentarily disappeared from view.

"Come with me if you want to live."

Richard stared dumbfounded at the man. At first blush he had taken the Englishman to be merely some kind of functionary, but the cold steel of his gaze and the quick efficiency with which he had thwarted the surprise attack told a much different tale.

"Amelia!"

Devine gestured furiously for the red-haired girl to join them and as she crossed the room, he stooped to retrieve a cross-shaped object from the rug. When father and daughter were reunited, the trio raced toward to exit door, still ajar from the killer's dramatic entrance. The girl gasped in horror as her eyes alit upon the spreading pools of scarlet, in which lay the lifeless forms of the first pair of guards. Devine's eyes however were scanning the far end of the hall; he didn't like what he saw.

Three more men were racing down the length of the corridor, silver crucifixes depending from their necks. The Englishman regarded the object in his hand; an ornate knife fashioned to resemble Christ on the cross. It seemed too beautiful to be anything but ceremonial, yet the dark stain on its scalpel-sharp edge bespoke a more utilitarian purpose, and something told him the fellows racing their way shared that purpose. He extended an arm to block the path of his new companions.

"Back inside!" When they failed to immediately comply, he gave them a firm shove, thrusting them past the scene of carnage and once more into the anteroom. As he pushed in behind them, he removed a handful of what appeared to be tiny glass marbles from his pocket and scattered them in the path of the attackers, before pushing the door firmly shut.

None of the three apprentices in LeMartre's murderous organization comprehended their blonde foe's final action, but the foremost of them got a quick explanation when his foot chanced to crush one of the glass spheres. Even as his shoe ground the fragile glass into sand, a cloud of white vapor swirled up in the hallway, rendering the trio unconscious almost instantaneously.

The gas, a potent anesthetic in aerosol form, was the signature tool of a man known only by the sobriquet: "Secret Agent X." That he was in fact a "secret agent" was not something that could be proven; no one knew his true identity, nor were his allegiances understood. According to the police, he was a master criminal, but many a criminal genius had been brought to heel by his surreptitious investigations, and not a few members of the press—Betty Dale foremost—publicly championed his cause. Yet no one knew if he was an American, working on his own behalf or on behalf of some government agency like the Secret Service, or if perhaps he was a foreign agent provocateur. The only thing that was known to be factual about "X" was that he was a master of disguise; he could literally be anybody. At this moment, X's true face was concealed beneath a thin layer of liquid plastic make-up, a blonde wig and pair of wire spectacles.

Richard halted abruptly inside the room and whirled on his savior. "We cannot get out. There is no exit from here."

"There's a window," X answered, his voice and accent perceptibly different.

Still crouched behind a sofa, Betty Dale held her breath in anxious anticipation. Shooting, murder and mayhem... she was smack dab in the middle of the biggest story of the week, if she could survive long enough to post it. As the fugitive trio approached the window, she sidled around the opposite end of the couch to stay out of their view.

"We're on the second floor," moaned Richard. "I can't make that jump."

X frowned, cast his eyes around the room, looking for a better answer, but there was only the long divan. "That's it!"

Richard and Amelia retreated from him as they might a lunatic on the sidewalk, but there was a method to X's madness as he grasped one end of the couch and hauled it toward the window. Betty choked back a squeal and scrambled behind a second piece of furniture, but her presence continued undetected. For his part, X scooted the heavy sofa toward the window, and with a mighty heave, pitched one end through the pane.

Amelia shuddered at the high-pitched crack of shattering glass, but X wasn't finished. He hastened back to the opposite end of the couch and lowered his shoulder to it like a football linebacker ready to meet the opposing team's charge. With a torturous sound of fabric ripping and wood splintering, the large piece of furniture began to slide across the windowsill and out into the air above the courtyard.

At just that moment, the door to the sitting room burst open again and two more men—ordinary looking fellows except for the unique accoutrement they shared with the stunned killer laying a few feet away—rushed in brandishing their knives. Their eyes roved the room, quickly alighting upon Richard.

X gave the sofa a tremendous shove and it scraped to the tipping point, where it slid of its own accord out into the courtyard. All the Secret Agent could do at that point was guide its descent in order to keep it positioned against the exterior wall. Once it was beyond his reach, beyond his control, he whirled to face the two killers and met them with his gun in hand.

The men were almost upon the defenseless Richard, brandishing their blades with murderous glee in their eyes. There was no time to warn them off; X aimed his pistol and fired. One of the assassins glimpsed the gun in X's hand, but before he could make a single move in his own defense, the weapon discharged.

There was no explosive report however; no eruption of flame and lead from the barrel of the gun. Instead, there was only a jet of pressurized anesthetic gas, which formed a narrow cone of white mist across the intervening space and swelled about the heads of the two would-be murderers. At the edge of the gas cloud, Amelia gasped and slumped to the ground, joining the senseless pair that had received the full dose.

X muttered a rare oath, then sucked in a deep breath and waded into the lingering haze of fumes in order to retrieve the girl. The gas was a substance of his own design—a vapor similar to nitrous oxides but which acted much more rapidly—and the gun an alternative to the lethal methods he had once employed in defense of freedom. The gas was now his preferred weapon of choice, and not merely because its employ spared him from the ghosts of those slain by his own hand—it was after all, much easier to gain essential information from someone who was merely rendered temporarily unconscious than from the dead. He had no doubt that Amelia Richard would be alert and on her feet again in a few minutes, but what had to happen in that period was what concerned him most.

"Out the window," he growled to Richard, hefting the girl's limp form onto one shoulder. The stately patron of the arts seemed rooted in place and it took a gentle shove from X to get him moving.

The silver haired professor swung one leg onto the windowsill, and then extended his head out into the courtyard. The couch remained tilted up against the wall, affording a flat surface upon which to stand, but the distance between the couch and the window was greater than Richard's full height.

"Go!" X urged. "There are bound to be more of them and they won't stop until you're dead."

"Who?" pleaded the older man. "Who wants me dead? And why"

"You mean you don't know?" X stared back, fixing the man with his unflinching iron eyes.

A strange look passed over Richard's face—it was neither terror nor confusion— and then he shook his head negatively.

X grimaced. "We'll sort that out once we're safe. Right now, we need to get out of here. Go!"

The command brooked no refusal and Richard surrendered himself to gravity. Once in motion, he seemed for more agile than his years, dropping onto the couch and then sliding down to the lawn of the courtyard. X cautiously hefted his burden through the window, and threw a final glance back into the chaos of the sitting room. The two assassins lay unmoving near one wall, while the first of their number writhed in agony near the center of the room, struggling to get his wind back.

Then X spied another form that he had missed in the confusion, huddling behind a divan. Though she did not recognize him, her face was well known to the Secret Agent; there was an unfathomable bond between X and Betty Dale. He met her gaze and, with one forefinger, traced two intersecting lines in the air to form an "X." Then he was gone.

❂❂❂

The tumult in the viewing room had not gone unnoticed by museum visitors idling in the courtyard. A small knot of them, mostly the clientele of the open air coffee shop situated against an adjacent wall, stared in mute disbelief as the fugitives made their escape, but none dared interfere. X steered Richard toward the crowd; there wasn't much chance of simply melting into the throng, not with the dazed Amelia slung over one shoulder, but perhaps it would be enough to hide them from the strange group of assassins.

The Agent felt the burden he carried shift abruptly and called Richard to a halt, just inside the cafe. Amelia had awakened with a start and her first impulse had been to struggle against an imagined captor. X eased her to the ground, allowing her father to soothe her rattled nerves. The anesthetizing gas was a powerful defensive weapon, but the Agent knew from experience that its effects could be short lived, especially when the initial dose was very small. The girl had breathed only a few wisps of the vapor, so her rapid return to consciousness was not surprising. X likewise knew that the assassins were likely stirring as well.

"We have to keep moving."

Richard held his daughter's hand a moment longer then faced their savior. "I have a car in the staff parking lot."

X nodded and gestured to the open archway that led into the museum proper. "Let's go."

A short walk led them back to the main lobby where they were no longer subject to the stares of amazed tourists. They moved briskly back through the maze of exhibits to a service corridor, and from there to the staff parking lot. X had maintained a constant vigil as they moved, but saw no more silver crucifixes, nor any indication that the group of assassins was monitoring their escape. As soon as they left the building complex however, his wariness increased.

"Where's Ashby?" Amelia asked.

"Who?"

"Our driver," Richard explained, slightly out of breath from the hasty egress. He pointed to a black Towne Car about fifty yards from where they stood. "He usually waits outside the–"

The Agent cut him off. "This is a trap. Quickly, to the street."

"A trap?" Amelia asked, but instead of explaining X simply grabbed her arm and directed her away from the parked vehicle. Immediately as he did, three menacing figures emerged from behind it and took up the pursuit.

X brandished his gas gun at the men. He had little thought of actually using it; in the open air, the concentration of gas would probably dissipate too quickly to be effective. Nevertheless, the mere sight of the weapon, which looked like an ordinary automatic pistol, was enough to send the assassins diving for cover. The Agent kept it trained in their general direction as he has trotted along behind Richard, easily keeping pace with the winded older man as they skirted the edge of the massive gothic structure and rounded onto the sidewalk opposite Central Park. There was no sign of the trio from the parking lot, but as they moved in front of the museum, a different group of men, led by the killer that had dispatched the guards, emerged at a near run, scanning the street for the fugitives. It didn't take long for them to spot their quarry.

"Head for the brown Tourer," instructed the Agent. "It's mine. We can make our getaway in it."

It was Amelia who seemed to respond first, grasping the old man's hand and tugging him along at a pace that was, for Richard at least, almost a dead run. It wasn't nearly fast enough.

"Keep going," X shouted, and then abruptly sprinted ahead of them, crossing the busy avenue and stopping onrushing traffic with a raised palm. He reached his parked car in a matter of seconds and slipped behind the steering wheel, but saw to his chagrin that Richard and his daughter were stranded on the sidewalk in front of the museum, unable to find a break in the flow of cars, and seemingly unaware of the malcontents closing on their position.

With a loud blast of the Ford's horn, X whipped out into the stream, triggering a sympathetic cacophony of screeching tires and horn blasts. The brown sedan carved a direct line across the macadam, still blaring its trumpet alarm, and bounced up onto the sidewalk, scattering tourists and assassins alike. He drew to a stop beside Richard and threw the door open.

"Hurry!"

The father and daughter pair barely made it inside ahead of their pursuers. The killer—LeMartre—caught the door before Amelia could pull it shut and attempted to wriggle his way inside. He would have succeeded too, but for the quick thinking of the man behind the wheel. X opened the throttle wide and the Tourer shot off the sidewalk like a rocket, yanking the assassin violently forward and spilling him into the street. The brown automobile fishtailed across the pavement for a moment, then straightened and charged forward.

Their elation at the narrow escape was short lived. A glance in the side mirror revealed a familiar looking automobile—Richard's Towne Car—bursting onto the main thoroughfare. X didn't need X-ray vision to know that it was being driven by one of the assassins, but when the elegant vehicle pulled up short to admit the leader of the group, his suspicions were confirmed.

"Hang on," he shouted and whipped the Tourer into a sharp right turn. The big brown sedan left smoking trails of rubber as it skidded around the corner. There was a loud crashing sound as the front end blasted through a short wooden barricade, and then the car was abruptly swallowed by the greenery of Central Park.

Under the strong guiding hand of Mayor LaGuardia, Central Park had been reborn, restored from a shabby wasteland into an emerald jewel on the crown of the city's collective pride, where children and adults alike played and relaxed in an island of tranquility. That tranquility was now about to be completely shattered.

X trumpeted the horn again, warning park goers of the relentless machine of destruction that was now charging down the service access road. About five seconds later, the bigger Towne Car crashed through the entrance as well, and its driver was far less concerned about running down innocents. That complete lack of regard for human life translated into an advantage of speed for the gang of killers; they were closing fast.

The mayhem continued unchecked. X kept one eye on the side mirror, watching anxiously as the Towne Car moved inexorably closer. He wasn't surprised at all to see a figure lean out from the passenger side and point a small dark object at the fleeing Tourer.

"Get down!"

Almost simultaneous with his warning, a tiny spurt of flame signaled the escalation from chase to running gun battle, followed immediately by a loud thump as something struck the rear of the Ford. The Agent wasn't overly concerned for his own safety or that of his passengers; the Ford was one of his specially modified vehicles—modified with, among other things, heavy manganese-steel armor plating and extra-thick window glass treated with a special chemical to make it bullet resistant. But every bullet that ricocheted from the impervious exterior of the car might very well strike an innocent hundreds of feet away. It was time to end the pursuit once and for all.

The spires of Belvedere Castle loomed ahead over the treetops, and X steered toward that landmark, a plan taking shape in his mind. The road they currently traveled would bring them abreast of the castle in a matter of seconds, and that seemed as good a place as any to make a stand against the assassins.

The Agent brought the car around a corner, momentarily removing himself from his foes' line of sight, and tapped the brakes. As the Tourer slowed, he flipped a switch under the steering column, releasing a smoke grenade from a compartment hidden behind the rear bumper. A cloud of white smoke began to billow in their wake, completely obscuring the roadway.

The smoke was just that—a chemical substance that burned rapidly to produce a screen to mask their escape. Yet the Agent continued braking and the brown car came to a complete halt about twenty yards from the roiling mist.

"What are you doing?" Amelia shrieked, still hidden in the well behind the driver's seat.

The Agent did not answer, but continued to watch the mirror, one foot resting on the accelerator poised for action. He was taking an awful risk, but if the gamble paid off....

A moment later, the front end of the Towne Car emerged from the smoke. In his eagerness, the driver had not eased off one bit. Now, as the sight of the motionless Ford filled his view, he reacted instinctively to avoid a collision, stabbing the brakes and twisting the steering wheel to the left. His panicked maneuver wasn't enough to prevent a crash, but as the rear end of the Towne Car sloughed around, certain to strike the Tourer, X stomped the gas and the brown car shot forward out of the path of danger.

The Towne Car went into an unrecoverable spin, leaving the paved surface to crash through the low stone wall that guarded an embankment. As it scraped over the rubble in a shower of sparks, the remains of the bulwark tore out the underbelly of the elegant vehicle, and in a nightmarish instant the spilled fuel ignited in a tremendous explosion of flames. The rolling pyre continued its doomed course, crashing down the steep rocky face into the reservoir below the castle.

The Agent saw very little of this as he sped away, but the roar of the explosion and the column of black smoke in the mirror adequately told the tale. He drove more cautiously now, searching his memory for the quickest route out of the park, where they would be able to blend in with the flow of traffic.

"It's over. You can come up now."

Both of his passengers complied cautiously, peering through the windows as if unwilling to trust their savior's declaration. After a few moments, Richard broke the silence. "Mister... ah, Devine did you say?... I am certainly grateful for you actions on our behalf, but I should like that explanation now. Just what the devil is going on? Who were those men?"

The Agent fixed him with a steely glare. "Those men are part of an organization called Fraternis Maltae—the Brotherhood of Malta. Does that ring a bell?"

Richard shook his head, a little too quickly, the Agent thought. "The Brotherhood of Malta is an old organization—they've been around for centuries—loosely tied to a monastic order based in France. They are mercenaries—spies and assassins for hire—but until now, they've stayed on the other side of the pond. Two weeks ago, Interpol received a tip that the Brotherhood was after someone they identified only as 'the Art Expert;' a man evidently living in the United States."

"And you think I am this expert?"

"Are you?" Receiving no answer, X turned his attention back to the drive, but continued speaking. "It is quite possible that the Brotherhood is unsure of the identity of their target. The museum theft might well have been designed to draw their quarry into the open. It seems plainly obvious that they believe you are their man, Professor, so I need you to be completely honest with me. Can you think of any reason why these men might want you dead?"

"This is outrageous," Amelia intoned from the back seat. "My father is a model of virtue; a man of the highest moral character."

"Good men are not exempt from the schemes of the wicked. Like it or not, the Brotherhood has fixed their sights on you. Until we can bring them to heel, you are going to have to trust me to protect you." X steered the car through an opening in the perimeter and waited for a break in traffic. "Uh, oh. Looks like we're not done running."

Honking the horn once more, he accelerated into the flow, cutting off a taxi that immediately swerved into a neighboring lane, sideswiping a second car. The accident caused a snarl behind them that allowed the Ford to quickly pick up speed, but it offered them only a momentary reprieve. The flashing of emergence lights and the blare of sirens quickly parted the way through the stalled vehicles, and black and white cruisers shot out in pursuit of the Tourer.

They may have escaped the assassins of the Fraternis Maltae, but now the Agent and his passengers were being hunted by the equally relentless men of the New York Police Department.

Chapter Three
Investigations of a Murder

Inspector John Burks had never visited the museum until the brouhaha with the stolen Rembrandt erupted, and now only a few days later, he was looking forward to a time when he would never ever have to set foot in it again. It was a dimly lit torch of hope; a stolen masterpiece was bad enough, but now the esteemed repository of art had become a slaughterhouse. Two shapes, indistinct beneath the heavy tarpaulins that had been spread over them, lay to either side of the door he now approached, and he had been warned that two more lay just inside. Yet, the first thing he saw in the sitting room was not the corpses of slain security guards, but the familiar face of Betty Dale speaking with Detective Malvern. Burks moved over to greet the journalist.

"How'd you get here so fast, Miss Dale?"

"I was right in the thick of it, Inspector."

"Betty saw everything," Malvern supplied. "A gang of thugs was after one of the art experts. Evidently the man from Lloyds was actually an Interpol agent. He whisked the art expert and his daughter out the window and to safety."

Burks looked at his detective as though the man were raving. "Lloyds? Interpol? What the devil are you blathering about?"

Despite the horror she had witnessed, Betty managed a rueful smile. "Better let me explain, detective." She quickly outlined everything that had happened from the time she and the ersatz insurance appraiser left the precinct house. She did her best to reproduce the strange oath the killer had uttered, and did not speculate concerning what it might mean. The only piece of information she withheld was the revelation made by the man she identified only as "Alec Devine of Interpol" just before he slipped out the window. Her discretion, however, was rendered futile as one of Burks' uniformed officers burst into the room, just as she was wrapping up.

"Inspector! Detective Keegan just fainted in the hall!"

A frown crossed the senior policeman's weathered visage, but before he could move out to investigate, a second constable shouted an update. "He's okay! It looks like he stepped on a glass capsule filled with knockout gas."

Betty's heart sank as Burks correctly deduced the significance of this discovery. "Knockout gas? I might have known HE would be in the middle of this."

"The Interpol fellow used knockout gas on the killers," Betty quickly supplied.

"Gee, do you think he might have been Agent X?"

"Impersonating an officer of the law is something he excels at," Burks snarled, recalling an occasion when X had actually impersonated the inspector himself. "By God, we'll get him this time, and he'll answer for his crimes."

Betty bit her tongue and let the ace detective rant. It was no use defending the Agent to the police; despite the many criminal schemes that Secret Agent X had thwarted, Burks was determined to prove that the man of a thousand faces was a villain of the highest order. Yet, the inspector's prejudices were of only secondary concern to the reporter. She was in a unique position to set the story straight in her newspaper, exonerating X in the court of public opinion, if nowhere else, but was that what her old friend would want her to do? Might she inadvertently spoil his clever schemes by stripping away his false identity?

When Burks paused to catch his breath, Betty jumped in. "Need anything more from me, Inspector? If not, I'd like to get back to The Herald. There just might be time to make the late edition."

The policeman frowned but then dismissed her with a brusque wave and Betty hurried off, her mind turning like a machine, to find just the right words to tell the city the real story.

✪✪✪

Although their methods were not as Draconian as those employed by the Brotherhood, the NYPD had a greater arsenal of resources at their disposal. The two police cars that dogged the Agent's sedan were in constant radio contact with a dispatcher who in turn maneuvered other patrol cars from all over the city to intercept the vehicle that had been spotted fleeing the scene of the museum murders. Secret Agent X had only one advantage over them: he knew where he was going.

Immediately as he had left the park road, he commenced navigating the urban maze to a secret location uptown. Getting there was going to be tricky – he knew the police were even now setting up road blocks in his path – but he still had a few cards up his sleeve.

They had only gone about twenty blocks when the first roadblock came into view, about 100 yards ahead. X scanned the street quickly looking for a means of escape but the police had chosen this location well. There were no alleys or cross streets the entire length of the block. By sealing the far end of the street, they had created a dead end from which it would be almost impossible for their prey to escape. But the Agent's steel-colored eyes saw something else that was almost as good.

"When I give the word," he said, never taking his eyes off the road. "I want you both to duck down."

Taking their silence as acceptance, the Agent immediately set his plan in motion. He thumbed the switch to release one of the smoke grenades, and as the white smoke billowed to fill the street with a cloud of impenetrable fumes, he pulled the handbrake and twisted the steering wheel sharply to the left.

Obscured by smoke, no one saw the brown Ford spin around 180 degrees, nor did anyone outside see the strange flash of light that burst from the vehicle. The Agent steered into the curb, slotting the car into an open parking space and hastily killed the engine.

"Now!" he shouted, heeding his own advice by laying flat across the seat. "Get down and stay that way."

It only took a minute or so for the smoke to clear. During that time, the passengers of the Ford sat motionless, hardly daring to breath, as the audible cry of nearby police sirens continued to assail their ears. Yet, the din of the claxons did not change during all that time; the patrol cars were wisely staying out of the blinding miasma.

"I don't understand," Amelia said, breaking the unbearable silence. "Why are we hiding from the police? We didn't do anything wrong."

The Agent had been wondering when one of his charges would pose that question; he wasn't surprised at all that it had been the daughter, rather than the father. Before he could answer, Richard jumped in. "It's better not to involve the local authorities in this matter, my dear. However sir, I fail to see how just sitting here will help our cause. The police are sure to recognize–"

"Just stay down," X reiterated in a tone that brooked no argument. The smoke had cleared now and the siren wails grew closer as the patrol cars slowly rolled up on them and then, inexplicably, went right past. The clamor of sirens was abruptly cut off and trio in the Ford could hear shouts of consternation from beyond their hiding place. After what seemed an eternity, there was a roar of engines and the din outside ceased altogether. The Agent cautiously raised his head, and then sat fully upright and switched on the engine.

"All clear. You can get up now."

To the amazement of his passengers, the street was now clear in both directions; there was no sign of the police. X pulled out from his parking spot and drove at a considerably more restrained pace through the urban jungle. Less than five minutes after escaping the roadblock, he pulled the car into a large brick building decorated with a sign that read: "Murphy Bros. Auto Repair." As he eased into the garage, a fellow in greasy overalls, chewing on the stub of a cigar, moved over to greet them.

"Howya doin', pal?"

"Never better," X said, smiling as he got out. He opened the door for his passengers as the mechanic walked slowly around the vehicle.

"What can I do ya fer?"

"I'd like to get it painted. Something bright." He turned to the girl. "What do you think, maybe a nice fire engine red?"

Amelia didn't answer. She was staring dumbfounded at the car – at the charcoal gray Ford – which had brought her to this place. "Wasn't it…?"

The Agent grinned. The special "flash paint" has worked perfectly. The brown paint that had covered the Ford had been impregnated with a special chemical, not unlike the flash powder used by stage magicians, and with the application of a small electrical charge, had vaporized completely, exposing the dark gray underneath.

"Red, it is my friend. Is there someplace we can relax while we wait?"

The grease monkey rolled the cigar to one side of him mouth and jabbed a thumb over one shoulder. "There's a little apartment upstairs. Make yourselves at home."

X steered Richard and his daughter toward the open staircase, then turned back to the mechanic and addressed him in a low voice. "Thanks a million, Murphy."

The other fellow just winked, and then drew a little "X" in the air with his finger.

❽❽❽

Typing like a woman possessed, Betty Dale handed her story to the copy editor a mere fifteen minutes after returning to the Herald Building, but she could not escape the feeling that the hasty recap of the events she had witnessed was merely a prelude to something greater. Her notebook lay open on the desktop, a page filled with scribbled shorthand notes recorded both on the scene and during the taxicab ride back to the newspaper office. Two items had been circled and despite her best efforts at deductive reasoning, remained completely foreign to her; in fact, she was almost certain that they were words from another language:

"FRATERNIS MALTAY"
"FORMONT SOCK"

Realizing that the answer to the riddle wasn't about to appear magically on the page, she snatched up the notebook and headed down to The Herald's morgue – the musty cellar where every single issue of The Herald, all the way back to its inaugural edition which announced the surrender of Confederate forces at Appomattox Courthouse, were filed, cataloged and cross referenced.

The archivist, Billy Hayes, remembered that first issue – a mere boy at the time, he had stood on street corners hawking the Herald to passersby. Though he had never received a formal education, he was one of the most knowledgeable people Betty knew; he not only read every column inch of The Herald, but also had dutifully cross referenced each article and filed them away for future reference. A kindly old fellow who always wore a red cable knit sweater, even on the hottest day of summer, and sipped continually from a chipped coffee mug – rumor had it that there was more than coffee in that cup – Hayes was Betty's best chance at unraveling the mystery.

"Heya, Billy."

"Ah, Miss Dale." Hayes was stooped over a large table where several issues of the newspaper lay spread out for his perusal. He took a swig of coffee then straightened to greet her. "Always a pleasure. What can I look up for you today?"

Betty flashed him a winning smile then showed him the notebook. The older man straightened his glasses, and then peered at the scribble intently. "Well, 'Fraternis' sounds kind of like 'fraternity.'"

"I thought the same. Some kind of secret society?"

"Hmm. 'Maltay.' That rings a bell." He scratched his stubbly chin thoughtfully, and then snapped his fingers in revelation. "Ever heard of the Maltese Cross?"

"I've heard of the Maltese Falcon."

Hayes winked at her knowingly. "In both cases, the word 'Maltese' comes from the island of Malta, and I wouldn't be at all surprised if your fraternity is somehow connected as well. Let's start there."

The old fellow shuffled down a row of card files to the beginning of the section marked "Ma." He flipped through it until he found a section of several cards all somehow pertaining to Malta. "Aha, this just might be the thing. There are several articles about the Knights of Saint John, also sometimes called the Knights of Malta."

He wrote the date of the most relevant articles on a piece of scratch paper then went off to pull those issues from the vault. In a matter of minutes, Betty was reading various news items pertaining to the Knights of Malta.

"Listen to this: 'The Knights of the Order of St. John of Jerusalem were at one time known as the Knights Hospitaller, owing to their practice of establishing hostels throughout the Holy Lands during the years of the Crusades. They amassed enormous wealth during this period. When the Knights of the Temple of Solomon were crushed by papal decree, much of their land holdings and vast riches fell into the hands of the Knights Hospitaller, who ultimately separated into several groups, including the Knights of Malta… etcetera… and the Fraternis Maltae.' That's it!"

"Is there anything about 'Montsock'?"

Betty scanned down the article. "Here it is. I just spelled it wrong. I think it's a French word. 'Most of the splinter organizations remain to this day, but some have fallen into ignominy, such as the Fraternis Maltae which was all but destroyed in the Tragedy of Mont Sacre in 1918.' Billy, we've got to look up Mont Sacre. That's the key to everything."

The archivist was already moving off to his card files and a few minutes later Betty was immersed in the tale of the siege and ultimate destruction of the French village of Mont Sacre. At first, she read aloud a few sentences that seemed important to their search, but after a minute, she fell silent and her eyes grew wide. When she finished, her initial elation had been completely sublimated. Now there was only a sort of horrified awe. She pushed the paper back to the archivist. "Billy, I need everything you can find about a man named Auguste Richard."

Chapter Four
INTO THE LION'S DEN

Murphy Bros. Auto Repair was just one of several legitimate businesses that served double-duty as part of Secret Agent X's vast underground organization. While they earned their daily bread providing necessary services for the residents of their respective neighborhoods, they also contributed to the war on crime and evil by using their skills to improve the Agent's arsenal of weapons and equipment, or to provide safe haven when the need arose. The Murphy brothers, for example, had worked to outfit several of the Agent's automobiles with flash-paint, smoke grenade launchers and several other useful accouterments. Like most of the men and women working on behalf of the Agent, they had little inkling of the scope of the organization; most of their contact came through a man named Harvey Bates, who was in fact, the director of the effort and answered only to Secret Agent X himself.

While Sam Murphy worked to refit the Tourer, Agent X was helping his charges get settled in. Richard had been strangely silent and Amelia had followed his lead, despite the curiosity burning in her eyes.

X however had little time to play the dutiful host. The Brotherhood's attack at the museum had been a big surprise; he had not expected something quite so audacious or foolhardy from an organization that had perfected the art of espionage centuries before. There had to be a compelling reason for their daring gambit and he needed to find out what it was. After encouraging Richard and his daughter to make full use of the amenities in the little flat, he excused himself and retreated to the tiny office in the downstairs garage. There, concealed behind a heavy bookshelf that appeared to be bolted to the wall, was the entrance to a small room, which contained only a special radio transmitter. The Agent seated himself before the radio and began tapping out a coded message summoning Harvey Bates. The reply came almost immediately.

"Chief, are you all right? The museum incident is already hitting the papers and they know you were involved."

Both men were as conversant in telegraphy as they were in spoken language and X responded without having to consult a Morse code chart. "Couldn't be helped Harvey. They struck without warning and it was all I could do to get Richard to safety."

"Then he is the 'art expert'?"

The Agent hesitated before replying, but not because of any uncertainty. "He's the one; no doubt about it."

"What do you need?"

"The location of the Brotherhood's headquarters in the city. They can't have pulled this together without some local help."

"Already got that for you. They're working out of the hall of the local chapter of the Knights of Malta. Here's the address."

X scribbled the street and number on a scratch pad. "Do the police know about them yet?"

"No," Bates replied. "They think this was all something you concocted to steal the painting."

"Good. That should keep them out of my way." X took out the cruciform dagger and studied it thoughtfully. "I need you to pull together everything we know about the Brotherhood and send it to drop point Violet."

"I'll have a runner deliver it within the hour. Anything else?"

Before X could reply, a chime sounded. It was a warning bell connected to the upstairs door; one of his guests was wandering. "That should do it. I'll be in touch."

He hastily signed off and crept back into the office just in time to see Amelia descending the stairs. He calmly exited the office and went to meet her. "Is something wrong?"

The girl averted her eyes guiltily. "No. My father… He's too old for this sort of excitement. He's resting. I wanted to… Well, thank you for everything."

"It's quite all right, Miss." He gestured to the stairs. "I think it might be well for you to rest, too."

"Are we still in danger?"

Something about her tone caught the Agent's attention. "Miss Richard, do you know something about all this?"

"Why on earth would I know anything?" she answered, but her reply came too quickly and she looked away again as she spoke.

"Amelia, I can't help you or your father if you're not honest with me." He placed a firm hand on her shoulder, compelling her to face him. "I think you want to tell me."

The pretty redhead sighed nervously and then fished a cigarette from her bag.

"You shouldn't smoke in here." He motioned to the stairs again. "Let's go up to the roof where we can speak privately."

A look of gratitude dawned on her face and for the first time, the Agent saw her, not as an empty-headed dilettante, but as a frightened and naïve child. Without another word, he guided her up the stairs, bypassing the apartment, and brought her to another set of steps leading to the open roof of the garage. The noise of the city was strangely soothing as they settled against the parapet, and Amelia waited only long enough to take a long drag from her cigarette before bursting into tears.

"When I was very young, he used to warn me that bad men might come someday… that we might have to leave everything behind. I thought he was just telling me stories to frighten me. We've always been so safe at the house."

X took her hand, soothing. "Start at the beginning. You weren't born in America, were you?"

"No. I was very young when we came here. I don't remember anything from before. Father told me that we had to leave because of the war. Everything was ruined there; America was the land of opportunity. After mother died, there was no reason to stay."

The Agent nodded and despite the urgency of his inquiry, kept his voice calm. "What about the 'bad men'? Did he ever tell you who they were, or why they might come after him?"

"I thought it might have something to do with his art collection. I may be young, but it wasn't too hard to figure out that he didn't come by everything honestly. But he's a good man; he's always used our wealth to help others. Anything he might have done in the past… well, he's not that person any more."

The Agent maintained his compassionate expression. "Don't worry, Amelia. I'm not going to let these scoundrels hurt you or your father. I'm going to go out and see what I can learn about them. I need the two of you to stay here where it's safe. Promise me that you will."

She nodded, stubbing out her cigarette.

"Good. Now go back and get some rest yourself."

He escorted her back to the apartment and as soon as she was stationed within, hastened down to the garage where Murphy had a second car ready, this one a 1929 DeSoto that looked ready for the junk heap. X slid behind the steering wheel with a wry smile. It might not have all the bells and whistles of his modified automobiles, but the old DeSoto had its own kind of natural camouflage.

He did not drive immediately to the address Bates had supplied. Instead, he traveled across town to his own residence, a brownstone dwelling on the west side. Taking care that no one observed his entrance, he went in and stationed himself before a large three-way vanity mirror.

He chuckled to himself as the unfamiliar face of Rhys-Reynolds/Devine stared back from the glass. He wore so many faces that sometimes he forgot which one was his own. But in the unending battle against evil, his ability to disguise himself was his greatest weapon; his true face, his true identity, meant nothing in that struggle.

Well, he thought, almost nothing.

He closed his eyes, searching his memory for every detail of the face he now chose to don: that of the young assassin. There was a black wig in his kit that would require only a few snips with barber's scissors to be perfect. The rest he accomplished with a variety of prosthetic pads and a special cosmetic putty that he dyed with pigments to mimic the olive complexion of the young killer. The finishing touch was a costume from his extensive wardrobe that approximated the garb the fellow had worn. The final result would stand up to all but the closest scrutiny.

Leaving as discreetly as he had arrived, the Agent next drove to the place where he had directed Harvey Bates to leave the information about the Fraternis Maltae. Drop point Violet was just one of many such clandestine locations throughout the city where documents and equipment could be covertly picked up. In this case, it was a simple newspaper kiosk and the file had been secreted within the pages of the late edition of The Herald. X did not pause to read the front-page story about the murders at the museum, but returned to the relative privacy of the DeSoto in order to skim the more important papers hidden within.

Much of the information was already known to him; the history of the Brotherhood – a long and violent tale of espionage and assassination for hire. Despite their origins as a monastic brotherhood of the Church, the men who had taken vows to be part of the Fraternis Maltae seemed much more devoted to secular interests. For centuries, they had used their skills to alter the face of Europe, often betraying former patrons in favor of new and more powerful allies. They had even aligned themselves with Napoleon, in opposition to the interests of their parent order, and in so doing helped the Corsican become, if ever so briefly, the most powerful man alive. He read also of their apparent demise at the hands of a brutal Prussian noble during the Great War; how the man had learned of their secret treasure storehouse and savagely slaughtered every member… or so it was believed. The Agent skipped over most of this; his interest was in the more recent events.

The Brotherhood had not perished as believed, but stripped of their wealth, they had retreated into the woodwork to nurse their wounds. It had taken more than a decade to rebuild, and even now, they were a shadow of their former strength. Yet, what they lacked in resources, they had more than made up for in ambition. Through the tireless efforts of their Grandmaster, Yves Ste. Jean d'Arc, and the Chevalier Premiere or First Knight, Armande LeMartre, the Fraternis Maltae was once more becoming a force to be reckoned with.

The last page in the document was a detail of the most recent information about the First Knight's mission to assassinate 'the art expert.' LeMartre was leading the effort personally, along with more than a score of apprentices – men who, despite their lack of seniority in the organization, were nonetheless hardened killers. The Agent's own experiences verified this last assessment; the Brotherhood had shown no hesitation in killing innocents who stood in their way.

X drove to within a block of the Brotherhood's headquarters and finished the journey into the lion's den on foot. Despite his outward calm, a tremor of adrenaline pulsed in his veins; he had often walked in the lairs of criminal masterminds, imitating their minions so perfectly that no one was the wiser, but this time it was different. He knew nothing about the young man whose face he now wore. But for the brief utterance in the instant before the attack on Richard, he had never heard the assassin's voice, nor did he know any of the man's mannerisms. He would not even be able to answer to the man's name, if called, and there was a better than even chance that he might come face to face with the young man himself. His only hope at success was to get in quickly and quietly, and leave just the same way.

His first test came at the massive wooden door to the old chapel hall. A monk, replete with tonsure and the chasuble of a Benedictine acolyte, stood guard there, but gestured for him to enter when X held up the dagger – the mark of an apprentice in the Fraternis Maltae. The hall beyond seemed deserted; he could only hope that the itinerate residents were out combing the city for their prey.

He bypassed an ornate, centrally located door – no doubt some kind of office – choosing instead a simpler, unmarked portal further along, which opened to reveal an empty guest room. The Agent closed and locked the door behind him, then moved to a window that overlooked an inner courtyard, which like the hall, was devoid of human presence. He popped the window open, then climbed out and ducked behind a row of arborvitaes that skirted the perimeter of the building. The window to the office was slightly ajar, and in a matter of seconds, he hoisted himself inside.

His initial assumption about the room proved correct. Not only was it an office, it was the temporary headquarters of the Fraternis Maltae. A large oak desk stood directly in front of the window, and on its surface, along with a scattering of newspaper clipping, an overflowing ashtray and a pack of Gauloises cigarettes, was an elaborate sheathed sword, with a hilt fashioned in the form of a crucifix. The Agent gently moved the scabbard to one side in order to get a better look at the papers beneath.

The articles trimmed from The Herald and other daily tabloids were a brief history of the theft of the Rembrandt, beginning with the obnoxious front-page headlines and finishing with a few brief columns concerning the decision to bring in a panel of experts to verify the painting's authenticity. The information seemed sparse – too little by far to prompt the Brotherhood to launch such an open attack on Richard. In fact, nowhere was Richard even mentioned.

"What am I missing?" he murmured, glancing over the desktop once more. Then his eyes settled, not on the documents, but on the sheathed blade weapon. But for its length, it was identical to the dagger… The Agent took out the smaller blade – the badge of the apprentice knight. The sword was reserved for those who had earned higher rank in the organization.

The attack at the museum was led by an apprentice, he realized. There was no grand strategy behind it. I've badly overestimated them.

He turned toward the window, eager to be away from the lair of his enemies, but it was already too late. The click of the door latch froze him in his tracks and he barely had time to compose himself in front of the open window before the creak of the hinges signaled that he was no longer alone. He turned, affecting a casual demeanor, to greet the newcomer.

There was no mistaking the identity of the man that now regarded him from across the room; it was Armande LeMarte, the First Knight himself. His dark complexion looked haggard, as if burdened with great anxiety or grief, but when his eyes lit upon the disguised countenance of Agent X, a strange sort of recognition flashed in his eyes.

"Andre? But you are…" His expression seemed to roil like a mirage, before finally hardening into an emotionless mask. "What are you doing in here?"

X sucked in a breath. This was the moment he had dreaded. He opened his mouth as if to answer, but then launched into a coughing fit. It was stalling tactic, nothing more, yet it might just be enough to explain away the difference in his voice when he at last answered. As the ersatz paroxysm continued, he spied the cigarettes on the desk and in a flash of inspiration, seized one and lit up.

LeMartre's face flickered with something that was not quite bemusement. "When did you start smoking cigarettes, little brother?"

The question had been posed in French, a language the Agent had no trouble comprehending, but the last phrase felt like a blow to the gut. The identity he had assumed in order to gain entrance to the headquarters of the Fraternis Maltae was none other than the First Knight's own brother. Now that the revelation was in the open, he cursed himself for not having seen the familial resemblance between the young assassin at the museum and the chief enforcer of the Brotherhood. He pretended to take a deep drag of harsh tobacco smoke, and then started coughing again.

"Today seemed like a good day to start," he answered in French, his voice gravelly between coughing spasms.

LeMarte nodded slowly, started brushing at threads or lint on his shirt front…

except that wasn't quite what he was doing. His eyes never left the Agent's face. "Indeed. It did not go well today."

"I believe I may know where the art expert is going next," X answered, taking a step toward the door. "I will make things right, First Knight."

The Chevalier Premiere did not move to impede him, but as he passed, LeMarte spoke. "A moment, Andre. Please, sit down."

X puffed on the cigarette again. "Yes, my brother?"

LeMarte did not meet his gaze this time, but moved toward the front of the desk, letting his hand rest on the scabbard of the sword. "Have you seen the late edition of the newspaper, my brother? A reporter has been kind enough to give us the name of the man we seek. Does that surprise you?"

It was a trap and the Agent knew it. "I have not had time to read the news."

"Oh, you should. There is a great deal of information about today's… debacle." LeMarte moved away from the desk and the Agent was relieved to see that the sword remained where it was. The First Knight continued moving about the room as he spoke. "Not just what happened at the museum. Oh, no. There is also news of men in cars racing through a city park. One of those cars crashed and burst into flames. All of the men inside were killed.

"You were killed, Andre."

The Agent started for the door, but something heavy crashed into the back of his head and night fell in the middle of the afternoon.

Chapter Five
The Tragedy of Monte Sacre

It was, he thought, like the surface of another planet.

Everything was alien. A strange pall hung over the world; not quite mist, not quite smoke, but a stench of burning and decay. The ground was ragged with craters and hastily dug trenches. There were no trees anymore; they had all been hewn down for firewood and makeshift buttresses. What few structures that remained standing were on the verge of collapse, shot full of holes or alternately reinforced with sandbags so that they no longer resembled the work of carpenters. And everywhere the eye looked, there was wire – a twisting sculpture of barbed wire that surrounded the entire village – denying entrance, or more accurately, preventing escape.

He turned away from the strange tableau to regard the young prisoner, suspended between two of his soldiers. Like the village, the man was also wrapped in a sheath of wire. The metal strands surrounded his torso and extremities and blood flowed from dozens of minor wounds where the sharp steel thorns had torn his flesh.

"We caught him on the outer perimeter," one of the soldiers was saying. "The dogs drove him to the wire and he got tangled up trying to flee."

A wry smile crossed the jailer's face – the grin of a sadist. "There is no escape, my young friend. I would have thought that you would have realized this by now." He turned to the soldiers. "Bring him before the other prisoners. It seems I have been remiss in explaining the futility of escape to those in our care."

Though his expression remained defiant, the young man – an enemy courier wounded in an ambush and brought to the Mont Sacre prison camp a week previously – was on the verge of collapse. The soldiers dragged him, through the labyrinth of wire and dropped him in a heap just inside the large holding area. The rest of the prisoners, an even mix of enemy captives and local citizens numbering about one hundred, had been marshaled in the yard and now stood under the ominous shadow of guard towers outfitted with Maschinengewehr 08 machine guns.

"Tie him to the gates."

The two soldiers hoisted the prisoner, still wrapped in his spider-web cocoon, onto the large swinging barrier spreading his arms wide like a crucifixion while the jailer gazed at the emaciated throng, allowing their collective dread to reach a fever pitch.

"Your attention, please. One of your number was captured this morning while trying to escape. Evidently, he did not understand the consequences of such an action. For this, I can blame only myself. Perhaps I did not make it clear to him, or to all of you, that such behavior cannot be tolerated."

He strode forward into their midst, barely able to contain his amusement as they shrank away before his deadly gaze. He made a circuit of the crowd, like a general inspecting the troops, then returned to stand before the captive hanging from the gate. Blood now oozed from the wire that dug into his wrists, but through the pain, the young man's eyes were clear and full of hate. The jailer's smile was as severe as the blade of a guillotine and although he spoke to the assembly, he held the prisoner's gaze with his own stare.

"It is fortunate for all of you that he did not succeed. You all know my standing order that, for every man that escapes, twenty of his co-conspirators must be executed. However, since he did not escape, it will only be necessary to punish ten."

The young man sucked in an agonized breath. "No! You can't…"

"Which ten shall it be?"

Despite his agony, the young man struggled against his bonds. "You can't do this. I'm the one who tried to escape. Kill me!"

The jailer affected a sad mien. "But how would that help you learn the folly of your ways? But I am merciful. You must help me decide which ten to choose. Shall I select ten of your brave comrades in arms? Or shall we take ten from among the villagers? Decide now, or I will rescind my generous offer and take ten of each."

The rage that suffused the face of the young captive was exquisite. At a gesture from the jailer, twenty souls were dragged from the crowd – ten wearing the torn and threadbare uniforms of three different enemy armed forces, and ten wearing the ragged remains of civilian clothes. The latter group included men and women, young and old alike.

"Which will it be, brave young soldier? I give you to the count of ten." He immediately began counting, his words metered to the tick of an invisible clock, each one falling like a scythe on the hopes of the prisoners.

The young man's hopeless anger quickly dissolved into helpless panic. "Please don't do this..."

"Six... Seven..."

"Choose us, lad," one of the British officers called. "We all knew this war might be the death of us. Spare the women and children."

"Nine... Ten."

"Yes," cried the youth. "The soldiers. If you have no mercy in your heart, take the soldiers."

The jailer smiled his sad, mocking smile. "I'm sorry, but it's too late. I gave you ample time to decide." He turned to his own soldiers. "Shoot them all in the back of the head, then hang them up on the wall to keep him company."

The cries of protest chased after the jailer as he walked away, leaving his men to carry out the grim task. After the fourth or fifth gunshot however, the wailing faded away to nothing. For his own part, the jailer had already dismissed the incident from memory; he had other matters to consider. The search....

"Mein herr!"

The shout reached him through the door of the office he had appropriated from the town mayor. It belonged to his chief lieutenant. "Come in."

The man burst into the room, his face covered in sweat and grime. "Mein herr, we found it! We found the treasure."

The jailer was on his feet. "Show me."

The pair raced through the deserted streets of the village, their steps haunted by occasional echoes of gunfire from the nearby prison compound. As they entered a small chapel across the town square from the mayor's residence, the twentieth and final shot reverberated like thunder across the hills.

The lieutenant directed him to the altar at the front of the nave. The mensa had been pushed aside to reveal a dark hole leading directly down into the dais. "The entrance was here all along, but cleverly concealed. We found it by undermining the foundation, but once we broke through, it was a simple matter to open the secret passage."

The jailer did not hesitate to lower himself into the exposed passageway, where his feet quickly found the rungs of a ladder. He descended into the utter night, more than three fathoms down, until his boots at last came to rest on the hard surface of a sub-cellar. The flame of his cigarette lighter cast a dim glow into the chamber that was immediately returned by dozens of glittering golden surfaces.

The lieutenant joined him a moment later. "Is it not magnificent?"

"It is everything I dreamed it would be," the jailer answered reverently. "Who else knows of this?"

"Only the laborers. I have already seen to them."

There was no ambiguity about the euphemism. Both men had always known that the treasure, if it really existed, would be for them alone. None of the soldiers in the camp knew of their tireless search. And of course, the jailer's plans did not allow for an equal division of the loot with his subordinate, but there would be time enough to deal with that when it had been safely transferred away from this hellish place.

"Excellent," he breathed. "Then we are finished here."

"What about the camp? The prisoners? There must be some among the villagers who know of this."

"We are finished with them as well. Give them all an extra ration of food tonight, along with a generous helping of rat poison. If any remain alive in the morning, we will shoot them. After that, burn everything."

"Mein herr, some of the men… They have doubts about the way we have treated the prisoners. If we command them to do this…"

"We cannot allow anyone to bring the tale of what has happened here to the outside world."

The dull firelight made the lieutenant's horrified expression seem all the more hellish. "You mean to kill our own soldiers as well?"

The jailer took one last look at the treasure piled up in the chamber. "The price of glory is often paid in blood. Kill them; kill everyone."

۞ ۞ ۞

Richard awakened in a cold sweat, gripping the cushions of the sofa as if they were the gunwales of a life raft, and he adrift in a raging sea. "Amelia?"

"I am here, father."

He sat up and searched the room to find his lovely red-haired daughter. "Where are we, Amelia? What is this place?"

"Mr. Devine brought us here, father, after those men at the museum tried to kill you."

Richard rose unsteadily to his feet. "Yes. I remember. I must have dozed off. Where is Mr. Devine?"

"He went out to investigate the attack. He made me promise to stay here."

The old man shook his silver head. "No, Amelia. It is too late for that. We must get to the house, quickly, before they do. Where's Ashby?"

A strange sad look crossed the girl's face. "Father, Ashby isn't here. I think those men might have killed him."

"We shall have to call a taxicab then. Quickly, girl; there is no time to lose."

For just a moment, Amelia looked as if she might defy her father and keep her promise to their mysterious savior. But she had known the man calling himself 'Alec Devine' for only an afternoon; her father had protected her for all of her years. "The man working downstairs may try to stop us. We should go to the roof and leave by the fire escape. That way no one will know we have gone."

"Very good," Richard replied, a gleam of admiration in his eye. "We will return to the house just long enough to gather a few essential things, and then you and I will leave."

"Leave? Where will we go?"

"Somewhere safe, Amelia. Somewhere where you will be safe."

❊❊❊

A slap brought the Agent back to consciousness, but also had the effect of exacerbating the throb of pain in the back of his skull. When he opened his eyes, he saw two of everything and despite his best efforts, the world refused to come into focus. Even through the blur however, he had no difficulty recognizing Armande LeMartre.

"Who are you?" the First Knight hissed. "Why do you look like my brother, who even now lies dead – burnt almost beyond recognition – on a coroner's slab?"

The Agent fought through the pain, rejecting the answers that came almost unbidden to his lips. A twitch of his cheeks confirmed that the mask was still in place; his captor had either chosen not to expose his true face or had failed to realize that the visage of his slain sibling was a construct of prosthetics and putty.

"Brother," he managed to say, slurring his speech to sound groggier than he actually felt. "What are you saying? It is I, Andre."

"Is that so?"

LeMarte's hands again moved, as if to pick at lint on his shirtfront, and it was only now that the Agent realized what the man was doing. The strange gestures were some form of sign language – a non-verbal method of communicating developed and used exclusively by the Knights of the Fraternis Maltae. His heart sank. "Brother, my eyes are not working. I cannot see what it is that you are saying."

"Your eyes were working fine before I hit you, pretender, but still you did not comprehend. Now I will ask you again; who are you?"

X blinked several times, willing the pain down to the level of a dull roar in his ears. His vision was clearing and he could now see that LeMartre had been joined by two other men, posted on either side of the bound Secret Agent. He further realized that he was now seated in a straight-backed wooden chair, with his arms bent around the upright backrest and his wrists bound together with what felt like packing twine. He also saw that his captor now possessed his gas gun, though it was unlikely that the man believed it to be anything but a common automatic pistol.

He evinced defeat with a heavy sigh, trying to distract his guards from what he was doing with his nimble fingers. "I am a policeman, LeMartre. We've been investigating the Brotherhood for some time now. We know all about what you've been up to. I was picked because of my resemblance to Andre, but we never meant for him or anyone to be killed. It's time to end this without any more bloodshed. If you kill me, you're bound for Old Sparky up at Sing Sing."

A corner of the First Knight's mouth twitched. "'Old Sparky?' I don't think so, detective... if you indeed you are a detective, which I very much doubt. We have allies in the police department, even in your government.

"No, I think rather that you are the man the newspapers call 'Secret Agent X.'" He held up a copy of The Herald. "It's all here. 'Secret Agent X Foils Murder Attempt at the Met.' You are the one who killed Andre, and now you are going to die."

As LeMartre had been speaking, X's fingers were working his watch crystal loose. The crystal was not a solid piece of glass, but rather a hollow capsule filled with the same anesthetizing gas as his gun. Yet it was not the vapor inside the crystal that he needed now, but rather the glass itself. Carefully transferring the disk to his thumb and forefinger, he went to work, sawing at his bonds, but he needed more time if he was going to get free.

"Tell me something," he said, seemingly oblivious to LeMartre's threat or to the gun barrel now pointing toward his face. "Tell me why?"

"Why?"

"Why are you after Richard?"

The hand holding the pistol wavered then moved away. "Richard? Yes, that is what he calls himself now. Back then, he had a different name."

One strand of the twine separated with a faint pop. The Agent shrugged his shoulders to hide the subtle release of tension. "You mean back at Mont Sacre?"

"Ah, you know about Mont Sacre? Then why do you need to ask? Von Reichardt razed our home to the ground, killed women and children, left us all for dead. We are mercenaries, true, but this is a matter of honor."

"Honor? Hah. Why don't you admit the truth, if only to yourself? You're after the treasure." Another strand parted… just one more.

LeMartre's eyes grew cold.

"Oh, yes," X continued. "I know all about the treasure. You're not after Richard or Von Reichardt…or whatever he's calling himself this week… for revenge. You just want the treasure so you can rebuild your criminal empire."

"The treasure is ours. It is our birthright. We will have it." LeMartre's righteous indignation simmered down to something more like grim determination. "The world is changing, Secret Agent X. New kings and powers are rising. The wise will seek the favor of the Fraternis Maltae, and in turn we will ensure that their dominion extends to every corner of the Earth."

The pistol came up again, mere inches from X's forehead. "Regrettably for you, it will not happen in your lifetime."

LeMartre pulled the trigger.

Chapter Six
FINAL FLIGHT

Instead of the recoil of a gunpowder explosion, there was only a hiss like that of air escaping from a tire valve, and a blast of knockout gas splashed across the Agent's forehead. Although the gas was most effective when inhaled, at close range

"Regrettably for you, it will not happen in your lifetime."

it could permeate the skin and cause localized paralysis. But the Agent had a layer of protective armor that prevented this from happening; the thin layer of cosmetic putty formed an impermeable seal across his face that kept nearly all of the gas from touching his skin.

In the same instant that LeMartre fired the gas gun, the final strand of twine parted under the relentless sawing of the watch crystal and the Agent's hands came free. He bolted from the chair, thrusting LeMartre aside, even as the First Knight and his men unwittingly inhaled a dose of the gas, and launched himself through the open window.

As he crashed into the hedgerow outside, the pain at the back of his head returned with a vengeance. To make matters worse, the area around his eyes – the only part of his face not covered by the make-up – was growing cold and his vision was starting to blur. The dose of anesthetizing gas he had received might not suffice to render him unconscious, but his vision was going fast and if he did not make his escape quickly, he would wander blind through the midst of his enemies.

Eschewing the indirect route he had used to gain access to the office, he charged instead toward the wrought iron fence that separated the courtyard from the street. Despite that fact that it was only late afternoon and the sun still hung low in the sky, darkness was closing in at the edges of his eyesight. He careened blindly into tree trunks that were directly in his path and tripped over flower boxes and benches that lined a path he could no longer clearly distinguish.

He thought he heard the sounds of pursuit from the Hall behind him, but it was difficult to tell through the roaring in his ears. He caromed from yet another tree, and then abruptly fell onto the spiky tips of the metal fence. The decorative spear points were not sharp, but they were enough so to tear clothes and skin alike as he tumbled over the barrier and spilled onto the concrete sidewalk.

The street might have been deserted or he might have been the subject of a dozen amazed stares; he simply could not tell. With one hand resting lightly on the wrought iron fence to feel his way along, he set off at a near run in the direction of the waiting DeSoto. In his mind's eye, he saw the street as before. It was his only means of navigating, for now he was almost completely blind; all he could distinguish was a bright ball of light, hovering just above the dark silhouette of the skyline.

When he reached the place he believed the DeSoto to be, he veered cautiously to the curb and extended a hand until he found the familiar outline of the car's fender… at least he hoped it was his car. He continued probing until he found the door handle and climbed inside. He had no thought of driving, not until the temporary blindness subsided, but to sit idle in the car was to invite discovery. He had to find a way to conceal himself.

Acting on a flash of inspiration, he tore the dark wig away to reveal his own wavy brown hair and similarly rubbed off the mask and prosthetics that formed the likeness of Andre LeMartre. Although his true face was now exposed to the world, he would at least look nothing like the man that the Brotherhood now chased after. Feeling some relief at the small act of camouflage, he felt in his pockets for the small first aid kit he always carried and shook out several aspirin tablets to combat the swelling of pain at the back of his head. The bitter pills grated in his throat, but the simple act of taking them seemed to help.

With a window open to allow some fresh air into the vehicle, the Secret Agent rested his hands on the steering wheel, and then after a few moments, leaned his forehead against the rigid circle and waited for his eyesight to return. It was not long before the darkness in his vision spread like a waiting blanket to completely engulf him.

✪✪✪

How long he floated in the embrace of sleep, he could not measure. When he stirred, his world was still in darkness, but now he could distinguish points of light scattered across his vision. His head still throbbed from the blow LeMartre had administered, but the pain was tolerable now. Nevertheless, it took him several minutes to realize that his vision was completely normal again. The darkness was natural; it was now nighttime.

He came fully awake in a state of near panic. Although he had escaped the clutches of the Fraternis Maltae, he had unwittingly given them a head start on securing their ultimate goal: the treasure of Mont Sacre. And now that LeMartre knew Richard's name, it wouldn't take long for the Brotherhood to reach the art expert's estate in the Hamptons and pillage his wealth. The Agent had a lot of catching up to do.

Through a supreme effort, he kept the DeSoto's speed at the legal limit as he raced back to his residence. He could not afford the delay of a police traffic stop nor did he wish to attract any attention to himself, unmasked as he was. He considered using the reserve of cosmetic putty in the heel of his shoe to don a new face, but rejected the idea; there simply wasn't time.

Upon reaching his brownstone, he moved immediately to his closet and removed a clear wave transmitter, identical to the one he had used at the garage, and called for Harvey Bates. The frantic pace of the other man's response immediately set off alarm bells in his head.

"Chief! Where have you been?"

"What's wrong Harvey?"

"Murphy contacted me on the emergency channel. That pair of birds has flown the coop."

The news would have struck him like a physical blow, were he not already so close to collapse from his earlier trials. "When?"

"Hard to say. He went up to check on them a couple of hours ago, and they were gone."

"I know where they'll go." Although he had taken a personal vow to defend the defenseless, the Secret Agent felt only ambivalence when he considered what would happen when the Brotherhood caught the man who now called himself Auguste

Richard. But Amelia was another matter; the daughter had no share in the crime of her father, and did not deserve the fate that LeMartre would unhesitatingly deliver. He had to get to Richard's house on Long Island ahead of the assassins, and there was only one way to do that.

"I'm going to need a few things, Harvey."

Despite his advanced years, Billy Hayes drove like a demon.

At a mere hint of a suggestion from Betty, he had bundled her into his old Model A Roadster and rocketed through the city as if the hounds of Hell were nipping at his heels. Once across the Brooklyn Bridge, he had somehow found a way to further increase the revolutions of the Straight-4 under the hood, until it sounded like it would break free of its mounts and shoot off into the twilit sky.

Under any other circumstances, the fearless blonde reporter might have found herself not quite so intrepid being whisked through the countryside by the elderly, somewhat near-sighted, and almost certainly inebriated archivist, but the information she had uncovered burned so brightly in her mind as to eclipse all her senses.

Her friend, Secret Agent X, was risking his life to defend one of the most horrible men that had ever lived.

It had not taken long for her to confirm her suspicion that Auguste Richard had sprung fully formed into existence at almost the same moment that Count Augustus Von Reichardt had vanished off the face of the earth. Von Reichardt, a Prussian warmonger directly descended from the Austrian Hapsburg's, had served with distinction at the head of an Austrian regiment during the Great War, but shortly before the signing of the Armistice, for reasons no one could comprehend, he had transferred himself to the command of a makeshift prison camp in the south of France – a small village named Mont Sacre, the Holy Mountain, which no longer appeared on any map. Von Reichardt was the reason Mont Sacre had been erased from both the Atlas and from existence period.

In the aftermath of the war and the defeat of Austro-Hungarian forces, the Count could not shield himself from the accusing finger of those who knew of his atrocities, both against innocent civilians and prisoners of war, so he had instead vanished into the night. A few months later, a wealthy Flemish art collector named Auguste Richard had purchased an estate on a remote corner of Long Island, and wrapped himself in secrecy and security.

It was fairly astonishing to Betty that no one had made previously made the connection; doubtless, Richard's wealth had served well to deflect the sort of inquiries that might have exposed him. Yet, while he had changed his name and nationality, the one constant in his life remained a love of European Renaissance art. In 1919, when the police had raided the Von Reichardt palace outside Vienna, they found that the entire collection of paintings – many of which were uncatalogued, and almost certainly priceless, early works from the Dutch Masters – was gone.

Betty felt a chill run down her spine when she thought about the silver-haired man she had briefly glimpsed in the museum. It was hard to believe that the reclusive art expert had at one time ordered the wholesale slaughter of an entire village, and she wondered what could have driven such a man – a nobleman and a lover of art – to such evil. Now, with the power of the printed word, she would bring Count Von Reichardt's crimes once more to the attention of the world, and more importantly to her friend, Secret Agent X.

Night closed in around them as they made the long drive to Southampton in Suffolk County. Despite Richard's penchant for privacy, he could do little to hide the fact of his ownership of a historic manor house where several of New York's earliest men of influence had at one time resided, and a quick search of the archives had turned up a lifestyle feature on famous houses of New York, complete with driving directions.

The estate was a few miles from the hamlet, situated on a bluff overlooking the Long Island Sound. Behind a forbidding wall of native stone, the property was dense with elm trees, creating an effective curtain to hide the residence from the eyes of curious passersby, but strangely on this night, the large iron gate stood wide open. Hayes pulled the Model A to a halt at the invisible line where the barrier would have crossed the drive.

"What now, Miss Betty?"

The blonde reporter shrugged. "An open gate seems like an invitation to me. Let's go in."

✪✪✪

In the cloak of night, the city hid its rough edges well. The squalid slums were swallowed up by inky darkness and only the glittering jewels of neon light remained, presided over by the towering spires of the Chrysler and Empire State Buildings in midtown, and to the south, amid the shimmering water of the East River, the majestic Statue of Liberty.

The effect was especially profound from two thousand feet above.

Secret Agent X lingered at the window of the Lockheed 10-A Electra until the city lights were swallowed up in the distance. With a pair of 450 horsepower Pratt & Whitney engines pulling the airplane through the sky, that didn't take long.

The plane was one of a small fleet of aircraft used by the Agent's organization, under the direction of Harvey Bates, primarily to provide aerial surveillance and reconnaissance for his clandestine activities. Their use had proved invaluable on countless occasions, but now he was using one of the camera planes for an entirely different purpose.

"Flight time is about forty-five minutes," the pilot had announced shortly after take-off. "Make yourself comfortable. Might be the last chance you get."

With the city now well behind them and the journey half-complete, X began making his final preparations. Using his portable make-up kit, he went to work, layering metal plates and plastic compounds to both conceal his true identity and present a face that would be familiar to Richard and his daughter. When he was finished, he once more wore the sandy-blonde hair and countenance of Interpol agent Alec Devine. But the disguise was the easy part.

"We'll be at the coordinates in five minutes, chief," the pilot called back.

The Agent acknowledged the timeline with a shout of his own, then went to work pulling on the rest of his costume – in this case a pair of heavy coveralls, a bulky backpack, and a flight helmet which he carefully pulled over his blonde wig. He was fitting a pair of goggles over his eyes when the plane began descending, prompting him to move forward to the cockpit. "How is it down there?"

"No wind, not even a whisper of a breeze. It's a perfect night to… well." The pilot chuckled. "Chief, you ever done this before?"

"Once or twice."

The pilot shook his head. "If the bird was on fire and both wings gone, I'd still try to set her down rather than strap one of those things to my back and jump."

The Agent clapped a hand on the fellow's shoulder. "Try it, my friend. It's an experience like no other."

"Thirty seconds until we're there." He pointed through the windscreen at the barely visible place where the waves of the Sound crashed against the bluffs of the island. "That's where you need to go."

X thanked the pilot and headed to the rear exit, quietly counting down the seconds. A rush of air filled the fuselage as he opened the door, and the wind of the aircraft's passage through the sky chilled him, even through the heavy garments. When he reached zero, he did not hesitate to step out into the night.

Chapter Seven
THE SWORD OF VENGEANCE

Armande LeMartre had not forgotten Mont Sacre; not one moment of the horror had slipped from his memory. No matter what the rogue Secret Agent might say, the desire for revenge against the destroyer of his village was an all-consuming fire.

He had been a young man and only an apprentice in the order when the war came to Mont Sacre. There had been opportunities to escape, but to flee would have meant abandoning both his kinsmen and the sacred treasure to the enemy, so he and his young brother had remained prisoners of the siege. And then Von Reichardt had arrived.

The Prussian knew of the treasure – how, LeMartre could not imagine – and was bent upon discovering its whereabouts by any means necessary. Senior members of the order were identified and culled from the larger group, never to be seen again. That they did not break faith was evident only by the fact that the horror endured. When all of the Knights had been taken, the scope of the torture shifted to other senior men from the town; by some miracle, the apprentices to the Brotherhood were overlooked. Ultimately, the young LeMartre brothers knew that they had not escaped their fate, but only postponed it. Yet strangely, the depths of despair had been their finest hour. They had kept hope alive for their fellow villagers, comforted old women and frightened children and often shared their meager rations with the weak.

The end came without warning. The soldiers guarding the prison had been generous that night, slopping an extra portion of gruel into their bowls, which the brothers, according to their custom, had surreptitiously divided among the youngest children. Only when Andre had roused him in the deep hours of the night, frantically reporting that the children were gravely ill, did LeMartre understand how Von Reichardt had turned his noble act of charity into the vilest kind of murder.

The next morning, the streets of Mont Sacre ran red with the blood of those who had not died in the night – villagers, Allied prisoners of war, and then in a cruel betrayal, even the young soldiers who had guarded the camp. The brothers had feigned death by poisoning and in the confusion of the mass executions, had found a place of concealment to weather the final storm, and so survived not because of hope, but because of a burning desire for vengeance.

And now, Andre was dead, another victim of Von Reichardt's machinations.

LeMartre's apprentices swept through the estate like wraiths, slaughtering the guards and domestic servants with the same indifference the torturer of Mont Sacre had shown nearly two decades before. They formed a noose, slowly tightening around the main residence, strangling every avenue of escape, but they did not enter the house. It was understood that the First Knight alone would administer the coup de grace.

LeMarte strode through the night and kicked in the heavy front door without even bothering to see if it was unlocked. The oak panels crashed inward and the assassin entered the abode of his enemy. A long foyer permitted access to several different parts of the house, but all of the rooms were dark save one. LeMartre moved toward that singular source of light; a great room on the opposite side of the mansion, which looked out over the Sound through an enormous picture window. There, as if poised for a final confrontation, the villain of Mont Sacre was waiting.

He was older now. Years of soft living had erased the lupine hunger that had once driven Von Reichart to the lowest depths of evil. The contemptuous sneer that twisted his patrician face now seemed merely laughable, but the revolver in his right hand could not be regarded with such indifference. "I always knew you would come. Did you imagine that I would not be ready?"

LeMartre hefted the sword in his right hand. "Even now, you are without honor. So be it. You will die as you have lived."

"Stop it, both of you!"

The outcry caught both men by surprise. But whereas LeMartre's gaze merely flickered in the direction of the voice, Von Reichardt appeared genuinely stunned. The pistol lowered as he turned to face the red haired girl that now stood at the far end of the room. "Amelia! You should have stayed in the–"

The old man's protest turned into a gurgle of pain as the First Knight sprang forward, stabbing the tip of his sword through Von Reichardt's right shoulder. The force of the thrust drove the old man backward, into the wall where the point of the blade pierced deep into the plaster, pinning him there like an insect in a child's collection. The gun fell from his nerveless fingers and clattered on the floor.

Amelia shrieked upon witnessing the sudden act of violence, and heedless of any peril, rushed to her stricken father's side. "Don't touch him! Murderer!"

LeMartre's hand was still wrapped around the hilt of his sword and he looked as though he might, at any moment, wrestle it free and drive it through the old man's heart. "Murderer, you say?"

"Let her go," Von Reichardt croaked. "Spare my daughter. She knows nothing…"

"Just as you spared the children of Mont Sacre? I think not. Your cursed bloodline shall be forever erased, butcher." The First Knight drew a deep calming breath to bring his passions under control. "You remain alive this moment for one reason only. I will not subject you to the torments of the damned, as you did to the noble Knights of the Brotherhood all those years ago; no, I will simply offer you this one chance at expiation. Tell me where the treasure is, and I will allow you to go to your final judgment with a prayer upon your lips."

"Amelia… Let her go. I beg you."

That LeMartre did not immediately refuse the wounded man's plea might have indicated that a shred of mercy yet remained in his tortured heart. But whether it was his intent to spare an innocent or not would never be known, for at just that moment, Amelia laid hands upon the gun that had fallen from her father's grip, and without hesitation raised the revolver and fired point blank at the assassin.

The bullet creased LeMartre's ribs, leaving a bloody but superficial wound; the First Knight had endured much worse. Though the impact had driven the wind from his sails, he struggled to his feet, closing on the girl with his hands curled into bestial claws. Amelia however was not intimidated. With more care than before, she aimed the pistol at the center of his forehead and thumbed back the hammer.

"Amelia, no!"

The introduction of a fourth voice onto the stage stopped everyone in their tracks. LeMartre froze in place, poised to strike if the red-haired girl's eyes left him for even a moment, but Amelia's sights did not waver.

"Who the devil are you?" she hissed, glimpsing a blonde head from the corner of one eye.

The newcomer moved cautiously forward. "My name is Betty Dale. I'm a reporter with The Herald. I saw you at the museum this morning."

A chuckle forced its way through LeMartre's grimace of pain. "Ah, Miss Dale. I very much enjoyed reading your account of what happened at the museum. I am grateful to you also for giving us the name of the good Prof. Richard."

Betty ignored the killer's barbs and focused her attention instead on the one person in the room who she reckoned might be worth saving. "Amelia, don't do this. We can call the police–"

"No police," croaked the old man. "Shoot him, Amelia. He'll never stop hunting us."

"Don't listen to him," Betty pleaded. "He may be your father, but you don't know the horrible things he's done."

"It is true," LeMartre intoned, straightening from his aggressive stance and raising his hands as if in surrender. "The blood of an entire village is on his hands."

"It was a war." Amelia replied, but her tone lacked conviction. "Terrible things happen in war."

"It was no battle, cheri. Women and children, poisoned. The survivors slaughtered and left for the carrion birds. And for what? To steal our gold. Your beloved father is worse than a killer; he is a thief."

"It was a terrible thing to do," Betty interjected. "But more killing won't change what's already done. The victims of Mont Sacre want justice, not revenge."

"What do you know of justice?" the killer spat. "Have you spent a night with the dead, daring not even to breathe, as the butchers spill the blood of children and old women before your very eyes. More than a hundred souls… poisoned… shot… slaughtered like cattle."

"Quiet! Enough of your lies!"

Amelia's gaze never left LeMartre but tears were welling in her eyes and her grip on the revolver no longer seemed quite so resolute. The First Knight pressed his advantage.

"Did he never tell you? A bedtime story perhaps? On the last day, before he found what he was looking for, he executed twenty prisoners because one young soldier tried to escape."

"Stop it!"

"He hung them up on the wall to rot. The birds ate their eyes–"

"Stop it! Stop it!"

LeMartre struck like a viper, springing across the room to hammer the girl with his fists. Amelia never got a shot off. The assassin scooped up the revolver and turned it on Betty.

"Thank you for the timely interruption," he said, panting. He aimed the weapon at her heart. "I wish that I had a better way to repay you, but alas, it is not our custom to leave witnesses."

But before he could pull the trigger, another player stepped onto the stage; a blonde-haired man that LeMartre did not recognize entered the room as calmly as if he was merely a curious tourist taking a stroll. His confident voice however was very familiar. "So the noble Knights of the Fraternis Maltae make war on innocent women. You must be proud of yourselves."

"Excellent. All of my enemies gathered in one place." LeMartre smiled, turning the gun on the newcomer. "Welcome to the execution, Secret Agent X.

Chapter Eight
THE DUEL

It had not escaped LeMartre's notice that both Betty Dale and X had somehow slipped through the noose of apprentices surrounding the house. In fact, 'slipped through' did not begin to tell the tale.

The Agent's parachute had deployed almost directly above Richard's residence. As he drifted down, he could not fail to notice the wave of assassins moving stealthily throughout the darkened estate. He was still more than two hundred feet from the ground when they dispersed in a ring about the main dwelling, and although they were unaware of his presence, he had little doubt that they would overwhelm him the moment he crashed down in their midst.

The capacious silk canopy had only one function: to slow his rate of fall to a survivable level. It was not designed for maneuverability, and while he anticipated a degree of drift, the windless night had kept him right on target. Now, he desperately needed to adjust to a different drop zone.

Twisting in the full-body harness, he gripped one of the heavy-duty nylon straps that secured his body to the web of cords blossoming upward to the parachute, and began to haul it in like a hawser. As that side of the chute was pulled down, the rush of escaping air cause him to lose lift and he began to plummet at an angle, away from the house and toward the dark woods. He held the line as long as he dared; knowing that to land at such speeds almost guaranteed serious injury. With the treetops seemingly brushing his feet, he released his grip and the enveloped snapped taut once more. An instant later, he crashed into the trees.

The elm branches were springy, bending rather than breaking, and while they formed a softer landing surface than the ground, the difference was negligible. The Agent was struck dozens of times, his legs slapped with repeated blows that felt like the swings of a baseball bat. Then, with a violent jerk that snapped him in his harness like the end of a bullwhip, his fall stopped. The parachute had become tangled in the treetops, leaving him suspended two stories above the ground.

There was no time to nurse his wounds. He cut free of the lines and made the bone-jarring drop to the forest floor. His eyes were well enough adjusted to the darkness now that he had no trouble navigating to the edge of the woods, and his dark overalls helped him go unnoticed by the apprentices of the Brotherhood who had now formed a defensive perimeter around the house.

He skirted the tree line until he reached the cliff overlooking the water. There were only three of the assassins, loosely spaced to guard what was probably considered the least likely avenue of escape for anyone inside the house. It took the agent only a few minutes to creep from man to man and subdue each one with a dose of his anesthetizing gas. He continued moving stealthily around the house, overpowering the apprentices and binding each one with wire restraints. He was in the process of taking down the last of the group when a shift in the shadows alerted him to the approach of a vehicle on the main drive. To his utter dismay, Betty Dale had emerged from the car, and before he could warn her off, entered the house unchallenged.

Moving swiftly but with caution to avoid detection by Betty's waiting driver, he gained the front entrance just as a gunshot broke the silence. He rushed forward in a panic, just in time to witness Betty's arrival on the scene. He held back as long as he dared, believing that Betty's appeal to common sense and decency might actually win the day, but when LeMartre turned the tables on Amelia and regained the advantage, there was no choice but intrude.

The First Knight brandished the revolver at the Agent. "You must be very brave. I almost admire your nerve. But you are a fool to come here."

"Nothing particularly brave or foolish about it," replied X, calmly. "The police will be here in a matter of minutes."

"You will not live that long." LeMarte's eyes narrowed. "In any case, I believe that you are bluffing. Secret Agent X is not a friend to the police. They would rather arrest you than me."

"Perhaps. But they won't simply turn a blind eye to the fact that you murdered four unarmed people, and before you tell me how swiftly you'll vanish into the night, let me just add that it will take you considerably longer to free your apprentices than you might believe." He moved across the room to stand beside Betty. "Your only chance is to surrender now. Betty's right; revenge isn't the answer. It is time for Von Reichardt to face justice. Let the world know the truth of his crimes; let him stand trial in a court of law."

Even as he spoke, the Agent knew that his appeal had fallen on deaf ears. LeMartre had lived too long with the fire of vengeance burning in his breast, and as a member of the Fraternis Maltae, was a true believer in the ideology of violence as a means to an end.

"There will be no court, no trial. It ends tonight."

"I can't let you do that."

LeMartre stabbed the pistol toward him. "And how will you stop me?"

X nodded at the firearm. "Not a very honorable weapon for a knight."

"So it is a duel of honor you want?" For the first time since confronting Von Reichardt, a smile cracked the assassin's hard visage. He abruptly stuffed the gun into a pocket, and then took hold of the cruciform hilt of his sword, which still pinned the Prussian pretender to the wall. He wrenched it free, eliciting a moan of agony from the old man, who slumped to the ground. "Excellent. You are correct, of course. A gun is far too crude a tool. This blade begs for your blood."

"If it's to be a duel, then you'll allow me to choose a weapon–"

The Agent's statement was cut off as LeMartre sprang forward, slashing with the long blade in a strike that would have taken off his head if he had remained where he was. The First Knight's concession to the so-called "duel of honor" did not evidently extend to the notion of a level playing field. He sprang forward again, this time with feint followed by another hacking blow.

Although unarmed, X was by no means defenseless. Even if the killer had elected to shoot him, the Agent's manganese-steel bulletproof vest would likely have stopped the round, allowing him a decisive moment in which to overpower his foe. Likewise, he was not completely vulnerable to an attack from LeMartre's blade. As an expert in the unarmed form of combat known as jiu-jitsu, Agent X was more than a match for any thug with a knife.

Except LeMarte wasn't merely a thug. He had not achieved the rank of Chevalier Premiere by default. On the day of the tragedy of Mont Sacre, he had been simply an apprentice in the Fraternis Maltae, but from that day forward, he had dedicated himself to the way of the sword and had studied under the tutelage of the finest saber masters in Europe. Against his blade, even a mastery of Oriental martial arts seemed insufficient.

Nor was the Secret Agent in top fighting form. He was still smarting from his earlier encounter with LeMartre, and added to those wounds were the numerous bruises and abrasions he had suffered during the parachute drop. Every time he dodged a thrust of the assassin's sword tip, he winced in pain. Fatigue was building in his muscles and he could feel his reactions growing slower with each attack.

But on the other side of the coin, LeMartre had failed to score a single hit against his unarmed foe, and the repeated stabbing and slashing was taking its toll on him as well. The wound to his ribs continued to weep blood and flashed with pain every time he extended his sword arm forward. He needed to end this fight quickly, before his own fatigue somehow gave the Agent the upper hand. It was time to change his tactics.

He launched a series of halting feints, designed to maneuver his foe's back to the wall – or in this case, the large picture window – and yet at the same time, lure the Agent into attempting a counterattack. When he had the man where he wanted him, LeMartre stabbed out in what appeared to be a foolish overextension, leaving his wounded rib cage exposed to his enemy. The Agent took the bait and when he launched himself at the assassin's unprotected flank, the First Knight drove his elbow down into the back of his foe's skull.

However, LeMartre had underestimated the canniness of his opponent. X was not fooled for a second by the swordsman's seemingly foolish attacks. When the other man gave him the opening, he took it, but not in the frantic desperate way that LeMartre expected. Instead of striking at the wound, the Agent instead wrapped his arms around the assassin, planted his feet firmly on the floor, and twisted the other man off his feet. Entwined together, both men crashed into the plate-glass and in an explosion of razor sharp splinters, tumbled out into the night.

The fall to the ground outside the house was no great distance – only about six feet – but it was enough to leave both combatants momentarily stunned. The Agent recovered quickly, perhaps because he had anticipated such a result from his attack, but LeMartre's hand closed on the hilt of his sword even as the former struggled to his feet amid a deadly garden of glass shards. In a matter of seconds, both men were up, and once more circling each other warily.

Removed from the confines of the house, the battlefield favored the Agent;

he needed only to avoid the reach of LeMartre's blade and there was nothing but maneuvering room on the expanse of lawn between the whitewashed walls of the mansion and the edge of the bluff some fifty yards away. Inexplicably however, X stayed close, barely out of the deadly circle described by his foe's increasingly desperate attacks, retreating toward the precipice.

The First Knight now fought two enemies – the Secret Agent, and his own fatigue. Yet through it all, he did not forget his hard won skills. Every inch that X ceded to him was a small victory; he was the one shaping this battlefield, not his unarmed nemesis. Step by step, like a Queen chasing the King around the chessboard, he pushed the fight toward the edge of the cliff and toward the inevitable checkmate.

A low wooden fence had been erected at the brink of the fall; a guard rail to keep anyone wandering close to the edge from falling over. The Agent knew it was there, but did not dare risk a backward glance to fix its presence. Nevertheless, the increasingly loud rush of breakers on the rocks below alerted him to the nearness of his approach. He was almost exactly where LeMartre wanted him, and when he felt the barrier against his legs, he froze in his tracks as if only now realizing his fatal error.

The First Knight did not hesitate. With a strike as fast as lightning, he stabbed the ornate weapon into Secret Agent X's heart.

Chapter Nine
THE SCORPION'S NATURE

Helpless to do anything to assist her friend, Betty Dale had watched in horror as the strange battle moved ever closer to the bluff. She had seen X fight countless villains with her own eyes, and while it was unthinkable that he would not also win this battle, those same eyes beheld a different outcome. Frantic, she began searching the ruins of the great room for some kind of weapon with which to aide the Secret Agent. Her hand settled on a piece of the window sash, jarred loose when the struggling pair had crashed through – it wasn't much, but it might just make the difference – and she hefted it in preparation to climb out the opening and rush into battle… and that was when she saw it.

Hanging on the wall, directly above the shattered window, was an ornate, jeweled sword that looked as though it might once have belonged to a Bedouin prince. The fearless reporter wrestled the decorative weapon from its mount and pitched it out into the night, following close behind. The weapon was heavier than she expected and she struggled to run with it on the springy grass. For every step she took toward the embattled men, they retreated a step away, closer and closer to the precipice. And then, when there was nowhere for them to go, she saw a sight that would haunt her dreams. LeMartre drew back his sword and rammed it dead center into her old friend's chest.

What happened in the next instant defied explanation.

The sword did not penetrate the Agent's body as it had Von Reichardt's. Instead, only the merest fraction of the tip pierced the fabric of his overalls, and then, with all of LeMartre's weight behind it, the long steel shaft bowed and with a sound like a gunshot, snapped in two. The Secret Agent's vest of manganese-steel armor was, it seemed, proof against more that just bullets.

The blade fragment against X's chest flipped into the air like the knife of a carnival juggler. The other shard, still attached to the hilt, which was in turn still held in the assassin's grip, lurched forward, gouging a bloody furrow across the upper surface of the Agent's shoulder.

LeMartre found himself falling forward into his seemingly impervious foe, but X was already twisting away from the fence and the collision that seemed certain to send both of them plummeting over the cliff. The assassin's flailing left hand managed to snare the fabric of X's clothes in the same instant that he pitched headlong over the fence, and just as with the window, both men crashed through the flimsy wooden barricade.

All of this happened in a split second. Betty Dale was still paralyzed by the horror of seeing the Agent stabbed, and it took the splintering sound of the fence collapsing under their combined weight to snap her out of it. She realized in that moment that X was still alive, but also saw that he was scant inches from what would surely be a fatal plunge. Throwing caution aside, along with the now useless sword, she dived after the men, grabbing hold of the Agent's foot as the edge of the cliff crumbled under him.

In that single fateful moment, everything changed. LeMartre's skill with a sword no longer gave him the advantage. His fate, and the fate of his enemy, was now beyond his ability to control. He hung, suspended only by his fierce grip on the Agent's overalls sleeve, a hundred feet above the craggy rocks of the shoreline. The shattered remains of his blade, the badge of his office as Chevalier Premiere, remained clutched in his free hand, a broken and impotent symbol of his failure. He stared up into the steely eyes of his enemy.

Although Betty's petite physique seemed as insignificant to the matter at hand as a feather on a rock pile, it was just enough to halt the Agent's slide and allow him to wrap one arm around a fence post. LeMartre clung to him with a death grip and the strain from the added weight was unimaginable. Every one of his myriad wounds now felt as though they had been ripped open with fiery daggers.

"It's over, LeMarte," he shouted into the other man's face. "Surrender now and live. Let go of the sword and give me your hand."

Even as he made the offer, extending mercy to an enemy who would most certainly never have done the same, he knew that the First Knight would refuse. Like the scorpion in the parable, he could not help but plant his sting, even if doing so meant his own death.

With a fearsome cry, LeMartre brought the broken sword up and hammered it toward the Agent's exposed back. Anticipating the treachery, X did the only thing he could. As he felt the other man's weight shift in preparation for the killing strike, he twisted away, pulling the fabric from the assassin's fingers. There was a flash of sparks as the steel of the blade struck only rock, and then LeMartre was gone, tumbling down the nearly vertical surface. The sickening sound of his impact on the rocks below was almost muted by the roar of the sea...almost.

Chapter Ten
FINAL JUSTICE

Amelia was huddled at her father's side, ministering to his wounds and offering what comfort she could, when Betty and the Agent returned to the house. She gave a little gasp when she saw them.

"The other man?"

"Gone," answered the Agent. He knew what had to come next, and for the girl's sake, he felt a twinge of regret.

The man who had called himself Auguste Richard stirred. "I am sorry... for everything."

The Agent knelt beside him. "Your apologies won't bring back the dead. Or change what you did at Mont Sacre."

Von Reichardt's face twisted defensively. "You don't actually believe that killer's lies–"

"He wasn't lying," Betty intoned. "What you did at Mont Sacre was... beyond human."

The old man sagged, his dignity in tatters. "You're right. I can't change what happened. I wish now that I could. I have tried so hard to atone..."

"It's not up to you to set the price for the blood you spilled," X answered unequivocally. "Lady justice will settle that account."

Dread overshadowed Von Reichardt's countenance. He glanced at his daughter who now sat as motionless as a statue opposite the Agent. "Please, let us go. You can have the treasure, all of it. We'll go somewhere far away... I'm an old man; what difference does it make if die in prison, or in exile?"

The Secret Agent looked at him for a long time before answering. "It makes all the difference in the world." Then he reached up with both hands and carefully peeled away a layer of his disguise.

Von Reichardt eyes widened in an expression of absolute horror. "No! It can't be. You're..."

A shudder passed through his body, and then another. The spasms intensified in a matter of seconds, and the old man's face drew into a rictus of pain as he clutched helplessly at his chest. "So," he gasped, forcing the words through clenched teeth. "You have your revenge."

"Not revenge. Justice."

Von Reichardt jerked once then thrust a hand out as if clutching at the last sparks of his life force. "Amel..."

The plea took his last breath. He did not draw another.

"No! It can't be. You're..."

The red-haired girl remained where she was, shell-shocked by the violence that had left her life in ruins, and perhaps more so by her father's awful legacy. The Agent wanted to comfort her somehow, but knew that such a gesture would be futile. Instead, he got to his feet and limped toward the door.

Betty hastened after him. "What happens now?"

"Now? That's for the police to decide." He kept walking.

"But Amelia? She has nothing now. She didn't deserve this."

"She has her life, which is more than Von Reichardt gave his victims. The innocent always pay the price for the deeds of evil men."

As he reached the front door, Betty placed a hand on his shoulder; a light touch, but enough. He stopped and turned to face her. "I don't think I've ever seen you so… hard. You were there, weren't you? At Mont Sacre?"

The Agent did not reply. His silence was answer enough.

"What do you want me to do? How should I tell the story?"

"Tell the truth, " he said simply.

"There's just one more thing I want to know. You're the one who stole the painting from the museum, aren't you?"

A corner of his mouth twitched in what might have been an agonized grimace. "I knew that Von Reichardt might emerge from hiding for a chance to see The Night Watch like that. Art was always his passion. But I never anticipated that the Brotherhood would act so openly and a lot of innocent people paid the price for it."

"It's not your fault. You said it yourself, the innocent pay the price for the deeds of evil men. You aren't evil. Justice is never evil."

"Justice," he echoed.

She reached up a hand to caress his cheek. "This is just another mask, isn't it?"

"There's always a mask, Betty." A faint smile graced his lips. He leaned forward to kiss her gently on the forehead, then turned and strode out into the night.

DISCOVERING SECRET AGENT X

When I got the opportunity to join the effort to breathe new life into some of the literary world's nearly forgotten heroes, I was faced with a choice – where to start? To be perfectly honest, I had never heard of any of these characters, but one name immediately stood out to me: Secret Agent X. That was the one for me. I didn't know anything about him, except that he must be some kind of spy. As someone who never misses an outing of a certain British spy with a license to... let's just say a penchant for causing mayhem, writing about a dashing action hero who keeps the world safe from evil megalomaniacs seemed like a perfect fit. As I was to learn however, Secret Agent X had more in common with the spies of the television series Mission Impossible, than with Ian Fleming's mythic hero, but discovering that proved to be the real journey.

My initial quest for information about the character took me down a false path. It seems that during the era when pulp magazines dominated the newsstands, secret operatives identified only by a letter, number or combination thereof were all the rage. At about the same time that perennial pulpster Paul Chadwick was breathing life into Secret Agent X, detective novelist Dashiell Hammett had teamed up with comic artist Alex Raymond to create a syndicated newspaper comic strip featuring a similar character with an all-too similar nom de guerre: Secret Agent X-9. Not fully comprehending the distinction, my initial impression of how to develop the character was based more on what little I could find about X-9. Ironically, the similarities outweighed the differences. Although Hammett's creation (his actual involvement with the strip was short lived) later became identified as Phil Corrigan, in his original incarnation, he was known only by his code name, and worked for a similarly anonymous government agency. His exploits were more in keeping with the private-eye genre than the sort of international adventures that would later come to be synonymous with Cold War era spies. Using this slightly skewed template, I began to brainstorm ideas for my first outing with Secret Agent X.

Fortunately, I learned of my mistake before too many egregious errors were made and to my delight, when I finally came across a copy of "Legion of the Living Dead" I discovered that my interpretation of pulpdom's greatest spy was not too far off the mark.

Since completing Masterpiece of Vengeance I have had an opportunity to read several more of the original Secret Agent X tales, as well as some of the new adventures chronicled in Airship 27's anthology series. If I've learned one thing, it's that the search to discover Secret Agent X never really ends. The scribes who brought this character to life more than seventy years ago, and now again in our own time, each reveal a different side of the nameless superspy who can look like anyone.

Whether this book represents your first exposure to the character, or you are a die-hard fan from long ago, I hope you'll enjoy this latest opportunity to discover Secret Agent X.

SEAN ELLIS is currently[1] (and unsuccessfully) undergoing treatment for adventure dependency. He is the author of several novels, including the supernatural thriller *Magic Mirror*, and a series featuring action-hero Nick Kismet. His interest in adventure is not limited to the literary world however. An avid outdoor and extreme sports enthusiast, Sean can often be found surfing and mountain biking in his native stomping grounds in the Pacific Northwest, unless of course duty calls; an infantry soldier in the Oregon National Guard, Sean was deployed to New Orleans following Hurricane Katrina in 2005, and to Afghanistan in 2006-07 where he discovered the dark world of Secret Agent "X".

For information on how to purchase any of the above titles, contact the author at: kismetbooks@yahoo.com

---

[1]   This description was written for the first edition of the book in 2008. Some details may have changed. For more information: http://www.seanellisauthor.com

Chapter One
GUN MOLL

Kneeling in the dark wet alleyway, Thomas 'Talker' Milligan mused that it was the last thing he would ever see. Given that, he examined it closely as it hovered inches from his face. The German-made, long-barreled pistol probably came stateside with a soldier in the Great War. He could barely make out the words its bearer seethed as Talker examined the sleek lines and intricate curves of the beautiful weapon. How could a thing of such beauty be an instrument of murder? Not really having the mind of a philosopher, Talker abandoned his consideration of the firearm and returned his attention to the gunsel pointing it at his face.

"Ya gonna play the nags with the big guy's jack, Talker?" Bobby 'York' Gallager droned. Talker got to use all his senses with York's words. He smelled the stench of his breath, heard the grating tones of his voice, saw the steam of his words in the cold night, felt the exhaled air warm his face, and tasted fear on his tongue. "Well, the boss thinks that's a mistake. That's a mistake yer carryin' with you to the cemetery!" Bobby didn't really have very many redeeming qualities. A bad temper and a face to match, everyone called him York after Sergeant York because he was a rifleman in the war. The comparison to Sergeant York, who'd captured dozens of German soldiers single-handedly, really didn't hold up that greatly with Bobby. He wasn't a very good rifleman, and he was from Hell's Kitchen instead of Tennessee.

None of this really stuck in Talker's mind for more than a moment, as he was more concerned with what would be stuck in his brainpan in a second. "Listen, York," he started, "Bobby...I was gonna put the green under big boy's pillow when Thundering Song hit the finish line—with interest! I'm tellin' ya, I'll put so much coin into Shiner Mack's pocket come noon tomorrow, he'll be jinglin' like Santa's sleigh! Just give me time, Bobby," he pleaded. "We've been friends since we were kids."

York shrugged. "You know the score, Tom. There's friendship—sure, but then there's business. Then there's talkin' to yer maker, and then there's answering to Big Boy. We can be friends in Heaven, and I'll ask for your forgiveness then." York tightened his trigger finger. "Put in a good word for me."

"Hang on, York."

York spun around, surprised by the sound of a voice behind him. He smiled crookedly. "Ah, geez, Hush—don't go sneakin' up on a guy like that!"

Tall, dressed to the nines under his raincoat and wearing a wide-brimmed fedora, Tom 'Hush' Johnson was a real killer. They would send Hush after people they never wanted anyone to hear from again, and Hush always obliged. Built like a huge linebacker, a pair of jagged slashes crossed over his chin and down his neck. "What's the deal, York?" Hush asked. "What're ya musclin' Talker for?"

"He's been usin' the swag from Shiner Mack to run the horses," York replied.

"Mack ain't happy 'bout it neither."

"Honest, Hush," Talker broke in, "I was gonna pay Mack back before he learned it was gone! I told ya—I was gonna pay out in spades! Thundering Song is guaranteed to win!"

"S'that so?" Hush's face darkened. "You're all wet to play with Mack's coin, Talker. He's climbing the ladder, and ya just made yerself a rung for him ta step on." Hush turned to York. "Why don't you let me deal with this yegg? I don't take kindly to someone what steals from others."

York's face fell. His eyes narrowed and his nostrils flared. "Look Hush—Mack gave me the job an' I need the money, dammit! You're not takin' the chicken off my choppin' block!"

Hush turned to York with a penetrating glance. York saw the look in Hush's eyes—the unmistakable eyes of a killer. Feeling a bit warm all of the sudden, York pulled at his collar. Hush sighed. "Lookit here, York—tell Shiner I said to pay you for the hit. I don't give a crap about the money. Talker's talked a bit too much in the past, an' I owe him for that stretch on the fed's dime I just whistled away from last week. You didn't know your squealin' to the swineherd was what put me in the monkey-cage, did ya, Talker?" He turned back to York. "What I'm sayin' is—I don't like Talker. Maybe you'd like to get on my Christmas list wid him?"

Smiling apologetically, York returned the gun to his jacket. "No, Hush. Thanks for the swag on this hit!"

With strong fingers, Hush grabbed onto the collar of York's jacket and lifted the gangster off the ground. York let out a quiet, involuntary yelp as his feet came off the pavement. "I said I don't care 'bout the green!" Hush spat. "Talker owes me one, and no amount of coin's gonna make up for a five-year stint with no wine, dames, or song! Unnerstand yet?"

York nodded as Hush put his feet back on the ground. York moved off quickly and said over his shoulder, "Yeah, I gotcha Hush! I'll give Mack your regards and let him know you're back in town!"

"Let 'em all know that Hush is back!" the gangster shouted through gritted teeth. "Let 'em know I'm up, and this town's coming down!"

Waiting until York was gone, Hush turned back to Talker. Talker considered the length of the barrel that came out from under the killer's raincoat. "Geez, Hush, that's a long cannon you're showin' me."

"It takes the bullet a long while to make it out the mouth when it spits, too. Gives you time to think about what you've done, Talker."

"Yeah," Talker licked his lips, "See, Hush, I've done a lifetime of thinking in the last few clicks. I'm real sorry I sailed you up the river—I didn't mean to. I know you're gonna kill me anyway, but I always thought you were like a movie star or something. Just don't make it hurt." Talker closed his eyes and waited for the bullet.

"Get up, Talker," Hush said. Talker didn't move aside from a tear leaving his eye. Why didn't Hush just kill him? "I said get up, dammit!"

Talker opened one eye, blinking a warm tear off his lashes. "Get to your feet!" Hush demanded once more. "I ain't sayin' it again!" Trembling, the thug stood up.

"Lissen Talker—and lissen good. I'm letting you go."

"What?" Talker asked, incredulous. "Why?" He fell silent when he realized he didn't want to talk Hush out of his decision.

"You're not lissenin'—maybe you need another ear canal in your head? If ya don't ya outta shut yer trap and listen. I want you disappeared, hear me? Do your best invisible man impression."

A long yellow-and-black taxi pulled up to the alleyway as Hush threw his thumb over his shoulder. "Get in that hack over there. The driver will give you plenty of cash and take ya to the airport, where you'll get on a private plane. You'll fly out of state and board a ship goin' to Brazil. If you ever come back to America, I'll drop everything I'm doin' to make sure ya disappear for good." Lowering his voice, Hush droned, "Ya hear me, Talker?"

Eyes wide with surprise and fear, the hoodlum nodded. Grabbing him by the collar, Hush dragged Talker to the taxi and threw him in the back. "You know what to do," he said to the driver. He slammed the door as the vehicle and it squealed its tires on the wet pavement. Talker tried the door, but there weren't any handles inside.

Pulling his coat closer, Hush began walking down the lonely street. Suddenly, a black sedan careened around the corner. An attractive, blonde woman wearing a red dress and hat leaned out the passenger's side brandishing a Tommy gun. "Here's dessert for ya, Hush!"

Hush jumped behind a parked truck as the bullets beat a staccato rhythm through the cold night air. The heated metal pierced the gas tank of the truck. The explosion pushed the engine out the front of the vehicle as fire licked the darkness. As the car squealed down the street, shrapnel from the blast peeled Hush's face away. He stood to his feet and yelled. "Betty!" He repeated the shout, but to no avail. The car moved too fast for him to be heard over the roar of the engine. Secret Agent X peeled away part of his artificial face made to look like the gangland killer Hush. Betty Dale had become a gun moll, and X knew it was not her nature. He had to know why.

Chapter Two
GANGLAND KILLER X

Groaning under the strain, the winch of the tow-truck protested as its steel rope pulled taut through the murky water of the bay. The back window of a waterlogged sedan appeared beneath the filthy liquid. Inspector John Burks looked on, indifferently holding a cigarette between his lips. Parked by the dock, several squad cars waited with uniformed policemen.

"I see ya got a bite, detective," Burks looked over his shoulder at Inspector Clyde Niehart. "What'd you catch?"

Burks pulled the cigarette out of his mouth and blew out a stream of smoke. "A

"Here's dessert for ya, Hush!"

giant Holy Mackerel that's been eatin' swimmers."

Niehart shrugged as he looked at the car now coming out of the water. "Sounds like a Red Herring to me. Nobody swims in this sewage. People are better off getting diseases the good old fashioned way. Who's the fish driving it anyway?" he asked as he pointed at the body in the driver's seat.

"Whoever it is, this is my catch, Niehart. Not even your jurisdiction."

"Just stopping to see if you need help gutting it. That's all." The pair watched as the face of the driver became visible. "You were right about the Holy Mackerel, John! That's Bobby Gallager!"

Burks nodded. "Yeah. A two-bit gunsel they called York."

"I just wanna know how you catch 'em so fresh! What'd you use for bait?"

Flinging his cigarette into the water, Burks replied with, "Got a tip by phone right early this morning. They said the fishing was good around here, so I brought my tackle box and put on my rubber boots."

"Good thing. Looks like it's gonna get pretty deep around here. York's one of Shiner Mack's gunners. He ain't gonna be happy about him getting offed so unceremoniously."

"Might've been Mack's idea," Burks reminded. "I've got an idea of my own, though."

"Yeah? What's that?"

Taking a cigarette out of its case, Burks placed it between his lips and lit it with a match. "That's something I'm not gonna tell you, Niehart. You can't hone in on my territory."

"Hey, I'm sorry if I ruined your morning."

Burks shrugged. "I don't blame you for that, Niehart. You were born with an ugly mug."

"Lissen Burks, we might just be workin' on related cases. I'm trying to track down the missing Dale woman. Word has it she's been seen hangin' with Mack."

"No law against bad taste, Niehart—just lookit who I'm hangin' with."

"That's just 'cause you're not good lookin'. I'll tell you somethin' else if you'll clean your ears out. I got a report of an attempted shooting in the Greenfield industrial area. The vic got up and walked away from the scene."

"Who was the victim?"

"The tip-off said it was Hush Johnson."

"Hush? Not a chance. He's making worry stones outta boulders upstate in the federal pen."

"Maybe not anymore. Anyway, I don't think it was Hush."

"Why's that?"

Neihart reached deep in the pocket of his raincoat and pulled out a piece of flesh-colored material. "Because, I found this at the scene. Something from a Lon Chaney make-up kit. Movie effects and all that. It's a piece of a mask that probably came from the vic's face. Who do you know what wears a different face?"

With wide eyes, Burks took the piece of material. He jaw clenched. "Secret Agent X!"

"Yeah, it looks like that X guy you're always going on about. Don't know why he'd impersonate Hush Johnson, but there it is."

Burks handed the piece of fake skin back to Neihart and returned his gaze to the dead body and the flooded vehicle. "Looks like York here knew why. Whatever he knew, X made sure he didn't share with us."

"What're you saying, Burks?"

"Isn't it obvious? X murdered York!" He punched his palm. "I've got him dead to rights!"

Chapter Three
BETTY DALE—MIND THRALL

'S hiner' Mack punched the old man in the face. The elderly fellow with the beard and tattered green suit fell to the floor. "You come over here from the old country, gramps, running from the politics over there. Now, outta the goodness a' my heart I agreed take you in, but you gotta be a good boy, you hear me?"

Professor Merrynk picked up his glasses and wiped them off on his shirt. "Mister Mack, I cannot work under these conditions!"

"You'll do like I tell ya, pal! You're gonna keep doing your messerschmidt mumbo-jumbo!"

Merrynk nodded as he stood to his feet. "It's called Mesmerism, you ignoramus, and it takes years to perfect." His finger danced in the air to illustrate his point. "You treat it as if any simpleton can perform it!"

"Yeah?" Mack replied. "You kin insult me any way ya want! You'd be best to do as I say, though. You know what's at stake for ya."

His shoulder's drooping, Merrynk examined the floor. "Yes, Mister Mack."

Mack laughed. "That's right, long hair! I got yer niece locked up in my dollhouse!"

Hatred seethed in his eyes as the professor looked up at Mack, but like a dog backed into a corner, his lips curled only slightly. "My Vanessa. Is she…?"

"She'll be jest fine, but only as long as you do what I say. She's a pretty girl, gramps, an' I'd hate to see her turned over to the guests at the dollhouse—they can be rough on pretty girls. Ya get my moll under control, an' ya get your niece back safe and sound."

The professor sighed as he stood up straight. He ran his fingers through his hair, pulling a few loose ones out with the action. "This is an abuse of my skills and my oath to the Mesmerists' Guild, but for the safety of my niece, I will do as you say."

Mack clapped his hands. "Good! Good!" He held his hands to his mouth and shouted toward the door. "Sonja, haul yer gorgeous gams in here!"

The woman who walked through the door carrying a cigarette smiled grimly. Betty Dale curled her lips as she blew smoke out the corner of her mouth. She wore a black dress and a black-and-white striped shirt. "Yeh, what do ya want, Mack?"

"It's time for yer etiquette lessons with the prof," Mack replied, flinging a thumb over his shoulder to indicate the aged man behind him.

"Ah geez, Mack—do I hafta?"

Mack took a cigar out of his pocket and lit it. "It makes ya a lady, cookie. Yer so much more polite than when I first metcha." Shiner gently patted her face with his rugged hand. "Do it for me, sweet-cheeks."

She pouted as she replied, "Okay, Mack—I'd do it for ya." She smiled as she flung her arms around his neck and kissed him roughly.

Mack smiled at the end of the kiss. "Thanks, doll." He moved to the door and opened it. "It'll do ya some good!"

When Mack was gone, Professor Merrynk moved toward Betty. "Hello, Sonja," he started, his eyes searching hers with a hypnotic stare. Her eyes began to glaze. "We will continue our lessons from yesterday." His fingers danced in the air in front of her eyes. Betty's lips fell apart. "You are not Betty Dale. You are Sonja Lace, a gun moll. You love Shiner Mack, and you are willing to kill for him. You are even willing to kill Secret Agent X."

Her eyes glazed, Betty nodded and affirmed the words. "I am Sonja Lace. I will kill for my love, Shiner Mack. I will kill Secret Agent X!"

Chapter Four
THE RAT-A-TAT RHYTHM OF JAZZ

Walking down the metal staircase leading to the Hurricane Lantern Club, Gerald Dake resisted the urge to plug his nose against the unsavory scents of decayed liquor and antique urine. Jazz music pounded through the night air of the squalid neighborhood, as hoots and howls livened the oppressive environ.

Holding each other up while they giggled, a black couple pushed past Gerald as he continued his descent. His brown pinstripe suit befitted that of a young tough, and Gerald hoped he would not be called to prove up the appearance. He grunted a surly 'heya' through his unshaven face to live up to the part of a young man trying to make it in the mob. A ready hand at fighting, he still found it distasteful. It did not fit in with his mission here at any rate, and he planned to serve out the mission Secret Agent X made for him.

He opened the door and was assaulted with a mixture of various unidentified smokes. The volume of the music leapt as he walked into the dingy establishment. On the stage a band battered and winded their instruments with glee and skill. The upbeat jazz song was infectious, even to Gerald. His tastes generally went toward country music, but good music was his highest preference. This was as good as any.

The trombone player just began an impressive solo on his instrument. Gerald resisted the urge to let himself do anything to indicate he enjoyed the music, as it wasn't befitting a young thug like himself. The Hurricane Lantern was truly a melting pot; with a variety of people from many races and origins enjoying a variety of vices—many of questionable legality.

"You are Sonja Lace, a gun moll."

Everyone who was anyone in gangland might walk in and strike up a conversation about a crime to come or a crime already done. It wouldn't do for anyone to strike up such a conversation with him. Luckily, he wasn't pretending to be anyone in particular, and Gerald had seen enough Edgar G. Robinson films and dealt with enough street banter to be a passable-if-generic street kid looking for an in.

Gerald walked over to the bar and ordered a whiskey on the rocks. A man calling himself 'Hush' had contacted him with orders from Agent X. Carrying all the earmarks of a tough and dangerous gangster, Hush made Gerald extremely uncomfortable during his visit. He said he owed X a debt, and paid part of it with the delivery. X had to keep all his regular contacts out of this as there was reason to believe they might be recognized. Hush informed Gerald he was to be the sole operative on the case. New to the agent game, Gerald could pass with simple make-up and not be spotted.

Hush told Gerald to be on the lookout for Betty Dale, although he surveyed the establishment and decided Betty wouldn't be caught dead in such a sleazy dive. He slugged back his whiskey shot, resisting the urge to cough, and thought he never expected to be hanging out in such a seedy establishment. He shuddered internally as he decided if he were discovered by these gangsters, he would be caught dead—literally.

Despite himself, Gerald flinched when he felt a large hand rest heavily on his shoulder. "What are you doing here?"

Gerald turned around to greet the lined features of police detective John Burks. "The kid from the museum, right?" Gerald's heart sank as Burks might well have blown his cover. "Hey kid, you don't want to mix with these types, you know? They're here looking for trouble. Is that what you're here for? Because if you are, I've got some trouble in the pocket of my jacket."

Standing to his feet, Gerald thrust his jaw out in challenge to the aging policeman. "Look here copper," Gerald said in his best gangster voice, "I ain't doin' nothin' wrong, see? You gonna arrest me for somethin' or not?" He had to stay convincing if he hoped to maintain some cover. His voice sounded like he was copying gangster films, which fit in well for a young kid trying to become a 'made man'.

Burks moved back slightly at the response. He was more surprised than afraid, although giving ground went against his training as a policeman and it surprised him even more. "Whoa, there son! I'm just trying to give you some friendly advice before you end up on the wrong side of the law! I hope you're not mixed up with that X criminal."

"What of it?" Gerald retorted. "It's my business, and none of yours if I go in with a partner or not!"

Burks opened his curled lips to inform Gerald of something, but he was interrupted. "All right, ya louses!" shouted the woman's voice. Burks and Gerald both dropped their lower jaws involuntarily as they turned to see Betty Dale, wearing a red dress that could scandalize an entire government. She carried a Thompson machine gun in her arms. "We're exterminatin' vermin today," she snarled, "so if ya ain't got six legs or a tail, ya'd better hit the floor or the door! Anybody goes for a gun, I'll know yer a rat!"

Panic began to trickle when she started talking, and when she stopped it flowed like heated mercury. People dived under tables and headed for the hidden exits left over from the days when the establishment was a speakeasy. The band members stopped playing and dove behind the inadequate shelter of the short bandstand.

"Miss Dale!" Burks shouted, holding up his hand. "Betty! Don't!"

Betty looked toward the bar, away from Burks and Gerald. "Don't know who ya think yer talkin' to, pal! I'm Sonja Lace!" she replied before opening fire on the bar.

Glass and liquid numbness decorated the air like a Christmas tree as the bartender found sense enough to hit the floor. Alcohol soaked a lamp broken by the gunshots and sparked into a brilliant red flame. Betty laughed as she began to slowly sweep the room, firing the gun wildly and causing chaos and destruction. The staccato sound of the bullets filled the air amidst incoherent shouts and screams.

Gerald took a quick survey of the room, scanning with his eyes the patrons leaping for cover. He glimpsed the bandstand being torn by bullets and pieces of wood flying around as the trombone player carefully and carelessly opened his trombone case to crouch behind it. Without thinking, Gerald rushed at Betty Dale, or Sonja Lace as she claimed, while she wasn't focused on him. He knew the trombone player would be killed if he didn't do something. His speed from playing football in school served him well, but Betty or Sonja or whoever caught a glimpse of him out of the corner of her eye and swung the gun around, a march of bullets leaving its nozzle in rapid succession. Gerald leapt from the path of the gun as boiling hot steel tore through the air. Gerald felt pain on his head momentarily, before falling to the ground to feel nothing at all.

On the now unattended bandstand, the trombone player retrieved a strange-looking rifle from his dented and tattered but intact bullet-proof trombone case. Decked in a tuxedo, Secret Agent X, disguised as the trombone player, pointed the odd weapon at Betty Dale.

Betty swung the weapon around to face this new assault, but a stream of orange gas permeated the air as X's face twisted beneath the makeup. "Stop this, Betty!"

Her arm went limp and dropped the machine gun to the floor. X began to move across the floor, stepping over the unconscious bodies of the patrons; the unwitting victims of the strange orange air.

X lunged toward the mesmerized Betty before finding an obstruction in his path. "I knew it was you, X!" Burks demanded. "You're the only one who uses those crazy gas guns! Luckily, I hold my breath when a machine gun's chattering like my ex! You're wanted for questioning about York's murder!"

X pushed the police officer aside as he continued his quest for the woman he loved. "Get out of my way, Burks!" The momentary interruption succeeded in stealing away the few seconds he'd had to retrieve her. The door leading to the street swung lazily in the smoke and haze. Rushing to the door, X heard the squealing tires of a sedan retreating from the scene. He knew he was too late, and that the well-being of his agent must be attended to. He knelt down next to Gerald. A bullet had grazed the young man's temple.

X shook Gerald as Burks looked on. "I don't know how you did it, X, but you're not gonna get away with destroying Betty Dale!" Burks pulled his revolver and aimed it at X. "Once you've made sure the kid's okay, I'm taking you in on a murder charge!"

Chapter Five
DEATH IN A DeSOTO

Gerald coughed and X smiled grimly. The young man would be fine. Burks waved his gun to remind the agent of his predicament. X put his hands up as Inspector Clyde Niehart walked brashly through the front door. "Who ya got here, Burks?" he smiled.

In a split second, X pulled on Niehart's collar. "Whoa!" Niehart offered his surprised protest as he involuntarily lunged into Burks. Both men fell to the ground.

"Get off me, you dunce!" Burks pushed Niehart off his chest and leapt to his feet. Swinging his gun around the room, Burks hissed. X had pulled his disappearing act once again. "Damn you, Niehart! Don't you have littering citations to dole out somewhere? That was X, and I had him in the palm of my good hand!"

"That was X?" Niehart chuckled deprecatingly. "I didn't know he was a colored man!"

"Shut up, Niehart," Burks said in a tired voice. He holstered his pistol. "That was a disguise, you imbecile. You screwed up a bunch of work for me! I was gonna take X in for York's murder!"

"Yeah," Niehart nodded as he took an open whiskey bottle off a nearby table and helped himself to a long, stiff drink. "He sure did a number on York, didn't he?"

Shaking his head, Burks replied, "No, he didn't. I don't know what game he's playing with Miss Dale, but he didn't kill York."

"You said you were gonna hang it on him!" Niehart protested.

Burks leaned over to see how Gerald was recovering. "No. He's innocent of it, I'm sure of that. He's got some other racket going on here, and I can use a murder charge to hold him until I figure out what he's really up to. But I'm not sending a man upriver, even a man guilty of the crimes X has committed, for the one crime he never did. I did some investigating, and I'm close to figuring out who offed York. I can pin something on the secret agent with my X files, if only I can hold him in the slammer for a couple of hours."

"Is that so?" Niehart drank down the last swallow of the whiskey. "Think yer gonna figure out who killed York?" The empty bottle pulled Niehart's hand into the air and then down again.

Gerald shouted, "Look out!" It was to no avail. The bottle broke over Burks' head, scattering glass and liquid everywhere. Burks slumped unconscious over Gerald. Blood poured from his head as Gerald looked on incredulously. "It's too late for ya to figure out now, Burks. You and I, we're going for a ride."

Niehart pulled a pistol out of his pocket and aimed it at Gerald. "Hey, ya brush ape, ya look a real strong farmer in the dell. Carry this chunk of bull-roast outside. No funny stuff or I'll tell ya a joke that'll keep ya in stitches for the rest of yer short life."

Gerald pushed off the unconscious officer and warily slung him over his shoulder. His head hurt like someone had hit him with a baseball bat, but he did not complain as he carried Burks' unconscious form out the back door, driven forward by the occasional painful prod of Niehart's gun in his ribs.

✪✪✪

Florsheim shoes slapped the wet asphalt as Agent X watched the car carrying the mesmerized Betty tear down the street while he ran. Even at the distance, he could identify the De Soto sedan swimming through the streets.

The rain poured in torrents reminiscent of Niagara Falls as the agent rushed to his car; a sleek, Stutz Bearcat resting on the other side of the street. A car antiquated in its appearance, it still had plenty of power and was not likely to be disturbed in this rough part of town.

Wiping the water from his disguised face, he got into the car. As soon as the powerful V-8 engine roared to life, the tires spit mud and water into the air as the Bearcat floated over the rain-drenched asphalt in pursuit.

Switching gears with the celerity of a race car driver, X pressed the Stutz onward, turning the corners with dangerous speed as he followed the sedan. Although starting out far behind the sedan, the Bearcat quickly closed the distance.

Shiner Mack offered a look of surprise as he and mind-controlled Betty Dale glanced over at the Bearcat pulling up next to them. Mack sneered angrily at the other driver and stepped on the gas. He would have driven faster if he knew there would be someone following them so quickly. "What's this colored guy think he's doin'?" Mack grunted. "I don't know what his game is, but I'm gonna ante-up and see what the stakes are!"

Shiner steered the De Soto over to try to hit the pursuing car. Although the tires on the De Soto were wider and offered more contact to the ground, the Bearcat's thinner tires sliced through the ever-deepening rain water. With lightning-fast reflexes, X easily steered out of the way of the sedan as he slowed his vehicle, leaving Shiner struggling to recover the De Soto's unobstructed path.

"What the hell!" Shiner exclaimed. "That guy can drive! He musta been on the dirt-circuit to drive like that. Sonja, doll; cut the man a piece of cheese!"

Betty Dale grinned wickedly through her artificially-induced stupor. "I dropped my machine gun back at the hole, sweetie."

Shiner gritted his teeth. "Don't call me sweetie! Ya think I only carry one Tommy gun with me? There's one behind the seat."

Sonja reached back, grinning with delight as her fingers wrapped around the cold steel barrel of the Thompson and pulled it out. She held it in her hands for a moment, lovingly checking out its sleek lines. She aimed it out the rear window of the De Soto.

"What're you doin'!?" Shiner demanded. "Roll down the window!"

"I'm not gonna ruin my hair," Sonja replied. "You know how long it takes me to look this good?" Laughing strangely, she pulled the trigger. The flashes of rapid gunfire lit up her face and accented the shadows as she giggled herself hoarse. The bullets shattered the rear window and littered the street with the death conveyed by tiny bits of burning metal. Fountains of water thrust through the air, indicating the points of impact.

The Bearcat continued under the onslaught. Bullets bounced off its grill and windshield. Sonja stopped firing. Her brow furrowed as a frown crossed her face. "Dammit, Mack—it's a regular armored car!"

Shiner Mack smiled. "Hell, that ain't no colored guy! It's Secret Agent X! Now, we've got him. Ya just fed him dinner, now offer him some dessert! Open up some a' them Jam-Tins behind the seat and spread some a' that sweet flavor on his toast!"

Sonja's lips curled into a wicked grin as she reached back and pulled out one of the British-produced, double cylinder Jam-Tin grenades from the Great War. She held onto the slender cylinder at the bottom of the device and gave it a flick of her wrist. The thicker grenade cylinder broke off and tumbled out the back window, leaving the stick-like cylinder in her hand. She shrieked with glee as the grenade exploded beneath the Bearcat and lifted it off the ground. Momentum and lack of traction caused the Stutz-engineered vehicle to reel out of control when it again struck the ground. On the passenger's side, the wheel broke off with a horrendous screech of protest. The Bearcat slid sideways despite the best efforts of its driver, and began to tumble about. It crashed into an electrical pole and caused it to fall over, live wires dancing against the rain. The vehicle exploded in a ball of flame to punctuate the disastrous events.

"That's the end of him!" Shiner Mack assured. "Ya killed Secret Agent X, sweetcakes! Now I get paid, and how!" He pulled out a gun and held it on Sonja. "An' it ain't just X who's gettin' a classy funeral. It's the end a' the line for you too, sister!"

Sonja's eyes widened. "But, Mack," she pleaded, "I thought you loved me!"

"You're fowled-up in the head, doll," Mack replied. "You'd have to be nuts to fire a Tommy inside a rolling tin can like this. My ears are still ringing like the bells of Saint Martins! That hipnotick stuff sure put a screw through your brain, but I think you hadta have some killer instinct in ya already ta get this fouled." He shook his head. "Thought maybe I could keep you around for fun, but yer too much of a spitfire for decorative purposes. Now that X is dead, I don' need ya for bait anymore, neither. I'm figurin' yer family will pay a ransom, but I don't need you alive for that. I'm gonna take ya back to the hideout an' tie ya up until I figure out how to get rid of ya."

Sonja pursed her lips. "Like hell ya are!" She brought the cylindrical stick portion of the grenade up and with incredible speed struck Shiner Mack over the head.

Shiner didn't expect the motion and fired on instinct before passing out. Sonja grabbed her left chest where the bullet struck her, trying to staunch the bleeding. In shock, she grabbed the machine gun and stepped out of the car. The rain poured over her as she stumbled directionless down the road past the burning Bearcat. She looked over at the burning vehicle, and felt a twinge of remorse. She'd killed Agent X like Shiner Mack said? Why should she care, anyway? He was just another bull in a different uniform, but she felt like he was something more to her. She just couldn't understand what.

Sonja tried to continue her walk, but the pain from the gunshot was too much for her. The street spun like a top while Sonja realized that she really was Betty Dale. She screamed in frustration before passing out in the thick water lining the street.

Cold mist wakened Secret Agent X. His breath came in white puffs as he opened his eyes. He lay on his side in a few inches of rainwater, pain shooting through his ribs. He looked out the cracked, bulletproof windshield at the battered hood of the Bearcat. Weakening flames struggled against the pounding rain. Only the freezing fire-retardant chemical sprayed into the vehicle from spray hoses installed around the interior of the car saved him in the inferno, and only the reinforced frame kept him from being crushed in twisted metal during the crash.

Coughing and spitting out blood, X tried to stand. Ignoring the pain from the lacerations and cracked bones, X pulled away his frozen mask. The oxygen in the cab was sour, and he needed to breath. He tried the door handle, coughing up more blood. No good. The door stuck fast. He searched the floor of the wrecked car. Finding a tire-iron, he used it on the distorted door. With some great effort and a few precious moments of breathing in noxious fumes, he finally pried the door open. Flashing lights of a fire-truck appeared far down the street. When the firefighters arrived, they found the wrecked and burning Stutz Bearcat curiously unoccupied.

Chapter Six
THE BITTER SCENT

The smell of hot coffee caressed her nostrils as Betty Dale awoke, no longer Sonja Lace. She remembered her entire disgusting ordeal with Shiner Mack and hoped she hadn't hurt anyone while under Merrynk's spell. A man she had never seen before stood over her drinking a steaming cup of coffee. A single light bulb struggled to stay alive as it grew brighter and dimmer at regular intervals. Surveying the rest of her surroundings, she discovered Detective Burks, a slightly-disguised Gerald Dake, the hypnotic Svengali named Merrynk, and Shiner Mack all tied up with rope next to her. The wound in her side throbbed, but the blood had dried on her dress and seemed to suggest the injury was not life-threatening.

Crates and other ephemera consistent with a warehouse setting rested around them. Beyond that an impenetrable darkness hung in the air. The fingernail sliver of a moon peeked through a high window, providing supporting light for the bulb.

"What's going on?" she demanded of the only unfettered man present. "Who are the hell are you?"

"Niehart," Burks spat. "You bastard! What the hell are you up to?"

"Yeah," Shiner Mack nodded. "What's the game, Clyde?"

Smiling sinisterly, Niehart took a sip of coffee. "Yes, of all of you who know me, you all know me as Inspector Clyde Niehart. I will tell you the entire story since your stories are soon to end, but first…" Clyde Niehart pulled out a long revolver and pointed it at Shiner.

Shiner's eyes widened. "No, don't" The exploding sound of the gunshot punctuated the sentence. Betty let out an involuntary scream as Shiner's brains portrayed an imitation of Van Gogh brushstrokes against the concrete wall and splattered across her dress. Shiner's body slumped forward, his broken skull cracking open with a sickening sound against the floor and relieving itself of a portion of its contents. A tear came from the corner of Betty's eye and she felt a river of the gangster's blood on her hands where they were tied behind her back. Even after everything Shiner put her through, she felt compassion for him.

Niehart wiped his hand with his kerchief where coffee spilled from the gun recoil and wiped his face where Shiner Mack's blood splattered across it. "Shiner Mack was always curious to know everything," Niehart explained. He took a sip of coffee. "I did not want him to know what I have been doing. It is just a spiteful bit of ill-humor on my part. That is why it became necessary to excuse him from the room."

The aroma of coffee and blood sickened Betty. She did not allow it to display on her face. Her expression remained stoical as she looked up at Niehart. "You didn't have to murder him, you know."

Niehart's smile strained the limits of his face. "You are right, Miss Dale. I did not have to kill Shiner Mack." He walked past his captives, examining their faces. "A show of hands now—who is sorry he is dead?" He took another sip of his coffee before throwing the cup at Shiner's broken skull and shattering them both. The black liquid mixed with the bright red blood. "It has gotten cold." Niehart commented. He looked down at Shiner's remains. "Nobody will raise a hand in your defense, Shiner? That is not a very complimentary eulogy. I do recognize that it is unfair since their hands are tied. Still, I doubt the sentiment would be much improved if unfettered."

"You're nuttier than a fruitcake, Clyde," Burks said. "What was your beef with Shiner Mack anyway?"

Niehart clapped his hands together. "I am so very glad you asked. You see, my name is not really Clyde Niehart. It is Arthur Kahller."

"Kahller?" Burks interrupted. "A blue-blood aren't you? From upstate? Didn't your brother use to run with the gangs as 'Cuts' Kahller?"

Niehart nodded. "Yes, my brother Charles had a taste for criminal adventures and low-class females. He worked hard to become a made-man. It proved his downfall when his own boss, Shiner Mack, crossed him and put him in the path of the individual known as Secret Agent X. While running from X, Charles befell a fate befitting a cheap crook. He was not, however. He was a well-bred victim of grievous error."

Betty's eyebrow rose slightly. "So, you're back for revenge?"

Niehart nodded. "Very Plebian, I know. It might have been beneath me altogether, except I intend to take over Shiner Mack's operations. Then I will begin a bloodbath in this town that nobody will forget. As people, gangsters are more ruthless than intelligent. I am a genius, and I say so with not an ounce of vain glory. I killed Bobby Gallager and placed his car in the bay." He turned to Burks. "I did not anticipate that you would side with your long-time enemy and obsession Agent X." Niehart turned his back on the captives. "Still, it was a mere setback for my plan. I have another plan to keep the police busy while I start a succession of gangland killings that will make Custer's Last Stand look like a Sunday picnic custard pie fight."

"How are you going to keep the law busy?" Burks asked.

Niehart smiled. "Simple. The unsolved murder of a police detective will engage the police force to a far greater degree than another of your Agent X snipe hunts. I am certain you will be missed, John. Your comrades will not leave your death unavenged."

Burks nodded grimly. "Yeah, but with these others it'll be a massacre. Me, they'll investigate. All of us will bring so much heat down that you won't be able to spit on the sidewalk in this burg!"

"Absolutely," Niehart replied. "I have arranged for the others. It is no massacre if they are not discovered. Disappearances happen every day." He waved his pistol at Burks. "Get up. We are going to take a pleasant ride."

"What are you going to do with us?" Betty demanded.

Niehart looked over his shoulder. "Oh, don't worry about that," he grinned. Three gangsters in long coats carrying machine guns appeared out of the darkness. Tilted fedoras obscured much of their faces. "These gentlemen will take care of you." He turned to the three thugs. "You remember the agreement, don't you? Give me a five count to get away from the scene before you start the fireworks display."

Niehart pushed Burks as they headed toward the door. The captives looked at each other as they heard the car start outside. They only had minutes to live.

Faced with impending death, Betty Dale shook her head. "Hey, ya yegg," she sneered at the nearest gunsel, "I kilt ya the udder night, din't I?"

The man kept silent beneath his fedora. Betty, the stress having caused the return of her Sonja persona, nodded. "Yeah, sure! Yer Hush, aincha? Can't believe I missed ya, ya two-bit yegg!" Her lips twisted. "Better make damn sure ya get me, kid. Ya won't get annuder chance!" Her expression changed again, this time to a quizzical look. "Can't figure why Clyde'd hire ya, though, when he musta wanted ya dead. Else Shiner wouldn't had me try ta kill ya."

It was enough to cause the other two gunmen to examine the man known as Hush. Hush glanced over at them. "Don't lissen ta her," he growled. "She knows damn well that it was X she tried ta kill, pretendin' ta be me. Youse guys have been in the racket long enough ta know X can look like yer mudder an' ya'd eat his homemade apple pie. Niehart sprung me from the pen ta bring me down so he could have some muscle to play against this X guy."

Paulie 'Lancer' Lancione chewed on a toothpick between his thick lips as he brought his machine gun to bear on Hush. The handsome and thin Vickie 'Sheik' Valerio followed suit. "Lookit, Hush, we ain't takin' no chances, see? Me an' Sheik came along for the ride, an' we jest figured you was playin' ball. Mebbe Niehart thought yew was too. Ain't worth yer life ta guess."

Hush looked sidelong at Sheik and Lancer. "Youse guys'd better lay down yer joybuzzers before ya make a mistake bigger than yer mouths. I got more friends than God."

"Yeah?" Sheik replied. "God's the only friend a dead guy like youse needs!"

Pulling back the trigger, Lancer opened fire. Hush dived behind a pile of bricks as the machine gun chewed up the red clay like a petulant toddler eating cake. Sheik joined in with his own Tommy Gun. In a few moments, the guns fell silent again, emptied of their bullets.

"I think ya got 'em," Sheik whispered. Then, with a little more bravado, he allowed a smile. "Nah—I think I got 'em!"

Suddenly, Hush's voice came from behind the pile of bricks. "Are you two lovebirds done yakkin'? Hope ya brought more sparklers to the cakewalk."

Lancer dropped his Thompson and pushed his hand under the long coat he wore to pull out a pistol. Lancer danced under the hail of machine gun fire as he collected the bullets flying from Hush's gun. Sheik spent the time leaping behind another pile of bricks. Lancer's body hit the floor in an ever-widening pool of blood. The acrid smell of gun smoke filled the air.

Gritting his teeth, Sheik yelled, "You just messed up big, X! I ain't gonna let ya drop a white sheet over my head!"

"Talk ta Lancer 'bout that, pal. Ya bought yerself all the blood an' sand you can carry on yer camel this time, Sheik. Nobody gets the drop on Hush!" Hush licked his lips. "I got a bucket full a' red paint I'll coat yer pyramid with!"

"Yeah?" Sheik replied as he leapt from behind the bricks with his reloaded machine gun. "How 'bout I play yer funeral march while you're whistlin' that tune, Hush?" Once again, the staccato rhythm of machine gun fire reverberated through the air as Sheik smiled broadly. Ricocheting bullets offered dangerous shrapnel as the pile of bricks diminished under the fire. "Them apples red enough for ya?"

Turning to head back before Hush could respond, Sheik broadened his eyes in surprise. "Hush," was the last thing he heard as the butt of Hush's Thompson smashed his face in. Hush stood over him and examined Sheik's broken and bloody face. "Yeah," he nodded. "Ya don't look so much like Valentino now, do you; ya candy leg?"

Hush stepped over the unconscious Sheik to a position where he could see the captives all tied up. "Bet you were hopin'," he said, "that I really was Agent X." He laughed. "Well, I ain't, an' your time's gonna be movin' as fast as my pal Tommy's bullets." He patted the barrel of his machine gun when he said this.

"How ya gonna dump all our bodies, Hush?" Sonja asked. "There's a bunch of us here."

"You could give me an hour in a graveyard," Hush boasted, "and you couldn't find a mole's corpse. Getting rid of the bodies is easier than Tiddly Winks for me."

"Yeah?" Sonja replied as she aimed a pistol, ostensibly Shiner Mack's, at Hush. Her hands were covered in blood and torn raw from where she used the liquid as a lubricant to slip her thin hands between the ropes holding them. "Let's see if yer hands work as fast as yer mouth!"

Hush wasted no time, but brought his Thompson to bear. Sonja's gun exploded and the bullet struck Hush's hand. He cursed and involuntarily dropped his gun to the ground.

"Good thing for ya dat I'm a lady, Hush. Never could stomach killin'."

"Dammit!" Hush howled as he held his injured hand under his arm. "Ya crazy dame!"

Sonja responded by shooting Hush in the left knee, causing the gangster to defy his nickname with a loud grunt as he fell to the ground. She sneered at his pain and kicked the machine gun away. "Geez, Hush—doncha ever shaddup? Yer whinin' like a little girl!"

"Good work, Betty!" a voice of acclamation sounded. Burks coughed a bit as he walked into the dim light. "You caught Secret Agent X. Now he'll pay for his crimes!"

He began to draw his gun, but Sonja raised her pistol at his chest. "I tol' ya before I ain't Betty, copper. Yer gonna realize ya got no reason for ticker tape parades. Drop yer heat."

Seeing no alternative, Burks dropped his pistol. It rattled over the concrete. Sonja sneered. "What'd ya do with Niehart? Figured that simpleton couldn't handle even an old bull like you."

Burks nodded. "Yeah, Niehart could've had me dead to rights. Gas came out of the keyhole when he started the car. Must've been X's doing, because he's the mad gasser in this burg. Anyway, I've seen that trick before, so I held my breath while Niehart went cold. He's wearing cuffs in his sedan now, and the spark plugs are missing. Now, we should get all these people to safety."

Sonja shook her head. "Nobody's goin' anywhere." She waved the gun to indicate the other prisoners. "You get over there, Burks. It's come full circle for ya."

Burks held his hands up. "What're you going to do with us?" he asked as she cocked her head at Hush, indicating she expected him to go sit next to the others.

"I think ya know," Sonja replied. "I'm gonna kill all of ya. I'll go drop that Daddy Warbucks Niehart into the municipal bay swimmin' pool. Then, I'm takin' over Shiner Mack's operation. The blood will flow in this town just like my man wanted!" Sonja let out a ringing laugh that made the mesmerist of the group cringe visibly. The others did not show signs of fear, but perhaps it affected them all the same.

Hush gritted his teeth as he slowly pulled a cigarette from his shirt pocket. "Lissen, Doll. You can kill us all, but it ain't yer expertise to dispose of the bodies. I know ya shot me, but I don't carry grudges. Grudges get people killed, but if

I worked for ya, we'd mop this town up like janitors in a floor-wax factory." He nodded toward the now-distant machine gun. "I'll open up that metal beehive on these boneheads, an' you won't hafta worry 'bout breakin' any nails. What'da say?"

Sonja considered Hush's proposition for a moment before nodding. "Yeah, get up an' give me a hand."

Hush grimaced as he stood on his injured leg, still holding his hand under his arm. He stumbled over to the machine gun and picked it up. As he stood to his feet, using the machine gun as a crutch, he felt the barrel of a pistol press into the back of his neck. He felt Sonja's breath on his ear as she spoke lowly into it. "Ya can't swing around and shoot me, even with yer uncle Tommy ta help. Go ahead and blast 'em all. Then, I'll kill ya an' the bulls will believe I was protectin' myself from a brute like you. Pretty clever, doncha think?"

Sonja pressed her body against his, sending a mixture of sensations into his skin. He hadn't felt a woman's warm flesh in years, but the danger he faced was palpable. It was almost worth dying for to have a beautiful dame so close again, but Hush refused to give up on the life he hated so deeply. He pushed back hard and fast against her, driving her into a wooden crate. The crate smashed under their combined weight and they both crashed to the ground. Broken pottery and straw littered the area under the impact.

Without being able to hold onto the machine gun with one hand as it hit the concrete floor and twisted around his fingers, Hush scrambled to retrieve it. A woman's boot kicked it away, and Sonja pressed the gun into his cheek as he looked up in pain from his injuries and the aggravation of the same from the fall. "Thought I could trust ya, Hush. I like a quiet man, ya know." Sonja pressed her full, red lips against his as he melted in pain and pleasure. "I know a way ta make ya even quieter, though."

Sonja moved away before Hush could muster a reaction, the deadly gleaming tube of her pistol constantly aimed at his face. He coughed as he attempted to remain aware.

"Sorry, fella. Guess I'm gonna hafta kill you first." She cocked back the hammer right on the spot. Hush watched his death come to him as her finger pulled slowly at the strip of thin, black metal. He always wondered how he would face death, but he found himself quite ready for it as he stared down the gun's black tunnel, soon to be filled with an onrushing seed of metallic death.

"Betty! Stop!" A shout came out. Her finger relaxed on the trigger as she turned to see Sheik stand to his feet. She looked at him, bewildered. She half-heartedly denied the accusation. "I... I'm not Betty..."

Sheik nodded; his handsomeness still appealing beneath the smashed and bleeding face. "Yes," replied the smiling gangster with a voice not belonging to Sheik—a voice that only Betty would recognize as Secret Agent X's. "Yes, you are. You are Betty Dale, and Betty Dale is no murderer." Agent X, disguised as the gangster Sheik, walked cautiously toward Betty.

"Yer not Sheik," Betty protested as he came closer. She raised the gun to point at his stomach. "And I'm Sonja Lace!"

"Betty! Stop!"

Sheik moved closer despite the threat. He allowed the gun to press into his belly as he wrapped his hands around the back of her head and drew her closer. She sighed with resignation and hatred. "Yes, I am X. And no, you are not Sonja Lace. You are Betty Dale, the woman I love. The woman mesmerized to kill me, the man you love."

Sonja's finger tickled the trigger as X stared into her eyes with understanding. "Sonja, you know you are Betty Dale," he said. "You know you are not a murderer. I know you are not. Killing a man in cold blood will change who you are forever. I know as well as anyone, and better than most. Trust me."

A tear came out of Sonja's eye as she bit her bottom lip. A trickle of blood appeared at the point of her tooth. She said nothing, but let the gun drop to her side. He pulled her closer into an intimate embrace. She kissed the bleeding X on his disguised mouth, long and deep. After long moments, she pulled X into an embrace. "I love you, X!" she exclaimed in Betty Dale's softer voice. "I will always love you!" The tears now fell from her doe-eyes in torrents.

"I love you, too," he whispered.

"Ah geez!" the complaining sound of Hush's voice echoed through the warehouse. "Yer gonna kill me with this syrup!" X and Betty turned to observe Hush carrying the recovered machine gun threateningly. "I gotta shut down this Romeo and Juliet stuff before ya murder us all! Don't lissen ta him, doll." His eyes narrowed and his grin widened. "It ain't no big deal to kill a guy in cold blood. Even four guys an' a dame for that matter. I was hired ta kill Secret Agent X and all a' youse. I always finish a job. It's about integrity, doncha know."

X moved with incredible celerity as he pulled the pistol from Betty's hand. Hush pulled the machine gun's trigger, but a shot from the pistol rang out and struck his unwounded hand. The bullets sprayed the wall as Hush involuntarily let the weapon fall from his grasp. "Dammit!" he shouted in defeat.

"It's back to making license plates, Hush," X said as he handed the pistol back to Betty. "Keep him and Burks covered while I leave. First, I need to talk to Professor Merrynk."

Betty obeyed as Hush sat down to nurse his wounds. X picked up Burks' pistol and walked over to Gerald. He untied the youth and shook his hand. "You've done well, Gerald," he said as he handed the gun to Gerald. "Help Betty cover Burks and Hush while I attend to the professor."

X untied the professor, who stared dejectedly at the ground as he stood up. "If you're concerned about your niece," X informed him, "you needn't be. I took the liberty of liberating her from Shiner's 'dollhouse'. She's safe and under the protection of a very trustworthy gentleman." He meant Harvey Bates, but felt the information was not necessary. "She will be returned to you as soon as we are finished here. First, though, I need to ask you a favor."

Professor Merrynk's eyes lit up at the news of Vanessa's safety. "Oh, thank you kind sir! Anything I can do to pay you back I offer as service for the safe return of my Vanessa!"

Secret Agent X shook his head. "This is not extortion for your niece's safety,

Professor. You are free to refuse the request."

"I will gladly do as you ask for a friend!" the professor replied.

"Thank you." X looked at Burks, then to Hush. "I need you to ensure these two forget the conversation Betty and I had. Let Burks think he is responsible for capturing Hush and Niehart, and everyone will attest to that."

"Say," Burks protested, "you can't make me forget!"

The kindly-looking Professor Merrynk turned to Burks and caught the policeman's gaze. "Peace," he said simply as his eyes seemed to probe Burks' mind. Burks instantly fell into a trance and remained quiet.

Merrynk turned to Hush, and the gangster said, "Oh no you don't!"

"Hush," Merrynk replied softly, and the gangster rocked back and forth, his mind drifting peacefully. Merrynk turned back to Secret Agent X. "Your request will be accomplished before I leave," he assured. He took the agent's hand and shook it. "You have my undying gratitude and fealty, Agent X!"

X nodded. "I hoped you would say that. I feel you can be trusted to say nothing of what transpired today, and perhaps I can utilize your abilities in the future. If you would be so kind, however, to help Betty recover from the trauma she has been through, I would appreciate it."

Merrynk nodded before X turned once again to Betty. She looked deeply into his eyes as she smiled and said, "Some day we will be together, X. I feel it in my bones."

"You shouldn't have to wait," he protested. "You have been through a lot for me."

Her eyelids fluttered as he embraced her. "I'll go through ten times as much for the hope of our being together."

The pair kissed once more, holding each other in a gentle embrace. X felt the heat of her body against his and cursed his luck that they might never be together. He hoped she was right. The agent reluctantly released Betty and walked out of the warehouse, leaving behind the mayhem and his one true love until duty called upon him, the ever-lonely Secret Agent X, once more.

BETTY, COPPER

One of the pleasures as a writer is putting references to other material in the stories. In the story included in this volume, I wanted to feature Secret Agent X's girlfriend, Betty Dale. I wanted to take X into the gritty underworld of Edgar G. Robinson and James Cagney gangster films. I wanted to reflect some of the stark stories told in the celluloid pulps of the era; Film Noirs.

When creating Betty Dale's alter-ego, Sonja Lace, I went back to one of my favorite Film Noirs. In the 1946 film Detour, Ann Savage plays a wicked woman named Vera. Savage's performance in the film is riveting, and she delivers a character unrepentant and yet seems very much looking for a better path. She is immediately striking as a personality, and this is the personality I wanted from Sonja Lace. Although Betty is mesmerized for most of the story, Sonja is the 'dark side' of Betty's personality. If things had gone differently in the young heiress's life, she might have become exactly like Sonja. Perhaps there is a dark side in us all, and what defines us is how successful we are in controlling it.

As far as the aforementioned references go, some examples include a line where Betty says, '...I'm not Betty, copper.' Sort of a pun on Archie's persistent girlfriend, Betty Cooper. Merrynk, the mesmerist, finds his name from the author of the famous novel called The Golem, and the mention of Svengali refers to a famous mesmerist character from films and literature. These are the types of references which are fun and quickly get lost in a story, as I sincerely hope the reader does, on top of enjoying the humbly submitted yarn of murder, mayhem, and mind control.

KEVIN NOEL OLSON lives and writes in Butte, Montana with his wife, their cat, and their pug-dog. A Quixotic eccentric, Kevin spends much of his time tilting against windmills and taking daily constitutionals to the local coffee shop. Living as a caretaker in a large, spooky building, he collects personal ghost stories to impress his friends with and to keep him from sleeping at night. An avid film and book collector, he enjoys horror, sci-fi, and esoteric material. He loves silent films and books that speak to the reader.

Kevin has written for several magazines and on-line websites, including Secret Sanctum, Strange Worlds, and SilverBulletComicBooks.com. Recently, Cornerstone Book Publishers released his juvenile novel, Eerey Tocsin in the Cryptid Zoo, perhaps soon to be a major motion picture, and Entopia. Cornerstone also recently published a sci-fi farce entitled Buk Bakus in Darn Near the Fiftieth Century. Upcoming projects include, but are not limited to, The Obscured Archives of Richard Fortean comic serial, slated to run in the back of the Witch Hunter comic book (http://witchhuntercomic.com), a Springheeled Jack: Gunfighter graphic novel, and a sequel to Eerey Tocsin.

Graytown was a steel city. Situated in the heart of the Midwest, on the shores of a flat and sooty lake, the brown spires of the metropolis' foundries and factories continually sent forth clouds of dense black smoke, cloaking the sky in foggy obsidian. Below, grime-covered and sweating in the unending summer of the crucibles, strong burly men slammed and shaped metal into flat sheets, set to become the frames of the mighty machines their beloved country needed to stay the greatest on earth. These were rough-hewn men in these factories, men whom perhaps gentler, more scholarly figures would step across the street to avoid. But proud. Proud of the shedding of their sweat and sometimes blood, for it was they that kept the country going Proud that at the end of the day, exhausted and grubby, their faces and hands filthy and raw, they had helped keep America strong.

But that was then. Now, as had been for weeks, the rusty parapets of the dilapidated citadels were still, their flow of insubstantial midnight muted. Now were the deep orange flames of the crucibles, so intense it seemed as if they were the birthplace of new stars, extinguished as if never lighted. Graytown lay in silence, a chill, expectant silence, as the strong men whose grim determination helped mold hot steel instead waited huddling in their homes with their families, listening intently for yet never wanting to hear that one dreaded word spoken now above all others in the city: Plague!

Plague! Bubonic plague, the dreaded Black Death that had nearly wiped out Europe in the 15th Century! No one could guess how it had come. All they knew was it had started quietly enough, as over a period of days a few men in various foundries complained of not feeling well and asked for time off until they got better. But they never got better. They simply grew worse. And as they sickened, so too did more and more men, and then women and children. The factories began to have to do a full day's work with only a skeleton crew. The schools shut down. Entire families took to their beds as fever wracked their brains and their strength left them. Finally even the foundries had no choice but to stop work. There simply wasn't enough men to run them.

Simultaneously, people began to notice the coming of the rats. Only a few here and there at first, particularly bold rodents that had somehow made their way openly onto the factory floors or store backrooms. Pest control agents were summoned to deal with them accordingly. But then, slowly, for every one rat there were now two. Then three. Sometimes they would disappear for days at a time. But then even more would show up. Flocks would appear in the back alleys, swarming over the garbage cans looking for tidbits. The vermin began to appear in the schools, hissing at anyone who approached and trying to bite the children. None appeared afraid of human beings and many were the screams and poundings of the broom as one would scuttle its way across a kitchen floor, chittering yellow teeth at the shrieking mother trying to strike it. And as their numbers grew, so did that of the sick.

Finally no one could deny it anymore. Graytown was under siege! In desperation the town fathers declared a city-wide emergency, shutting all but the most necessary services down. Doctors—those who had not been struck down themselves— converged on the hospital, bringing their heads together for some idea on how to deal with the pandemic. National assistance was requested. And on just about every house and apartment building in town went the dreadful placard: QUARANTINE. A curfew was declared No one was allowed in or out of the city. And coroners prepared for a run the likes of which they had never seen before.

In a well-to-do district of the city, a meeting was being held. Unlike the neighborhoods of the working classes, this part had been little touched so far by the Black Fever, as it had come to be called. So in the comfortable home of Franklin Moss, owner of the largest foundry in Graytown, lights blazed as five of the most influential men in the city met to discuss their options.

A grave butler served the brandy in reserved silence as Moss lit his last cigar and sighed He was a large, florid man possessing a hard, determined face. As well he should Every cent he possessed he had earned twice over, for as a boy he had swept the soot from the floor of his own foundry. He had grit his teeth and saved his money, earning promotions and buying shares in the company bit by bit, until he had finally had the funds to purchase it outright from its previous owner. Under his leadership the foundry had expanded to three times its former size. He knew every bit of work his men did, for he had done it himself. As a result they loved him for his strength, and everything that happened to them concerned him personally. "So the state is saying what?"

Dr. Wilbur Scott, city councilman, shook his head. A painfully thin, unattractive man, he was more scarecrow than man. "The state is sympathetic, of course. Supplies of food and water are being rushed in as we speak. But their primary concern is to prevent the Black Fever from spreading further than Graytown. The entire town is to be considered closed until the Fever burns itself out."

"Impossible!" snapped Alvert Messington, owner of Graytown's second largest foundry. "We've barely recovered from the economic slump as it is! Do you know what would happen if Graytown closed down again? We'd lose millions!"

"Actually, I was thinking more of the men we're losing now," Moss shot back. "People are more important than profits, Messington. Nevertheless, I'm forced to agree. We all know America is bound to enter the European war sooner or later. If and when that happens, Graytown will be on the forefront of war production. If we cannot cure this plague soon, we shall lose hundreds of men. And damned few will come in to replace them, if we can't prove the Black Fever's gone for good! If only for the sake of the country's safety, something must be done! What about the Federal Government?"

"Unfortunately, much the same reaction," replied Robert Grohmann, mayor of Graytown. Older than the rest of the men in the room, he wore his silver hair and kindly face with dignity. "They have doctors working on the situation now. But aside from basic supplies, they're keeping everyone out. They don't want a national epidemic on their hands, and I can't say I blame them."

Tucked away in a corner, the last of the participants groaned. No one could say Tyrone Ebersol was a colorful man. He was small and pinched, gray as the lake the city bordered, and quiet. If you didn't already know he was there you could easily forget him. But beneath the bland exterior lay a first-class brain, which is why he served as lawyer for the entire city. 'So we're stuck, in other words," he said grimly. "The only thing we can do is wait it out."

"If such a thing is possible," said Moss, "But I'm not certain we can simply 'wait it out.'"

"What do you mean?"

Jabbing his cigar into an ashtray, Moss stood and regarded his audience grimly. "Gentlemen," he said, "I am not certain we're dealing with a natural plague. It is, in fact, my belief it has been intentionally introduced!

"Hear me out. We know Graytown has always had a problem with vermin; every industrial city does. But to this extent? Impossible. There are more rats in the lower city now than can be accounted for by any normal birthrate! Why, you can barely go outside without seeing families of them crossing the street! Our pest control officials exterminate literally hundreds every day but more keep appearing! This goes beyond any natural rise in numbers, gentlemen! These creatures are being deliberately introduced!"

"That's ridiculous!" Messington exploded with a gnash of teeth. "Why would anyone intentionally breed rats to release a plague? Why, not only that—it's not rats that carry the Black Fever, it's the fleas on the rats. Whoever's doing this would have to breed them too, and purposely infect them with the Fever!"

"I suggest that is precisely what someone is doing. As I said, Graytown will be the first line of any wartime production; what potential enemy of our country would not want to remove it from the scenario if he could? You could sabotage the foundries, of course—but buildings can always be rebuilt. But you cannot rebuild people. To slaughter those who work in those foundries—that may ultimately be a better means than mere explosions."

His four listeners regarded his theory thoughtfully. Then Mayor Grohmann released himself from his chair and put out his own cigar.

"A frightening thought, Franklin . Very frightening, and one I confess I never considered. If you're right and the Black Fever is being deliberately introduced into this city, then we are faced with an enemy the likes we have never seen before. But the State and Federal authorities are certain that this is simply some fluke of nature and will burn itself out soon. Your evidence, though strong, is still circumstantial. But... I will put the idea to the authorities I am in contact with. I doubt they will believe it, but it may give us some room for thought on how to deal with this. For the rest of us, I suggest we say goodnight The curfew is almost due, and I for one hate the idea to be found breaking my own laws." Hizzoner chuckled a bit but no one felt like joining in. They agreed to adjourn, and to meet the next night for more discussion. The butler helped each on with his coat, and the four dignitaries took their leave.

"Will there be anything else, Sir?" the butler asked as he gathered up the remains of the drinks.

"Hmm?" Moss, gazing out the window, was startled. "No—no, Tom. You may retire. I'll lock everything up."

"Then good night, Sir."

For a long time Franklin Moss sat in his favorite chair staring out the window. Against the black of night he could just make out the silhouette of his foundry's funnels. He recalled the first day he came to work there, alongside his father and grandfather. Messington and his contracts! Moss had contracts too, and stood to lose just as much from the Black Fever as he. But Moss knew of those who were losing much more—the wives and children of the workers who could only sit and watch as their husbands and fathers lay in bed dying. His theory was right, he was sure of it! If only he could find more evidence; could advance even the name of a suspect!

The telephone, sitting on a counter across the room, rang. With an irritated snort, Moss climbed out his seat to answer it. "Moss residence."

"You are entirely right with your premise, Franklin Moss." The voice on the line was hollow, sepulchral. Lacking even the barest modicum of human mercy. "Although not your motive. The Black Fever upon Graytown has indeed been intentionally introduced. By me. But I care nothing for war or what purpose this city would serve in one. I seek to destroy this city because it amuses me to do so! Still, it is time to let myself be known. You have already done so by advancing your theory to the proper authorities. Now must come a show to indicate how helplessly in my power your city is."

"W-what is this? Who are you? What do you want? Money?"

"I have no demands, Franklin Moss, save that this city be razed to the ground. That its people die like the rodents infesting it. As for my name—you may call me the Plague Doctor. I would wish you farewell, Mister Moss. You might have made a worthy enemy. But, alas, I must nip that possibility in the bud." With a sharp click the connection was canceled.

"Hello? Hello? Operator! Trace that call! I–" Franklin Moss stopped at the sound of the shrill squeak behind him.

The rat was waiting for him, beady red eyes peering up evilly. It was nearly as big as a cat. How it had gotten in Moss could not say—damn it, wait! He had not locked the front door yet! Someone had opened it and slipped the rodent in!

Moss remained very still, hardly daring to move. So did the rat. It seemed to be waiting for something. Slowly, very slowly, Franklin's Moss's hand carefully began moving toward a large paperweight. The rat hissed. Moss withdrew his hand hastily.

And then it came. The whistle. A strange, long and shrill sound, biting like fangs into Moss' spine. The rat pricked up its ears. Then, rising to all fours, as if obeisant to some telepathic command, it advanced, bounding the few feet between it and the human in moments, gripping the hem of his pants with tiny claws and scrabbling up his leg!

"No—no!" Moss screamed as he tried to wrench the wicked thing from his leg. But it sank its incisors deep into his hand, forcing him to let go, and started climbing up his arm instead. Like a demonic monkey it slipped up to his shoulder, even as a bloody hand went for it again, and this time buried its teeth into the tender flesh of Moss's neck. The human screamed as the jet of crimson fluid fountained from his veins and toppled backwards to the floor…

After a moment the rat paused, sniffed the body curiously as if inquiring why it was no longer moving. Then another of the peculiar whistles rang through the air, slower, lighter in tone than the first. The rat immediately dashed out of the room, back toward the front door of the fine house. Once there, it stopped. On silent hinges, the door opened—from outside, just enough for the rodent to pass through. It did so, and the door carefully closed again.

✹✹✹

The moon was but a dim crescent against the clouds. Across the fresh-tilled fields, the lone, haunting cry of an owl rang out. And, slumping down low in the seat with a cigarette hanging from his lips, PFC Dick Wilshire was bored stiff. It had been a dull night. Sentry duty always made him sleepy. But orders were orders, and every road leading into Graytown, no matter how remote, was to be guarded, lest the Black Fever extend further than the city's boundaries. And this road was damn remote. Just a bunch of scattered farms, with everyone snuggled safe in their beds. Except him. Oh, and Sam, his Army German Shepherd, who lay panting happily in the back of the sedan. Nothing ever bothered Sam. So when he heard the singing, PFC Wilshire snapped right to attention.

Wobbling unsteadily out of the darkness the bum came stumbling down the road, clothed in rags, two-day old beard filthy with grizzled hair and soup stains. His shapeless hat was plopped firmly over stringy white hair. But he seemed happy enough: the old-timer was bobbing along without a care in the world, grasping a wrapped bottle in his grubby hand and belting out Bing Crosby. Fans of the Crooner did not have anything to worry about.

PFC Wilshire hopped out of the sedan. "Hold up there, Gramps."

The bum paused, crooked yellow teeth into a grin. "Howdy-do, Son! Nice night, inn't it? Say, fine-lookin' dog ya got there." He reached out a friendly hand toward Sam, who sniffed at it curiously.

"Thanks, Pop, but you can't come down this road. Graytown's closed. "

"Closed?" The bum blinked. "Whatcha mean, closed? I'm lookin' fer work, and—"

"Just what I mean, closed. So just do yourself a favor and turn around, huh? I'm sure you can find a barn or something where you can sleep."

"Well…" The bum scratched his head. "I s'pose so. Ain't the first place I got run outta. But, say, boy—why don't you have a quick snort with me?" He held out his bottle. "Warm ya up on a night like this."

Wilshire frowned, gazing at the grimy flask. It didn't look like something he

The rat paused, sniffed the body curiously...

particularly wanted to drink out of. But, if it would get Grandpa on his way…
"Okay. Give." Wilshire twisted the cork and with a pop it came out of the neck. So did a strange, cloudy gas which curled up into the private's nostrils. PFC Dick Wilshire collapsed like a puppet.

Instantly two strong arms flew out to catch the soldier as he fell. Even as he did, the bum turned toward Sam, who was growling and bristling at the sight of his master's fall, and a peculiar, sharp whistle emitted from between his lips. Instantly, Sam's fur went down, and he wagged his tail, panting contentedly The bum scratched behind his ears. "That's it, boy. He isn't dead. Just asleep." Then, instructing the dog to stay, the bum gently dragged the unconscious solider to the side of the road and gently lay him upon the ground.

Then a most strange thing happened. From within his raggedy jacket, the bum removed a long, flat case. Opening it, he flipped on a tiny light to reveal a dozen miniscule packets of makeup, and all the equipment needed to apply it. The bum's hands went to his face and, astonishingly, began peeling off his features. The white wig gave way to thick, dark hair. The false bridge slipped out, revealing rows of perfect white teeth. In the moonlight the face of a man appeared every newspaper in the world would give its yearly profit to have a picture of. The face of Secret Agent X!

The Agent wasted no time in his task. First, he carefully examined PFC Wilshire's face, memorizing every detail. Then, bending low over the case, he applied such makeup to himself that he appeared an exact double of the soldier. A wig, packed in with others in a section beneath the makeup, provided the hair style. And lastly, a full exchange of clothes perfected the ensemble.

"You won't freeze," the Agent told the sleeping solider, now in his clothing, with a smile. "That's all thermal." Once again he patted Sam. "Why don't you stay here, boy, and look after your master? He'll wake up in a few hours." Obediently, Sam lay down next to his handler, thumping his tail. "Good boy." Moving to the Army sedan, Secret Agent X climbed in. Then he started it up and backed out into the road, vanishing up the gravel in moments. Up toward Graytown.

Captain Roger Anderson sat in his office tent, barely listening as his orderly went over what paperwork had to be signed where. Outside, the makeshift Army camp set some three miles outside Graytown, just one of a full dozen forming a perfect circle around the city, went on about its business of keeping all traffic out of—and inside—the city. But it was a grimly silent business, for all knew what it would mean if they failed in their attempt to keep the Black Fever from escaping its cordon. The death of the city! For Major Randall, the officer in command, had full orders to fire-bomb the city with planes if even the slightest case of the Fever should be found outside the city limits!

Personally, Anderson prayed it wouldn't come to that. The last thing he wanted was the blood of hundreds of thousands of American men, women and children on his hands. Thank God the final decision didn't rest with him. But if things continued the way they were going…

He glanced irkedly up as some commotion or other rustled outside his tent, then stood up as some private he didn't recognize pulled back the flap to make his way in. The private's hand flew up in a salute. Feeling a bit miffed at the interruption, Anderson automatically started to return the salute—then, for just a fraction of a second, his expression froze. Whipping around to his orderly, he barked: "Dismissed!"

The orderly blinked. "Sir?"

"Get out," the Captain snapped. The orderly hastened to obey, looking puzzled. He had not noted, as the Captain had, that as he had saluted, the forefinger of the private had just barely traced an 'x' over his forehead

"So. It's you.' Captain Anderson sank slowly into his chair "I thought you didn't really exist."

"I'm not sorry that you're wrong," smiled the Agent

"Ideally, I should arrest you," the Captain snapped. "Agent of the U.S. or no, as far as the public is concerned you're wanted for about every crime in the book. If I'm caught with you, it's my career. But my superiors were told by your superior that I had to work with you, so I'll do it—despite my better judgment. You're here for a debrief on the situation so far, I take it?"

"I am," the Agent replied, "And don't worry. My orders are specific. I'm to work alone in finding out who is spreading the Black Fever in Graytown. I only require such information as to get me updated, and then I'm on my own."

'So they do think it's intentional, then.'

The Agent nodded.

"I agree. What's the word on this possible cure?"

"So you heard, then." From his pocket, the Agent removed a small glass flask; not the flask he had used earlier. He set this on the table before the Captain. "What you're looking at is the only sample of a very theoretical, and very expensive, serum that might cure the Black Fever. Or at least prevent me from contracting it. Two days ago, Hazzard Laboratories received a strange telegram from an unknown source. It claimed that the Black Fever infesting Graytown was designed, and gave the formula it said may be the only possible antidote to the plague. Experts are even now trying to trace where this information came from. Whether it can cure the Fever or not is unknown; what is known is that, without more data, it is too expensive and risky to mass-produce. I have a radio; if by some chance the serum does keep the plague from affecting me, I am to contact Hazzard to begin mass-production immediately. If I do contract the Fever.–" The Agent shrugged.

Captain Anderson shuddered. "I don't envy you. All right. Nothing in the situation has changed, save one thing—Franklin Moss, one of the most influential men in the city, was killed this evening by, of all things, a rat. No, it doesn't make sense to us, either. But his butler found him after coming downstairs to investigate a strange whistling noise, and found Moss dead; his neck arteries pierced by what definitely was a rodent's bite."

Agent X frowned. "Interesting."

"Yes." Captain Anderson stood. "Personally, I hope you can get to the bottom of all this. Major Randall, the commanding officer, seems to believe the only way to prevent the Fever from spreading is to fire-bomb the whole damn city—and he'll do it, if something isn't done soon. Oh, he has full permission. All it would take is one massive outbreak, and–" He broke off, craning his neck toward the opening. "What on earth is going on out there?" The loud roar of approaching trucks were beginning to drown out his voice.

Soldiers milling about their fires glanced up as, from out of the darkness, two canvas-topped trucks suddenly pulled up to the edge of the camp, turned, and backed up to a stop. Immediately Uncle Sam's boys began to stand. Trucks coming to the camp were strictly scheduled; for any to arrive this late meant something was amiss. Captain Anderson and the Agent emerged from the tent.

From out of the cabs and the back of one of the trucks came men. But what men! All were masked, and each one was clutching a sub-machine gun in his arms! Instantly, the soldiers raised their weapons. The invaders did the same. For a moment electricity crackled silently in the air as each side waited for the first to move.

But then from the back of one truck emerged another figure. Like the other men, his face was hidden, but instead of a simple face mask, his head was entirely covered by a full black cowl. He bore no weapon in his hand, but the ramrod-straight back and the way the others stepped to the side to let him pass let everyone know he was the dominant figure of the group.

"Men of the United States Army," the hooded man suddenly spoke in a booming, yet strangely dead voice. "I am the Plague Doctor. It is I who has brought the Black Fever to this city. Therefore I say this, and I say this only once—leave here immediately. Graytown is mine, to do with as I see fit. There is no place for you in my city. If you do not go, and go now—I will not be responsible for the consequences."

"Consequences, hell!" Anderson was racing forward. "I don't know who you are, but nobody goes around telling the United States Army what to do! And if you're responsible for this plague, then by God, I'm going to–"

The Plague Doctor made no movement. "Very well," he stated calmly in his sepulchral voice and nodded to two of his men. Instantly they twisted about, yanking down the door to the carriage of the second truck.

It seemed to the Agent that a black cloud, more ebon than even the night around it, swirled within the body of the truck. Then it swarmed forward, out onto the grass! Rats! He gasped. Hundreds and hundreds of rats!

From the hood of the Plague Doctor same a strange, shrill whistle, like and yet unlike any the Agent had ever heard before. The ocean of rats darted forward, right for the waiting soldiers! Anderson screamed to fire and the harsh popping of rifles filled the night air but for every rat a bullet took down two more took its place. They swarmed, up and over each solider the could find, slicing their evil teeth deep into their flesh!

The Plague Doctor and his men calmly turned their backs on their enemies, reboarded the trucks. With a rumble the engines started and began pulling away. With the speed of light Agent X rammed himself across the camp, kicking away any rodent that tried to hop on him, making for the last truck in the line. Barely—just barely—his hand gripped the canvas body of the truck and he hung on for dear life. He might not be able to do anything to help the poor soldiers fighting off the vermin behind him, but he had to stop this truck!

It was only due to the cloth top, and the fantastic strength of the Agent, that he was able to hold on. As quickly as he dared, knowing the slightest slip would mean his life, he forced himself along the side of the moving vehicle, hand over hand, moving every closer to the cab.

Up front, the man in the passenger seat glanced out the rear-view mirror. "We've got company!" he snapped, reaching for a revolver. An awkward rifle would do him no good here. Opening the passenger side door, the gangster leaned out and glared up at the solid metal roof of the cab.

The Agent had climbed to the roof of the truck, clinging tightly as he made his way to the cab. The gangster clambered up after him. Just as the Agent reached the cold metal, the gangster fired. The shot went wild. Scrambling onto the roof, he grappled with the Agent, trying to throw the latter from the truck. Two men wrestled with the wind blowing violently against them, each knowing to fall would be to be caught under the heavy tires of the truck!

The Agent felt the sharp hole of the revolver barrel next to his chest, knew his masked foe's finger was tightening on the trigger. With a sudden thrust he managed to cast the gun down to the roof as the bullet went off—and suddenly the truck lurched wildly. The bullet had penetrated the thin metal, entering straight into the brain of the driver. Already the truck was veering uncontrollably. The Agent kicked out, and the gunman suddenly fell over the side. There was an awful crunch! as the wheels ran over his body. But the Agent wasn't safe yet, for even as he looked up he could see the fast-approaching side of a bridge. The truck was headed right for it!

In desperation the Agent leaped from the cab, as far as his powerful legs would carry him. At the same time he went absolutely limp, allowing his momentum to carry him as he rolled over and over again upon the hard pavement. With a roar of its engines that seemed like a scream, the truck broke through the metal railing of the bridge and plunged downward, exploding as its gas tanks ignited into a ball of flame!

After long moments, the Agent painfully rose to his feet. Fortunately there were no broken bones, but there would be many bruises. But at least he was better off than those poor wretches in the truck. Still, the Plague Doctor, the man he really wanted, had been in the first truck, and it was long gone by now. Nor was there any sense in returning to the camp—whatever happened there, Anderson would have to take care of it himself. With a grimace of pain, the Agent forced himself to walk. Two miles up the road, Graytown was waiting.

✪✪✪

Like an evil little tyrant on his throne, the rat crouched on top of the garbage can, tearing into a rancid, four-day-old ham it had found. In its wicked little mind, it had found heaven. For days now, the Big Ones had cowered behind locked doors and windows, ever since so many of its Kin had suddenly appeared in the streets. It knew not why—it had been born in this alley, and knew nothing of the Black Fever his cousins carried upon their backs—but was prepared to take advantage of the situation. Never before had it eaten so well. Never before had it had no fear of Big Ones with their sticks and traps to drive it away; never before had it had no predators, the stray dogs and cats of the city, to worry it. The latter had almost all fallen to the hunger of swarms of his brothers. Yes, this was paradise, and if they could, all its Kin would have agreed. But even the most mindless of them could sense something in the air; some taste of great expectation, impatiently waiting, yearning for the order. They knew not what it was, but they awaited it. It would come soon. It would come soon.

A sudden noise caused the rat to cock its beady eye. Down along the alley, a large shadow slipped furtively. The rodent instinctively tensed. But the shadow grimly ignored it, choosing instead to pass by silently. After a moment the rat returned to his meal. One lone human was no danger to it.

The shadow moved cautiously out of the alley onto the street. But not before looking every which way to make certain it hadn't been followed. Swiftly it stepped off the sidewalk, crossing the cracked asphalt in rapid strides. As it did, it stepped out of the dawn shadows long enough to slip through the violet rays of the just-rising sun. Its halo surrounded a middle-sized plain man in a tattered, cheap trenchcoat, possessing the curly dark hair and eyes of one of Italian descent. He was by no means handsome, but the features upon his face revealed at once an honest, hard-working personality. Yet his black eyes bore a look of utter desperation. Once on the other side he paused before a storefront. The painted words scrawled across the window were brief and to the point: WALLACE'S DRUGSTORE. A hand slipped into a trenchcoat pocket. It withdrew, clenching in its grasp a crumbly ochre brick The man took a deep, uncertain breath, as if trying to gain the strength for what it must do. Then he lobbed the brick straight at the clear glass.

The morning air rippled with the shattering echo but the vandal paid it no mind. He was too busy pounding at the remaining glass with a shoe, battering it away to seize upon the display of medicines on the counter. "Come on, come on." Rapidly he began placing any—all!—of the prescription bottles in his pockets. There had to be something here, he thought, something that can help save my–

"HEY! YOU!"

The man wheeled around. Slowly he drew his hands out of his pockets and raised them over his head. The gun the policeman was pointing at him left him little choice.

"P-please," he began nervously, darting a glance back at the broken window. "I'm no thief. My name's Al Vittoro. I know I'm breaking curfew. But my daughter—Stephanie. She has the Fever. She's dying. Please. I'm no rich man. I've got to find something to help her–"

"Shut up!" Something whirled before his face and suddenly there was a spurt of red upon his cheek. "Just shut up!" the cop roared again, pulling back the butt of his revolver for another blow. "Stinking foreigner! Think you matter more than a real American? Come to this country to take our jobs, and then think you can loot whenever you want? Probably brought the damn Fever with you! It never showed before you people started arriving!" The wild gleam in his eyes told the man called Al Vittoro all he needed to know. Perhaps, during better days, this would have been the most honest and law-abiding of policemen. One whom—under ordinary circumstances—would never dream of brutalizing even the most vile of criminals. But this was a city under siege. The law department was under pressure like never before. Here were looters everywhere, taking whatsoever they desired without thought for the law; here were policemen, running shifts up to eighteen hours a day without sleep. Many of them with families suffering from the Fever. Little wonder some policemen were beginning to crack under the strain. The butt came down again and smashed the would-be vandal across the forehead. Vittoro tumbled back, reeling, but dared make no move to defend himself. Sweat running down his face, in spite of the cool morning, the grimacing constable drew back, now pointing the barrel of the gun down at the prone figure. "Maybe I should just save the court the expense of a trial…" With wide eyes, Vittoro saw his nemesis' finger tighten on the trigger…

Then the cop's neck bent back with a choke as a white hand suddenly reached around and yanked it. Simultaneously, another knocked the gun away at an angle. The bullet tore through the concrete sidewalk, but not Vittoro's flesh. Indeed, he just had time to register the unremarkable features of a man reaching down to pull him to his feet as the latter hissed: "Come on! Run!"

He did. Together the two strangers raced through alleys and down empty streets, leaving the unconscious body of the policeman behind. Somewhere in the background they heard a siren wail. But neither stopped until they were a good ten blocks away from the scene.

"Mister," Vittoro panted gratefully, leaning over to catch his breath, "I don't know how to thank you. Another moment there, and I woulda been a goner."

The fellow in the nice suit and blandly handsome features didn't seem impressed. "Well, to begin with," he said, folding his arms, "you can tell me why you were breaking into that drugstore in the first place."

"My—my daughter. Stephanie. She's all I got left, and she's got the Fever. She—she was one of the first. She'll die if I don't do something. I thought—I thought maybe the drugstore… she's all I got left…" His voice trailed off. A tear gently began streaming down his face.

Secret Agent X regarded the man thoughtfully, putting his remarkable judgment of men into play. This was a good and honest citizen. It was desperation that had driven him to his crime, not evil. And perhaps this Al Vittoro was a heaven-sent help for him.

Because for once, the Agent was at a disadvantage in this case. For all his many aides, he had not dared send any to Graytown for fear they might catch the Fever. Nor was the city one in which he maintained one of his many headquarters—he had foolishly believed Chicago was near enough. That would have to be rectified.

"My name is A.J. Martin," he introduced himself. Once entering the city, he had divested himself of the identity of PFC Wilshire. A quick break-in of a men's clothier provided the appropriate suit, and the Agent had left money behind to pay. "I'm a reporter, investigating the Fever."

"A reporter? Then you're in a jam, too, Mister. Reporters aren't allowed in the city."

"Then perhaps we can help each other, Mr. Vittoro. I need a place to hide while I investigate this story. You need something that might cure your daughter. And I–" Carefully he withdrew the flask of experimental serum from his pocket. "I have something that may help. Are you interested?"

The Italian's eyes lit up at the sight. "Mister," he said, "In the name of Mother Mary, if that can help my Stephanie, I'll fight the Devil himself for you!"

✪✪✪

Al Vittoro was one of the many ironworkers in the city, living in a fifth-floor walkup near Graytown's heart. Not many blocks away stood, black and shrouded beneath the dawn's tepid light, lay the foundry owned by Alvert Messingham. Vittoro worked there. His wife had been dead for some years. And his daughter, Stephanie, was one of the prettiest little girls the Agent had ever seen. Yet she lay in her bed, perspiring, glands swelling, her sweet blond head wracked with pain. She didn't even seen aware her father was there.

"Please, Mr. Martin." Gently, Vittoro wiped his daughter's face with a damp rag. "She's all I got."

The Agent looked at him seriously. "You realize this serum is entirely experimental? That it may not help her at all?"

Vittoro nodded. "It's still more than the rest of the doctors here are doing. Go ahead."

With a grim face the Agent gently tipped the child's head back and lowered the bottle to her lips, forcing a bit of the thick, evil-smelling serum down her throat. Stephanie choked, but nevertheless automatically swallowed the bile. The Agent carefully rested her back upon the pillow.

"Now what?"

"Now we wait."

More than a hour passed. Vittoro made some coffee. Both men sat at the bedside of the little girl, intently watching. The clock ticked on relentlessly. Then, just as Vittoro felt it was all in vain, his daughter moaned softly and turned upon her side, sighing as if in relief. Instantly he felt her forehead. "The Fever," he breathed. "It's broken."

The Agent slumped back in his chair exhaustedly. But he smiled.

"Give her a warm bath and change her sheets," he suggested. "That'll make her feel even better. I'll be back momentarily." Silently, but triumphantly, he stole out of the room as Vittoro turned to his daughter's ablutions. It was some time before he came back in.

Al Vittoro looked up eagerly at the man he knew as A.J. Martin. "You work for Alvert Messington?" the latter asked again.

"Yeah," Vittoro's voice was bitter, and he suddenly spat. "Half the city does. The lucky half works for Moss."

"Messington's foundry isn't a good place to work then?"

"Hell, no. Fifth-rate equipment, no wages to speak of, and an accident at least every day. The government's told him to improve things a million times but he never does. He's too important to the city… and he knows it. If he closed, half the town would be out of work. Graytown can't afford that. The Mayor doesn't dare touch him."

"I see. Would you happen to know where he lives?"

'Sure. Biggest house in town."

"Give me the address. I think I'd like to pay a visit to Mr. Messington"

✪✪✪

The black, featureless car took its time, crawling slowly through little-used back streets, pulling over and the passengers ducking down whenever a police car showed itself. Beyond that, there was very little traffic in the city. Even so, with the delays it took more than an hour for it to pull up in a green, well-treed two-laned street, not far from a immense brick mansion looming majestically over the rest of the well-to-do neighborhood.

"You don't have to do this, Al," the Agent cautioned as he slipped out of the passenger side. "It could be dangerous."

"Mr. Martin, like I told ya," Al Vittoro softly shut his own door. "You helped save my Stephanie. So now, I'm gonna help you save my city."

Agent X could only smile; impressed with the man's courage. "All right. But keep down and do exactly what I do." Silent as a wraith, the Agent slipped into the dense shrubbery surrounding the high wall of the Messington estate. More noisily, but no less gamely, the ironworker followed.

With infinite patience, Agent X made a complete circuit of the wall, examining every inch. As he had expected, the top was criss-crossed with barbed wire, and every entrance was armed with motion detectors. He suspected guard dogs within the grounds, as well. Alvert Messington was obviously very paranoid when it came to thieves. Finally coming to a pause very near the main gate, which remained closed, he mused on the situation. He knew he could get into the estate easily enough; he had breached far more formidable edifices before. But Al Vittoro had no experience in these matters, and he instinctively knew his new ally would not be left behind. He could see no way they could both get in. The Agent was about to suggest they return to the car to plot a later attempt when he heard the noise of an approaching vehicle. Quickly he gestured to Vittoro to get down, and the two crouched low in the bushes, waiting.

An expensive gray sedan pulled up to the gate and a thin arm reached out to a console to punch the buzzer. After a second, a voice rang out of the speaker harshly. "What?"

"It's Scott, Messington."

"It's about time! Ebersol is already here. We're just waiting for Grohmann. I'll buzz you in."

With a shrill whrrrrr the iron gates parted automatically and the sedan rolled in. The gates clanged back shut almost immediately. The Agent tapped Vittoro. "That's our way in. We just wait a few minutes."

It was almost ten full minutes before the new car arrived. As its companion before, it came to a stop before the gates and Mayor Robert Grohmann reached out to tap the buzzer. As he did, the Agent jerked his head toward Vittoro. Now! Crouching so low they could not be seen from the rear-view window, the two men hastened nearly on hands and knees to the back fender of the car, clutching on with strong fingers Even as they did, they heard the gates swing open and Grohmann's car pulled ahead, down a long, black driveway to the mansion proper, where two other cars were parked waiting for it. The Agent allowed himself to be carried nearly one hundred yards down the drive before he dropped off the back fender and darted for the safety of nearby underbrush, followed immediately by Vittoro. Grohmann, entirely unaware of his unintended passengers, parked and stepped out of the car, to be met by Messington, who held the main door for him.

Agent X scanned the premises. From where he waited in the shrubbery up to the mansion there was little but green, well-kept grass. A window? Would take too long to open and undoubtedly would have alarms. The servant's entrance? A possibility... carefully the Agent fingered a small glass capsule in his pocket. This contained a very concentrated gas, developed and given to him by the owner of Hazzard Labs, which would harmlessly put to sleep any who breathed it for hours. That would certainly take care of any servants, but there was a problem—the gas would not work on animals.

For example, the two guard Dobermans snuffling boredly right outside the servants' entrance. Blocked from the wind by the building, they had not yet sensed the strangers on their master's lot. But it would not be long. He would have to take care of this now. "Stay here," he whispered to Vittoro. Then, before the Italian could protest, the Agent stepped directly out into the open before the dogs!

Two furry heads rose, four triangular ears pricked up in alarm. Growling low, the Dobermans crouched, showing wicked white teeth, then with snarls darted forward, barking furiously. The Agent remained where he was. He made no move. Pounding across the turf the dogs advanced, opening wide jaws meant to rend the Agent's flesh from his body and were just about to pounce when the Agent pursed his lips together. A queer, shrill yet strangely musical whistle emitted from them, the same peculiar sound he had used upon Sam, the soldier's dog. With the same result. Immediately, both Dobermans acted as if they had not been about to rip to shreds this man they had been running hell-bent toward. Ears came down, tails wagged, and two oversized puppies panted contentedly as the Agent smilingly scratched between their ears.

"Ho-how did you do that?" asked Vittoro, coming out of the brush.

Growling low, the Dobermans crouched, showing wicked white teeth...

The Agent smiled but said nothing. Al Vittoro would not have understood the years of study with so-called "primitive" peoples who lived freely among the wild beasts of jungle and desert, of the secrets they held in dealing with the creatures that lived among them. He would not have known the English Lord living in Africa the Agent had met under an assumed name, convincing him to teach him certain means of basic communication with animals the former had learned. Through these means, the Agent had mastered a whistle of a certain pitch that, while it could not directly control an animal, would allow it to instantly recognize the Agent as a friend. That, as well as certain special studies in the uses of sound and sonics…

The Agent's eyes went up. "Of course."

"What?" asked Vittoro.

The Agent shook his head. "Later. Let's get inside before we're seen." With a wave of the hand he dismissed the dogs, who pranced happily away. Moving to the door, the Agent listened for a moment for the sound of any movement. There was none. Swiftly but in complete silence he picked the lock, daring to creak it open just a bit. No one was waiting in the kitchen it lead to Motioning for Vittoro to follow, the Agent moved inside.

Outside the kitchen, the side hall proved as lacking in staff as had the kitchen. Alvert Messington must have had little use for expensive unnecessary help. "I always knew Messington was a sparrow," Vittoro muttered under his breath

The Agent looked at him.

"Cheap, cheap, cheap."

Agent X forsook groaning aloud, instead motioning for his companion to follow quietly. Like shadows across a lawn two figures slipped mutely down the carpeted corridor. At each door they came to, the Agent listened carefully, then moved on. It was near the final door that the Agent no longer had to eavesdrop, for the sound of Messington's raucous voice came to them.

"–require protection!" they heard the florid businessman snarl belligerently. "Who does this 'Plague Doctor' think he is, anyhow? I'm an important man, the most important man in this town! He wouldn't dare touch me!"

"He touched poor Moss right enough," someone said.

"Moss was a fool, Ebersol," Messington's voice was cold. "Besides, what proof do we really have the Plague Doctor was responsible? Yes, Moss was killed by a rat. But the city is crawling with vermin! How do we know one didn't just get hungry and attack him?"

"In his own home, Messington? Where the rats hadn't even been seen yet?"

"Oh, shut up, Scott. The man doesn't know who he's fooling with."

"And don't we all know it," another voice muttered just loud enough to be heard.

"What was that, Mr. Mayor?"

A long sigh. "We all know how important your foundry is to the economic health of this city, Messington. You never let us forget! That's the only reason the city council agreed to absolve you of any crimes when–"

"Oh, for god's sake, Grohmann! When are you going to let that go?"

Listening from behind the door, the Agent could nonetheless practically see the

Mayor of Graytown's face redden and he slowly rise to his feet. "One never forgets one's son, Mr. Messington," he practically spat through his teeth, "No matter how long it's been. Gentlemen, the rest of you must forgive me. I feel that my continued presence here would only be a deterrent. I ask you to excuse me. Perhaps later I'll be in a better mood to continue this discussion." There was the sound of heavy footfalls, and a door slammed.

"Well, that could have gone better," the voice of Ebersol said.

"Ebersol…"

"Gentlemen! Gentlemen!" The blunt voice of Dr. Scott interrupted. "This is getting us nowhere! Messington, I know you say you don't need protection, but I'm telling you I really feel we all ought to have the police–"

Brrrr-ing.

"Telephone," said Tyrone Ebersol unhelpfully.

"Obviously, you idiot. Pick it up!"

The Agent heard the click as Ebersol lifted the receiver and for a second all was quiet. Then Ebersol spoke, and even his voice was pale: "It—it's him. He… he wants me to put him on the speaker." There was the slightest of pauses, then the Agent tensed as he listened to the coffin-dark tones of the evil voice he had heard in the Army camp.

"Gentlemen." Cold and dead, the words boomed monotonously out of the tiny box. "It would seem that Moss's death has failed to teach you your lesson. You still persist in meeting in a pathetic attempt to thwart me. Rather you should have spent your time with your loved ones. Alas, it seems that is not to be."

"Who are you, you monster?" Ebersol roared toward the speaker.

The Plague Doctor gave no answer, continuing remorselessly in his hollow intonation. "All your attempts to stop me will come to naught, gentlemen. Moss discovered that. The Army discovered that. Graytown is about to be razed to the very ashes and not one of you will be able to prevent it. Not even that mysterious interferer you seem to have contacted. I am not certain who he is, but it matters little. He, too, will die like the rest of you. But for one of you, I have a very special punishment reserved. Oh, yes. As for the rest—I shall not say farewell. Merely—die like men."

The line went dead.

Just outside the door, Agent X and Vittoro waited with drawn breaths. The ironworker was just about to whisper to his companion if they should leave. But just as he was about to put his lips to the Agent's ear it seemed as though the entire mansion reverberated beneath the clanging noise of smashed metal even as they heard Ebersol suddenly cry: "THE GATES! THEY CRASHED THROUGH THE GATES!" and a hurricane explosion buffeted them from their feet while the very door was knocked from its hinges by the force of the blast. Agent X tumbled, rolled, and with the litheness of a leopard was back on his feet even as the plate-glass window of the room beyond was filled with the elephantine sight of a canvas-back truck, zooming up the manicured lawn at top speed to smash through, pelting them all with shards of glass and brick and metal!

Before the truck even came to a stop the doors were open; two masked men toting tommy-guns hopping out. Four other men poured out of the back of the trailer, all equally armed. The Agent waited no longer. Crying to Vittoro to stay down he leaped into the room, drawing his own, much smaller revolver. He knew it would hardly suffice against the more powerful weapons of his antagonists, but he could stand by no longer and let these men die!

Surprise was on the Agent's side and his first bullet met the forehead of one of the Plague Doctor's men and sent gray matter flying. Instantly three of the remaining men moved in front of the other two, returning fire. The Agent dropped to the floor, rolling behind a davenport. Ebersol was screaming, making for the door; someone fired but must have missed. He plunged past Vittoro as if he hadn't even seen him and was vanishing down the hall in an instant. The courageous little Italian paid him no mind. Despite the Agent's orders he burst into the room, sweeping up a vase in one hand and pitching its heavy base right toward one of the gunmen. His aim was true. Bone shards from a smashed temple pierced the brain, and the gunman fell, dead instantly.

But even while the lead flew, the two attackers behind the others were moving like well-oiled machines. Under cover of their companions, they made their way to Messington, who had taken cover cowering upon the carpet. A swift blow of a blackjack and the florid industrialist made no protest as they lifted him like a rag doll. Hastily they retreated back to the truck, tossing Messington into the back like an old sack. With him so close, the Agent did not dare shoot them. One yelled, and the gunmen suddenly pulled back, darting once again into the cab. With his companion providing covering fire the driver hopped backwards into the cab and pulled the truck into reverse. It groaned backwards out of the destroyed room back onto the lawn. The driver jammed the stick forward and before either man could move its wheels were tearing back down along the grounds, out the gate it had simply crashed through moments before. Messington had been kidnapped!

"That ain't good," muttered Vittoro simply.

"I thought I told you to stay down," snapped the Agent. Then, at the working man's hurt expression, he couldn't help but smile. "Never mind. You fought well." Swiftly he knelt by the two fallen gunmen and checked their pulses. Too late for either of them.

"Should we go after Grohmann or Ebersol?" asked Vittoro.

"No." The Agent shook their head. "Let them be. Messington is our primary concern now." But behind his seemingly calm exterior, the Agent's mind was a stew. Why should the Plague Doctor kidnap Messington when he could simply kill him like Moss? What was he planning when he said Graytown would be razed to the ground by morning? How would he do that?

A sudden groan interrupted his thoughts. "Scott," he said and led the way behind the davenport. Lying awkwardly on the floor behind, his chest a sea of red, the prone figure of Dr. Wilbur Scott gazed almost blankly up at them. It took the Agent only one look to see he could not help.

"G-gone?" the dying man managed to cough.

The Agent nodded. 'It's all right, old man. We'll get you to a hospital–"

"No—no. Don't… don't bother. Listen. Not much… time. I know… I know who he is."

"The Plague Doctor?" gasped Vittoro. "You know?"

Painfully the doctor nodded. "Always did. But couldn't tell anyone. Never… mind how. Take… too long to explain. But he… he had hold of me. Made me… made me develop the Black Fever for him."

"You?"

Coughing, the dying doctor nodded again. "Thesis was on… on variant strains of plague in the tropics. Knew all about them. He found out. Made me create it while he bred the rats and fleas. But managed—managed to secretly send out a possible cure…somewhere…"

"Hazzard Labs," the Agent breathed softly. "You were the one."

"Y-yes. Did it—did it work?"

"Yes, old man. It works perfectly."

For a moment Scott grinned. "G–good. Didn't want to do this. Didn't want to see my city… die…"

"But why?" the Agent demanded. "Why is he doing this? What's his plan?"

"Pl–plan is simple. Has thousands of rats just waiting in breeding dens beneath the city. Thousands. All with the Fever. Just waiting for his call. As for Messington, he–" Suddenly Scott gasped, a bit of blood spilling from his mouth. "Not only one he has hold of. Army major. Ga-gambling debts, I think. Promised me I'd survive… but I—I knew he lied. So sent out cure…" A fit of coughing spouted a geyser of blood. "Lu—Lucinda.." he managed to spit out. Then Dr. Wilbur Scott breathed no more.

"That damnable traitor!" sputtered Vittoro. "He created the Fever!"

"I agree, Al," the Agent quietly, "but he was still only a pawn. And don't forget he also sent out the cure for it. Whatever hold the Doctor had on him, however weak he was, in the end Scott still tried to get out of it. He still tried to put things right."

"Who's Lucinda? His wife, maybe?"

The Agent shook his head. "I doubt it. As I remember, Scott has always been a bachelor." Quickly he stood. "We should get out of here. The police will arrive any moment. I need to contact someone again. But in the meantime–"

"Yeah?" said Al eagerly.

The Agent smiled grimly. "I need you to set out a mousetrap to catch a rat."

Vittoro's jaw dropped incredulously. The Agent laughed.

"Oh, don't worry, Al. This is just the beginning. We'll need that rat to catch another kind of vermin. A very, very human kind of vermin."

Alvert Messington felt sick from the gentle rocking from beneath his blanket-less bunk and his arms and legs were stiff and sore. His head throbbed from the blow it had taken. He longed to get up, off this ridiculously tiny bunk he had spent the last few hours lying helplessly on; to stretch his cramped limbs until they cracked; but dared not do so. The rats would not have let him.

They waited patiently, like devilish guard dogs, two dozen or more, crouched on the floor of the small, windowless cabin, gazing up at him with red, hungry eyes. He could see the ribs clearly sticking out from their scruffy sides. Yet not one of them made a move toward him: they hissed, bared their sharp yellow fangs, but made no advance unless he attempted to put a foot off his bunk. A quick gurgle of hunger, and Messington hastily drew it back again.

He wondered if these verminous sentries carried the Black Fever. Somehow, he didn't think so. Something told him these wicked little creatures were to be used for something far more concrete than passing disease.

A creak of a door and a sudden breeze, and the scarlet light of the setting sun blinded his eyes as someone entered. Instinctively Messington turned his head and blinked; even as he did he could hear the stolid, measured footsteps of someone climbing down into the makeshift brig. He dared take a peek, peering through nearly shut eyes; the intense aura of the coming evening made the figure a shadow to him. The rats had all turned, silently, regarding their master.

But Messington knew that voice. He knew it all too well.

"Hello, Alvert. Welcome to the Lucinda. I don't believe you've ever been aboard before."

The Plague Doctor was still wearing his silken hood, but Messington knew who it was.

"You. Why?"

From beneath the hood, a pair of cold gray eyes suddenly blazed with rage. "You truly dare ask that? You dare? For thirteen years I've waited for this moment and you have the audacity to sit there and ask me what it's all about? You haven't forgotten, Messington. You could never forget."

Very slowly, a look of pained realization—and disbelief—dawned across the industrialist's face. "Darrin. Darrin Grohmann. After all these years—dammit, man, don't you remember the trial? I was completely absolved of wrongdoing!"

"Oh, yes." The Plague Doctor's voice took a bitter keen. "You were absolved. Because you knew the right palms to grease. And if you didn't, someone else did. Someone who knew just how necessary you were to keep this city alive. You were the second largest employer in Graytown—and the Depression was just about to begin. Never mind the shoddy equipment that could—and did—rip a man's arm off. A man who just happened to be gathering information to take to the authorities on substandard equipment and lax safety standards in your factory. And a man who just, somehow, happened not to get any medical aid until it was far too late!"

The Doctor stepped forward. Like obedient waves, the rats parted a path for him. "Graytown might have been able to forget that for you, Messington—but not me. I never forget the town that didn't care, as long as their financial future was secure. For a while I thought Moss might actually do something about it, perhaps even buy you out, but he didn't. He didn't want to. Even he stood to lose too much.

"So I swallowed my pride, hid my anger and got into politics to try and stop you.

I tried legal ways, at first. But I soon realized that that was not going to work—how could it when everyone in Graytown would just bend over backwards to continue to accommodate you? Even if there was a legal way to hurt you, they'd never let it pass. The city itself was as equally responsible for Darrin's death as you were. And that's when I realized that it wasn't enough just to kill you, Messington. Graytown itself must be punished!"

Messington shrank back as the hooded figure loomed over him but it was doubtful if the Doctor even noticed. His voice cracking with madness, he was too involved in explaining himself. "But how? To simply blow up the city would not work; too many people would survive, too much money would come pouring in from the government to rebuild And I didn't want Graytown rebuilt. I wanted it totally destroyed. No, to do what I wished, Graytown would have to be ignored—something would have to happen that would make the entire country wash its hands of it. But what? A disease? Yes—but not just a disease. A plague. A plague as deadly and dangerous as the Black Plague that nearly destroyed Europe over four hundred years ago!"

With an intense, insane glare he gazed down at his unwilling captive. "That fool, Scott, created the Black Fever for me. I had certain… indiscretions on him from his past he could not let become public. Also, being who I am, maps of the city and its sewer system were easy for me to obtain. I found entire dens just abandoned down there, Messington. A perfect place to breed my vermin. And fleas—I needed fleas to actually carry the Fever. Even so, a bunch of feral rats infected with the Black Fever still wouldn't be much good to me. I needed the plague spread in certain ways. Workmen first, to raise the alarm. Then doctors and other government workers, to prevent anyone from finding a cure immediately. So I knew I would actually have to train the rats; to make them respond to me and go where I wished. And I found a way. It's like dogs responding to whistles so high-pitched humans cannot hear them—I discovered that the rats could be trained to obey commands when they hear a sound at a certain pitch. I could make them simply infest a factory or a store—or I could make them attack and kill a specific person. And I have thousands of them, Messington—thousands and hundreds of thousands—all waiting in the secret dens beneath Graytown, all infested with fleas, all infected with the Fever. All just waiting for my call.

"There is an antenna on top of this boat. A very special antenna. When I turn it on, one burst will emit the summoning call that all my rats have been trained to respond to. They will come—pouring out of the sewers, of the garbage dumps of this city; more than there ever has been before. And every one of them will carry the Fever. Whereas dozens died earlier, hundreds will die now."

"You're mad," Messington sputtered. "Absolutely mad. The Army will –"

"– will do what I wish them to. I have the commanding officer in my pocket as well. Once he 'hears' of the massive flood of vermin in the city, he will have no choice but to 'order' a complete air strike upon Graytown to prevent the Black Fever from spreading further. Graytown will be reduced to rubble and ash. Those who don't die of the Fever will die from the fire. Except us, of course. My men and I are out here on the Lucinda. And you…" The Plague Doctor smiled. "Well, let's just say after the fireworks, I will take great joy in watching you re-enact the saga of the Christians versus the lions in Ancient Rome. Only, instead of lions–" He swept an arm out over his pets.

"Boss! BOSS!" At the frame of the hold's door a man appeared "We got company, I think."

The Plague Doctor glared at his prisoner. "You shall remain here. If you try to move from your bunk, my pets will attack you immediately." Swiftly he climbed the steps to the deck above. "What is it?"

The gunman pointed beyond the starboard of the expensive yacht, across the gray waters of the flat lake. "Take a look." He handed his master a pair of field glasses while the rest of the crew—about ten in all—gathered about.

"Mmm." The Plague Doctor muttered, peering through the lenses. About three miles out, he could see the rusty towers of Graytown nestled along the shore Beyond that the lake rested still, turning to black beneath the drooping sun, until the glasses picked up what seemed to be a hump rising from the surface only a few hundred yards away. It bobbed closer, revealing itself to be the bottom of an overturned rowboat.

"You've got to be kidding me," the gunman said. "Nobody falls for that old gag anymore, Boss."

"Indeed, they do not." The Plague Doctor lowered the binoculars. "All right. Do as you must." Nonchalantly he waved a hand.

Ten hard faces smiled, ten sub-machine guns came up. An explosion of bullets roared out over the waters. Splinters threw themselves up from the rowboat as more and more giant holes appeared in the side and water swirled in, pulling the wooden craft down until it vanished beneath the surface, leaving only a ever-widening circle of ripples in its wake.

The crew burst out in evil hyena-laughter.

"Enough," the Plague Doctor snapped. "There's work to be done Jenks, Wilkins, Taft—take your usual posts. Davidson, you're with me. I have to warm up the equipment and need a hand. The rest of you may go below." Turning his back upon the sunken vessel, he climbed a short ladder to the yacht's bridge.

The rest of the men did as ordered. One, Taft in particular, moved to the stern, slumping down against the hull and lighting a cigarette. More intent on getting his stubborn match to light, he failed to notice the shadow that fell over him until the fingers themselves were against the nerve centers in his neck.

Secret Agent X caught the body as it fell, pulling the tommy-gun from the unconscious man. Peeling off his goggles and snorkel, he turned to Al Vittoro, who was doing the same. "If this guy's so smart, won't he figure out we just used the boat as a diversion?" Vittoro whispered.

"I'm certain he will," the Agent hissed back. "But it gives us time to find Messington and possibly gain an advantage. Look there." He gestured toward the top of the boat. A lengthy, thin, but odd-looking antenna jutted from the roof of the bridge's cabin. "That must be how the Doctor will summon his rats. Take this gun.

Follow me—and be careful."

Silently the two men slipped cautiously along the side of the yacht, slipping behind cover whenever they could. The Agent tapped Vittoro on the shoulder. Another guard, Wilkins, was leaning casually before an closed door. From a pocket the Agent removed one of his glass balls. Carefully he rolled it down the deck.

Wilkins didn't note anything until he felt his foot crush something that felt like glass. He had time to look down curiously before the gas knocked him cold. Secret Agent X pulled him into cover and swept up his gun. "I'm going to check the hold. Messington might be in there."

Carefully, Agent X creaked the door open. A short flight of steps revealed a small makeshift brig. Messington was lying as still as he could upon the bunk, hardly daring to breathe. He glanced up at the sight of the Agent; no recognition lit his features The Agent brought a finger to his lips.

"Hold your breath, Messington."

By now the rat guard had noticed the stranger in their midst and turned, long scrawny forms tensed, mouths open in terrible hisses. The Agent pursed his lips. Slowly, a strange, shrill whistle came from them. And the rats froze, confused, uncertain of how to react.

It gave the Agent enough time to lob yet another glass ball to the floor. But this one did not hold tranquilizing gas. Hastily the Agent took a deep breath as the ball shattered; even as the rats paused, trying to reason how the stranger knew their master's call, they collapsed as their tiny lungs took in the poison. Messington, cheeks extended like bulbs, widened his eyes.

After a second the Agent exhaled, swigging back in good air. "Are you hurt?"

"N-no," the industrialist panted, still a bit afraid to breathe normally "You—you've got to stop him! He's mad! He'll destroy the whole city if he isn't stopped!"

"I know," was the terse reply. Quickly he gazed back up toward deck. It was rather too silent out there. "Vittoro!" he hissed. "Where are you?"

Vittoro's short, burly form framed itself in the doorway. With his hands raised. Slowly he trooped down the steps, followed by three men bearing sub-machine guns. With the wrong ends pointing towards him. Behind them, moving silkily, was the Plague Doctor.

"Sorry, buddy. They snuck up on me."

"That's all right, Al," the Agent said, carefully lowering his gun to the floor. Al's appropriated one was placed next to it.

The Doctor regarded the Agent thoughtfully. "Good evening, sir," he said. "I take it you are the gentleman who killed my men after the Army base incident. As well as the man who tried to interfere in my kidnapping of Messington. I thought at first you might be an Army agent—but now I tend to doubt it. I believe you must be one of those vigilante do-gooders that have been showing up on the East Coast with such ridiculous regularity. Who are you? The Phantom Detective? The Eagle? Hammond? No? Not going to say? Well, I suppose it doesn't matter. At any rate, you won't be around long enough to pass this story along to any of your friends. But tell me—how did you find me out?"

"It was very simple, Mr. Ebersol," Secret Agent X replied calmly. "Scott lived long enough to tell us your plan. And a bit of research by a friend of mine, Jim Hobart, revealed that you were the only one of the major influences in this city that owned a yacht called the Lucinda."

Slowly the Plague Doctor raised his hand to the top of his hood. Within a moment the weak, colorless face of Tyrone Ebersol smiled coldly out at him.. "Good, sir. Very good. And if you have discovered that, you must also have discovered my reasoning."

"I did. I heard Grohmann and Messington arguing, and it was clear there was something between them. A little checking, and I discovered that Darrin Grohmann, Robert Grohmann's son, worked in Messington's foundry for a while—until he was killed in an accident. An accident caused by Messington's third-rate equipment and lax safety standards. I also learned that you, at the time, were his best friend. Both Grohmann and you wanted revenge, but, as Mayor, Grohmann's hands were tied. Messington was far too important to a city about to go reeling under the economic crisis. The courts had little choice but to let a man of such influence go. So you blamed Grohmann as well as Messington. And since Grohmann represents the city…."

"Graytown, too, must die," finished the Plague Doctor with a smile. "And it shall. Even now the machinery is warming up. All I shall have to do is throw a lever, and the call will go out to bring the rats from their dens beneath the city. Then Major Randall, at my summons, will begin firebombing to prevent the Fever from 'spreading.' My revenge will be complete."

"Save for one thing. Scott told us about Randall. I have already contacted Captain Anderson and told him how you offered to pay Randall's gambling debts in return for an order given, as far as his superiors were concerned, under extreme conditions. The Major has already been arrested. There will be no firebombing of Graytown, Ebersol. The city you hate so much will continue to live."

At this news Ebersol's face twisted; so utterly and horribly Vittoro knew that whatever good man may have once been there was lost forever. "You may think! But I still have the rats! I can still give the order to release them and the Fever will decimate Graytown! You dare think you can stop me? Just try! I will see your dead body at my feet before Graytown falls to me!"

Before Vittoro's astonished eyes, the Agent didn't seem a bit perturbed. "Fine," he said casually. "But before you kill us, perhaps you might tell me one thing—do any of these rats here on board carry the Fever?"

The Doctor seemed startled by the question. "What? Do you think I want the plague?" He chortled. "Certainly not. All the rats on this boat are clean."

"Really?" the Agent replied. "Too bad. This one isn't." And like lighting the Agent's hand flashed into his pocket and back out again, darting the rat clenched in his fist right at the Plague Doctor.

The creature had been caught in the trap set by Vittoro at the Agent's instruction. Its neck had been snapped instantly; it was in fact long dead. But the gunmen didn't know that. Instinctively they yelled and jerked back; automatically loosening their hold upon their tommy-guns. "NOW!" cried the Agent and he and Vittoro hit the floor, sweeping up their own weapons. Messington screamed and dove beneath his bunk as lead filled the air. Bullets exploded into bodies, jerking them around like broken puppets and causing them to tumble to the deck. But the Plague Doctor, shielded by his men's bodies, was already pelting up the steps.

"Come on!" yelled the Agent and he and Vittoro dashed after him. Already the rest of the Lucinda's crew were darting up onto deck. Lead spat, sending them flying before they could fire back.

"Martin! Up there!" yelled Vittoro.

The Agent looked. Ebersol had made the bridge and was even now bending over what looked to be some huge awkward radio, full of dials and knobs, flipping switches with savage fury. As he did the air was suddenly filled with a wailing banshee screech that seemed to cause the very air to shudder; sending agonizing waves of pain down the mens' vertebrates. Vittoro dropped to the deck and covered his ears.

Agent X, however, ignored the pain. Shutting out the whining cacophony as best he could, he hauled himself up the ladder to the bridge. "Turn it off, Ebersol!" he cried, lowering the tommy-gun's barrel toward the lawyer. "I won't tell you twice."

Slowly, with great care, Tyrone Ebersol, the Plague Doctor, turned to face his adversary "No," he said. "You won't have to." The Agent stepped forward. But even as he did Ebersol's hand had flown into his sleeve, coming out with a pistol. But he did not aim it at the Agent.

"You'll never stop the Fever now," he stated remorselessly, placing the barrel to his own temple. "Graytown is finished."

The following boom nearly drowned out the machine's wail.

The Agent forced himself to ignore the body; to ignore the crimson pool his feet were stepping in. He swept up a pair of binoculars and peered out toward Graytown. Then he turned toward the radio device.

"There's only one chance," he muttered, and immediately began turning more dials.

Al Vittoro finally looked up, only to wince more as the antenna's screeching grew louder. But the Agent pointed toward the far shore.

Al looked. For a long time, nothing seemed to happen. But then he saw. It started small, so small even binoculars couldn't bring it out at first. But gradually, the beach so far away began to have what looked like black specks seem to slide across it. Then more specks. And more, and more, until they started merging into globs. And the globs continued to grow as more specks, then streams, of black joined them, forming a branching river-pattern along the sand. As the minutes rolled by the river-pattern filled out, solidified, into a rolling midnight sea of tar trundling unendingly down toward the water. An ever-moving, endless sea, swirling out from holes and chinks and gaps from sewers and buildings and docks.

"The rats!" Vittoro breathed. "You're calling the rats into the lake!"

The Agent turned dials, altered pitches. The great furry sea continued to pound their way into the lake, unable to resist the hypnotic siren call. For hours the eerie

"The rats!" Vittoro breathed. *"You're calling the rats into the lake!"*

migration continued as more rats than Vittoro felt could ever exist in the world swarmed out over the sands, marching implacably into the waiting waters only to gradually split back into specks; tiny, pathetic drowned figures floating helplessly in their liquid tomb.

At long last the beaches turned from black to its sandy gray again. The tar sea shrank back into rivers, then specks. Throughout the lake collections of the dead rats could be seen, like furry rafts bobbing in the waves. The Agent turned off the summoning machine.

He lowered himself to the main deck. And instantly Al Vittoro had enveloped him in a joyous manly embrace. "You did it, Mr. Martin! You save my Stephanie, and you saved my entire town!"

"We did it, Al," smiled Agent X. clapping the ironworker on the back. He had become deeply impressed by the man's decency and courage. As they shook hands, he ref   lected perhaps he could use him on a case again some time. But that was for another day.

"One thing I can't figure out, though—if Ebersol was the Plague Doctor, who was on the line when he picked up the phone at Messington's house?"

"A simple phonograph recording, played by a flunky no doubt. You'll recall the message did not respond to any questions; it simply said its piece and hung up. He had recorded it earlier to be played back and throw suspicion off himself."

"And his men trying to shoot him?"

"They never intended to—Ebersol would have miraculously 'escaped' the attack, I'm sure and Scott and the others would be dead, save for Messington—who would have been here on board."

"So what now?"

"Now?" grinned the Agent. "Now I leave. I can't be found here."

"But–"

"Sorry, Al. It's better this way. Use the radio to call the authorities to come pick up those two who are still alive. And contact Captain Anderson of the U.S. Army and tell him to tell Hazzard Labs to get cracking on that cure. If they hurry, a lot more people should be saved. The full credit for stopping the Plague Doctor will go to you. You should get quite a reward. Your daughter has a secure future ahead of her."

"And me?" The voice of Alvert Messington,who had finally dared venture up from his prison, sounded unaccountably humble. "What about me?"

"Ah, yes. You. Alvert Messington, it was your greed and callousness that directly led to all this—your lack of care about your substandard equipment and your equal lack of compassion for your employees. I cannot arrest you for your crimes, but I can say that I will be keeping a close eye on you from now on. I will expect to see great improvements in your foundry in the future, Mr. Messington. If not, I will know. And I have contacts that make yours seem like pool-hall race touts. Do you understand me, Mr. Messington?" Swallowing hard, Alvert Messington had no choice but to nod. A lot had been taken out of him in the past few hours

"Very good. Now, if you don't mind, I'll borrow that life-raft I see over there."

As the inflated vessel was tossed over the side, Al Vittoro could not help asking one last question "At least tell me who you really are!" he begged.

Lifting the oars, Secret Agent X smiled. "Let's just say I'm a patriotic American doing his best, just like you." He pushed out from the yacht. "Take care of yourself and Stephanie, Al! Goodbye!" Al had no choice but to watch as his mysterious ally began to row away. "Huh," he said at last to Messington as the Agent became smaller and smaller in the distance, "Imagine a yegg like me workin' for none other than Operator F–"

Yards away the man on the raft threw back his head and laughed and laughed. Vittoro evidently didn't know sound carried over water. He felt very peaceful. The night was cool and the stars were out. Using his advanced knowledge of astronomy and navigation, he set course for the not-terrifically-far city of Chicago. There, perhaps, he might receive a few days respite from his adventures. But if not, he would remain as he always was, Secret Agent X!

G.L. GICK

I'm a thirty-eight year old[1] native of Lafayette, Indiana and have been a pulp fan ever since a random pick-up of Phillip Jose Farmer's Tarzan Alive turned me on to the book and introduced his wonderful Wold-Newton Universe to me. Up until then my only real exposure to pulp heroes were the Filmation Tarzan cartoons (which I later learned were actually quite faithful to Burroughs' novels; as much as a Saturday morning cartoon in the 1970's could be, anyway) and a Sherlock Holmes appearance on an episode of Scooby-Doo.

Yeah, yeah, taste escaped me back then. I admit it. Hey, I was eight years old! (Besides, only the first two seasons of Scooby were any good, anyway.)

Then, after reading Farmer's next, **Doc Savage: His Apocalyptic Life**, I was hooked for eternity (Thank you, Columbus Indiana Public Library!). My love for pulp took second place only to my love for the Oz books of L. Frank Baum and his successors, (see? I did have SOME taste, even back then!), although movies like **King Kong** and TV series like **Doctor Who** and the original **Star Trek** vied for my attention. But I credit Farmer with not only developing my love for pulp adventure, from Dent to Grant, but for classic adventure novels of all sorts, from Dumas to Leslie Charteris to Doyle's "non-Canon" tales. And imagine, I would never have even known about these wonderful worlds if I had just kept sitting in front of the television!

Even so, the tales of Secret Agent X remained unknown to me until I happened to attend the University of Denver's Publishing Institute in 1991. My then-idea of becoming a book editor came to naught; but on a Saturday I wandered into a SF bookstore tucked away in a side neighborhood and found (along with reprints of Operator 5 and Dusty Ayres) a reprint of X's adventure "Octopus of Crime." Well, I thought, it's not Doc Savage, but I'll give it a try.

And once more I made a new hero.

Since then I've read a few more X's, and enjoyed them just as much. So, when Ron Fortier invited me to scribe an original adventure of my own, I jumped at the chance. As my first real short story with a very specific amount of words assigned, it was tough going at first but Ron's kind encouragement and support kept me at it, and for that. I am forever grateful that he gave a newbie a chance—and stuck with him. For what's it's worth, this one is for you, Ron.

As for the tale itself, I wanted to try something where the Agent was at a bit of a loss. In the novels, Agent X seems to have apartments and safe houses everywhere; I wanted to see a bit of what might happen if, for once, he was assigned to a town where he didn't have a ready hideout. Nor did I want him to have any of his regular aides at the ready—what would the Agent do, I wondered, if for once he didn't have anyone trained to fall back on? Even so, I still would need someone for the Agent to explain things to—so enter Al Vittoro. I was curious what might happen if an ordinary civilian wandered in on one of X's adventures—and wouldn't go

---

1   This was written in 2008.

away. Al Vittoro is inexperienced, volatile and a little clumsy—but he's got a big heart and sense of decency that all good sidekicks have. Of course, now he's happily taking care of his daughter and enjoying the perks of being a hero. So will he ever encounter the Agent again? Only time will tell....

Chapter One
Another False Face

Fat Benny Drago drew the line at a lot of things but easy work wasn't one of them. And kidnapping was easy work. As long as he didn't have to cross the state line and bring the feds into it. He would definitely draw the line at that. Fat Benny had drawn a lot of lines in his life. He didn't know it, but he was going to be forced to cross a stranger, darker line before this night was through.

About a month ago Benny had been scheming to scrape up money for back rent, when his friend Dwight had come stumbling into O'Leary's Tavern and asked if anybody needed a temporary job. Since every job Fat Benny had ever worked at wound up being temporary, he had raised his hand.

Benny hated work but he was about to get evicted, and nothing any easier had come along. Besides, Dwight had assured him it would not be hard. Dwight knew Benny was no great admirer of the law, and after swearing he could keep a secret, Benny had been given the job on the spot. And, boy, was he glad. Other than having to show up on time and stay till dawn, it was the easiest job he'd ever had.

In the past two weeks all Benny had to do was come to an abandoned building in the warehouse district, every night, and watch an old man chained to the wall inside a tiny room. Every once in a while Dwight, or a swarthy man named Davidson, would come in and check on the two of them and that was it.

All Fat Benny had to do was heat the old man a bowl of stew on a hot plate, mix in a tablespoon of powder from a shaker, and feed it to him. For this Benny was making a hundred dollars a week.

Initially, he had been taken aback by the fact that the old man was being held prisoner, and, that this was most likely some kind of a kidnapping plot. But when Mr.. Davidson gave him his first weeks pay up front, and then guaranteed him more just for showing up, there was no way he could turn it down. Not only had Benny paid his back rent in the first week, but he had paid the next month in advance! And he was still rolling in the old dough-ray-me.

Fat Benny got the impression that Mr. Davidson was not the kind of man people said *no* to, anyway. He was definitely not the kind of guy you could just turn down. There was something intense about him, a scary, kinetic energy waiting to explode beneath all that calm.

Benny had spent his entire life crossing undefined moral boundaries, and kidnapping had been just one of them. He'd worry about crossing the next line when he got to it.

Fat Benny nudged the old man in the corner with the toe of his boot. The old man rolled over slowly, glancing through the cracked lenses of his wraparound eyeglasses, his eyes rolling back in his head as if battling for consciousness. When he was awake, the old man shook and glanced around the room wildly, as if frightened by things that weren't there. Mostly he just slept. Benny thought it was probably something in the powder that made the old man sleep. But he didn't think about it too much.

The fact was, Benny didn't think about anything too much, really. Barely smart enough to worry about kidnapping, he hadn't bothered to notice he might be tied up in anything newsworthy. If he had, he would have been aware that in the past two months two United States Army Generals, and a physicist working under government contract had been kidnapped. The police had assured the family of the first General that the kidnappers would be easily apprehended and there was no need to negotiate. The first General had never been seen again.

After the kidnapping of a second General, the police had made the same statement. This time, the second General's family had been only too happy to comply with the kidnapper's demands. After the second General's ransom had been paid, the trade was made—money for hostage—and the General had returned home with his family, only to disappear within the next twenty-four hours. Neither of the two Generals had ever been seen again.

If Benny possessed any intellectual curiosity whatsoever, he might have at least glanced at a newspaper and recognized the old man from the pictures emblazoned across the front page. For chained to a darkened wall in front of one the most incurious minds in the western world was one of it's highest intellects. Dr. Phineas Bledsoe, world renowned theoretical physicist.

Benny kept nudging the imprisoned doctor, trying to make him talk in an effort to keep himself entertained. The doctor remained silent. Bored, Benny thought about eating the rest of the old man's stew before he remembered it was most probably drugged. He almost took time to find it odd that the old man had hardly touched his food that night. Usually, he lapped it up like a stray dog. Benny wouldn't have thought anything of it at all if the stew hadn't been sitting on the floor right there in front of him.

He was supposed to make sure the old man ate all of it, but he really didn't feel like keeping the old man awake anymore. To top it all off, Dwight had come into work with him that night, and then, as soon as they got to the warehouse, made him go out and get cigarettes. Like he was some kind of errand boy!

The more he thought about it, the angrier Benny got. Not only was he going to let Dwight have it when he came back to check on him, but he was also going to let him know that Fat Benny Drago was nobody's gopher. Benny decided not to force feed the old man. That'd show 'em. Besides, why bother? He was an old man for crying out loud. He was chained to a wall, helpless.

The door to the back of the warehouse creaked open and a sliver of light cut into the darkness, slowly broadening. There were two voices. Dwight and Mr. Davidson. The broad light dimmed back down to the single bulb hanging from the ceiling, as the door snapped shut behind them. When Fat Benny's eyes readjusted to the light he almost jumped in surprise. Standing before him was an exact duplicate of the frail old man chained to the wall. Benny pivoted back and forth, staring first at one, and then the other. The old man's double stood centered in the circle of light and spoke—in the voice of Mr. Davidson.

"Good evening, Mr. Drago, Dr. Bledsoe. You'll both be glad to know that the doctor's family and friends have decided to pay our ransom money."

Fat Benny smiled as the physicist rolled over his chains to face his doppelganger.

"Unfortunately, for you good doctor," Davidson's voice echoed. "There's been a change of plans. While myself and two associates collect the ransom, *you* will be unable to make it. Not to worry, I'll be taking your place."

Benny continued to swivel his head back and forth, confused. The real doctor merely sat there, staring into space.

Mr. Davidson placed his hand on Benny's shoulder, displaying an array of fake liver spots, and patted him on the back. "That's right, Dwight and Benny here are going to take great care of you—in your last hours."

Benny watched the impostor shuffle to the door in a gait he imagined the old man might use. When the outside door closed Benny and the old man remained staring at it with the same blank glaze. Dwight stood shadowed in the corner darkness, his position only visible from the manic light in his eyes.

"You hear that, Benny? You're moving up."

"Moving up? I don't get it."

"Don't you see, Benny? You're moving up. A promotion!"

"A promotion?"

"That's right, a promotion." Dwight stepped out of the corner, his eyes glaring even more in the light. "All's we gotta do is remove the evidence. But if I shoot him, you gotta clean it up."

"You mean we gotta kill him?" Benny stammered.

"Look at him, Benny. He's a little old man. His best years are behind him anyway. We do this one thing, and we're in like silk. All we have to do—is remove the evidence."

"Now *waitaminnit*. I didn't agree to no murder. I could get the chair for that."

"Everybody dies, Benny." Dwight's voice rasped. "It's just a matter of when."

"What's that supposed to mean? Really, Dwight, you gotta stop this. You just keep getting weirder and weirder. First you make me go fetch cigarettes and the next thing I know it sounds like you're saying—"

"He's saying, that if you don't kill me, Benny. He'll kill you," the old man on the floor said through dry, chapped lips. "My guess is he'll kill you regardless. Because dead men can't be live informants."

Benny's mouth opened and stayed that way, dumbfounded. The old man hadn't said that much in two weeks. Fat Benny slowly turned to face Dwight. "Is that what you're gonna do?" Benny looked heartbroken.

"No, no, not all, Ben." Dwight approached him, his head tilted to the side as if in sympathy. His hands outstretched like he was almost going to hug Benny, except for the gun still in his hand. "Don't you know the old man's crazy? Listen, I'll take care of him if you want. I'm starting to think we're all gettin' a little stir crazy in here. I mean, I never sent you out for no cigarettes." Dwight shoved the clip into his automatic and started to approach the old man.

"Yeah you did," Benny said. "Not an hour ago, after we came in together."

"I never sent you out for no cigarettes." Dwight glanced up angrily at Benny and the old man spoke:

"He's right, Benny. He didn't. I sent you out."

Dwight's eyes widened, not in manic glee, but surprise. The doctor's voice didn't sound like that. It wasn't Davidson's voice, but it wasn't the doctor's, either.

Benny stared between the two of them, still confused. "Waitaminnit—"

"Oh my God! Benny! It's him!" Dwight yelled, and raised his automatic. "It's Secret Agent X!"

Benny watched the old man roll, seeming to spin in the air, as the shackles flew off his wrists and rattled against the chain. Dwight's gunfire hit empty space. There was nothing but a bullet hole in the wall where the old man had been. Still spinning, seeming to almost float in the air parallel to the floor, the escaped prisoner ground Dwight's shoe into the ground with one foot as the other kicked him behind the knee. Benny could hear Dwight's head thump the concrete as he went face down on the floor. The old man leapt across the body like a striking spider and came up with the automatic. Fat Benny was only now beginning to reach for his gun.

The old man fired over Benny's head. The light bulb popped and Benny screamed as the room went pitch black. Flames shot from Benny's gun barrel illuminating the room in stroboscopic fashion as the escaped prisoner seemed to disappear, and reappear somewhere else with every flash of light. Benny fired off his last two rounds, seeing only a blur to his right, and then a fist hurtling at him. He wouldn't truly feel the pain of the blow that knocked him out until he woke up later, chained to the wall next to Dwight, and cursing Secret Agent X.

Up above, on top of the warehouse, a man stood sheltered from the moon by one of the dome-shaped vent-covers that sprang up from the roof seemingly at random. Even dressed entirely in black, he was occasionally revealed as a rugged man with a square jaw, his mouth set straight. He checked the glowing dial of his radium watch face and looked down on the comatose form of the real Dr. Phineas Bledsoe. Only for a moment did a look of compassion cross his features, to be quickly replaced by the stern, broad shouldered stance of a man on guard. A strange whistle, eerie and musical at the same time, wafted up from the ground below.

Harvey Bates, chief operative of Secret Agent X, had often wondered if the strange, almost directionless tone was created with some kind of mouthpiece like a bird-caller might use, or if it was merely another one of the seemingly endless talents of The Man of a Thousand Faces. Bates walked to the edge of the roof and threw the rope-ladder over, reminding himself that he knew more about the man of mystery than probably anybody—and since he didn't know squat, he'd have to be happy with the mystery.

Seconds later the Secret Agent appeared over the parapet still in the guise of Dr. Bledsoe sans glasses. "There are no X's in the word intrigue," he said.

"I never sent you out for no cigarettes."

"Except Secret Agent X," Bates responded. It was part of a well worked out and constant series of codes between the two of them, without it Bates would never have known if he was actually dealing with the real Agent X. If need be, the dialogue was designed to continue until they were both sure. In this case there was no need.

"Change of plans, Mr. Bates. We've got another false face on this one."

"Thanks for telling me. I thought it was you. I saw him walking out with the goons, so I figured I'd just sit still until you radioed in and told me different."

"Listen, we have to move fast. You still have those two operatives monitoring the payoff?"

"Of course."

"Let them know the doctor's a fake. They are by no means to let him out of their sight—even if it means not following the money. His family may be in danger."

"Check."

"I'll lower the doctor down to you on the ground and then throw down the rope-ladder. I need you to take him back to your office if you can. Keep him comfortable until I make radio contact."

"Aye-aye, sir. One question."

"Yes."

"How are you going to get down?"

Agent X gave him a look for which there is no disguise: Bates would have to learn to be happy with the mystery.

Chapter Two
The World's Most Secret Agent

Agent X was on the ground within five minutes, and tearing off the old man's tattered shirt as he approached a low-slung, black sedan. The windows were tinted so no one could see inside. X sat down behind the wheel and tore off the gray wig he was wearing. Pulling a hidden shelf out from under the passenger seat, an elaborate array of make-up and accessories was revealed. His long, nimble fingers were kneading himself a new face before he even adjusted the rear view mirror. It was one of the numerous anonymous aliases the Agent used all the time—low maintenance and not a lot of detail. It wouldn't pay to get pulled over looking like a famous kidnap victim. X pulled a clean shirt out of the back seat and hit the starter.

Luckily, he had already done his research on Dr. Bledsoe and knew the details of his family. Father, mother, son, daughter. He knew the address and headed there to set up a stake-out ahead of time. The way he saw it, even with the ransom having been paid the police would still have to be involved somehow. There would be a short debriefing, and no press; so his alias of reporter A. J. Martin was out of the picture.

Or was it?

Martin might be the perfect cover to get in close to the Bledsoe family. As the somewhat aggressive, headline-chasing journalist he might be able to charm his way inside the house. Or at least get his foot in the door. The Agent parked a half-block away from the address, and decided to wait, gathering all the information he could before acting.

He opened a secret compartment in the dashboard to reveal a short-wave radio set. Pulling a bullet shaped microphone from the holster inside, he hit the button to broadcast on his own private frequency.

"Station X. Come in, Station X. What is the status of our guest?"

Station X was only a short distance away from the warehouse district. In reality it was the office of The Colonial Research Foundation, managed by operative Harvey Bates. A legitimate charity organization, The Foundation also acted as a business front for the investigative work of Secret Agent X. Bates was more than just a dedicated, fiercely loyal operative. He also maintained a communications network with operatives all over the world. If everything was going according to plan, Bates should have already arrived safely with the real Dr. Bledsoe, and would be seated in a secret, state of the art, radio room.

"Station X acknowledging. Guest has arrived physically safe. Appears however to be suffering from delusions. Other than that, all systems are go."

"It may be the after effects of some solution our competitors were using," X answered. "Continue trying to question him, but cause no discomfort. Make him aware you're responsible for his safety. Try to gain more information. Also—I need as much as you can give me about a Mr. Marcus Davidson. It may be an alias, but that's the name the kidnappers used to rent the warehouse. Are our operatives still on the tail of our guest's family?"

"Answer that affirmative. They're currently leaving police headquarters and headed home."

"Let operatives know I'll be working in the area. They are not to interfere unless it's for the safety of the family. X out." The Agent placed the microphone back in its holster and sealed up the dashboard.

X had been right. The police were involved, and, as yet, none of the press. A story like this would be quite a scoop, a good reason for any reporter to get involved. His hands flew to his face once again. Quickly, nimbly, he massaged his features into that of an Associated Press Reporter. The A. J. Martin disguise was an easy one. For Secret Agent X.

A sudden rapping startled the Agent as he put the finishing touches on the nose of his reporter alias. X took the time to check his face in the rear-view mirror as a large man in a suit continued banging on the tinted window—the Agent was well aware that overconfidence in his skill could someday get him killed. He took his time. After pushing a lock of hair off his forehead and readjusting the rear view mirror, X rolled the glass down.

"Well, well, well. If it ain't Mr. Martin, my number one argument against freedom of the press. And what would you be doing, skulking around the house of a recent kidnap victim?" the large man said. It was Inspector John Burks, probably on stake-out. X knew Burks more than he cared to admit. Since no public recognition had ever been accorded to the Agent's battle against crime, Burks had long ago made it his personal mission to catch Secret Agent X.

"Inspector Burks, how are you this evening?" X said, sugarcoating the sarcastic comment. While the Agent had the utmost respect for the law, A. J. Martin did not. He had to walk a tight line between irreverence and respect.

"You didn't answer my question, Martin, you just asked another one." Burks's black eyebrows jutted menacingly over the crack in the window as his eyes pierced inside the car. It was obvious the ace detective didn't enjoy this assignment, and even more obvious he felt like he was wasting his time when a shady character turned out to be a reporter. "While you're at it, you mind telling me how a muckreeking journalist like yourself is driving around in such a respectable vehicle?"

"That's muckraking, I believe, Inspector. And I think you know the answer to that already. I'm looking for a scoop."

"It's muckreeking if I say it is, Martin. And if it's a scoop you're looking for this ain't the place. Maybe you ought to try the stockyards. They got plenty of stuff there for a guy like you to scoop."

"Funny you should mention that officer—I mean inspector. I was just on my way." X hit the starter and the finely tuned engine began to purr. Inspector Burks backed away as The Agent hit the gas and took off before the detective had time to ask any more questions about the car. X made a mental note that Martin had been spotted in it, just in case Burks wrote the license down. It wouldn't do to have the intrepid reporter tied up with any of the Agent's other identities.

Meanwhile, it was obvious the neighborhood was crawling with police. After the disappearance of the last kidnap victim it was only standard operating procedure for the authorities to maintain surveillance. What they didn't know was that the man they were trying to protect was an impostor. Traffic blurred outside the Agent's windows as he sped to the closest of his numerous hideouts in the city.

After pulling into a private parking lot beneath a tall, brick building, X parked the sedan next to three other cars that were currently at his disposal. The parking lot's rear entrance led him up six flights of stairs. He was barely winded when he unlocked the door to the only room on the floor and walked into a large studio apartment. Its Spartan furnishings consisted of a bed, desk, chair, bathroom and two closets. The Agent checked the coat closet, the bathroom and under the bed before striding briskly to the closet in the far wall. Reaching inside, he felt beneath the shelf for a small distended knothole toward the back. X pressed the camouflaged button and the entire back of the closet slid away to reveal another, much larger room.

It was the walk-in wardrobe for a thousand different characters. Over a hundred suits of varying style and size lined the back wall. Shoes, belts, ties, watches. Spring, summer, autumn and winter. A full length mirror covered the entire left wall. A vanity sat before it containing enough make-up, putty, and hair attachments to disguise a small army. File cabinets and another room stood to the right. The Agent slid the back of the closet back into place and effectively sealed himself inside the secret room. Another room behind the wardrobe contained an amazing array of gadgets and weaponry, a hospital bed and medical supplies.

All of this was only a small part of the Secret Agent's arsenal in his one man war on crime.

Shortly after the war, X had been recruited into the Government Intelligence Division, and been given complete *carte blanche* as an independent Agent. A one man agency, he was licensed to operate outside the restrictions of authority, dispensing justice as he saw fit. Secret Agent X was guaranteed a virtually unlimited fund to draw from, provided for him by an anonymous group of ten men. When the fund was depleted, The Group of Ten replenished it through a bank account in the name of one of his many aliases. Their identity was unknown to him. His identity was unknown to them. The world's most secret agent didn't even have a code number. He was X.

The Agent pulled a film projector out and placed a newsreel on it. He shut the lights off and began to watch the projection on the wall. His subject was a big man, figuratively and literally.

X observed the way the man in the film moved, both while making a speech and in an interview. He began to imitate the man's speech, finding the right tone and pitch, the rhythms he talked in. He detected the minute trace of a drawl. The subject's voice came from the back of the throat, and not the sinuses or diaphragm. He was the kind of man that was used to giving orders. Within seconds the Agent sounded exactly like him.

He watched it a second time, all the while mimicking the subjects gestures, tics, and smallest mannerisms. When the light came back on he walked toward the wardrobe wall with the large man's gait.

Running his hand along the coat rack, X removed a padded, brown suit from the hanger and pulled a foam padded belt from a drawer to use as a prosthetic belly. The Agent then donned a large, specially tailored shirt. Designed to look too tight around the neck and sleeves, the shirt provided the illusion that its wearer had recently gained weight.

Reaching into his weapons case, he grabbed several of his favorite gadgets, along with a handful of incendiary pellets and smoke bombs. He checked to make sure his gas gun was still functional, and shoved it into a shoulder holster along with several reload cartridges. He hadn't liked having to abandon the non-lethal weapon back at the kidnapper's warehouse, but it had been necessary for the sake of disguise. As weapons go, the gas gun was his standby. An expert shot with any gun, X left random slaying to cruder, less skillful investigators.

The Agent faced the mirror, inhaled and then exhaled strongly as he began to pull the putty off his face. He sat down at the vanity, and stared at a face that most of the people in his life had never seen. It was the face of a young man. Yet at closer perusal part of it seemed old. Small scars from numerous battles became visible only when the light hit them just the right way. Wrinkles had begun to form around the eyes, eyes that had aimed machine-guns through propellers in aerial combat. Eyes that had witnessed massacres on missions for Lawrence of Arabia, and the brutality of the Tong wars while stationed in China. Suddenly, a fierceness began to burn in those eyes. And a defiant grin began to curl at the corners of a set, determined mouth.

It wasn't that the disguise he was about to attempt was a hard one. It was, in fact, relatively easy for the Agent. It was one he had done many times before. But it was one that led him into the perusal of men that would love to catch him. One that left him in constant danger of being discovered.

The only way the Agent could get past police surveillance was to become a policeman himself. The only way to move about detectives and patrolmen, unhindered, and with the ability to investigate was to outrank them. And the only policeman that could outrank every other cop in the city was Commissioner Charlie Foster. Not only would X have to play the part perfectly, but even if he were to escape detection by men trained in investigative techniques, he would still have to expose Dr. Bledsoe's impostor without being exposed himself.

Yes, X would be in danger, but the Agent had been in danger many times before. The doctor's family had not.

Once again, deft, swift hands grabbed for the specially formulated face putty. Ten minutes later Police Commissioner Charlie Foster was walking to a roadster licensed in the name of The Colonial Research Foundation.

Chapter Three
Gateway to Fear

X parked on a street backed by the alley behind the Bledsoe residence. In case of trouble it would make for a clean getaway. The Agent then hailed a cab and came around the block, exiting directly in front of the doctor's house. There was a squad car parked in front and a man stationed at the front door. Probably a man stationed in back, and two more, watching from a window or rooftop in the distance. He hoped his own operatives were watching the stake-out as well as the house.

"Commissioner Foster," the officer stationed at the door said, sounding a little surprised. X watched the man's posture improve as soon as he recognized the Commissioner.

"Evening, Sergeant Murphy." X recognized the veteran beat cop. Murphy had tried to keep reporter A. J. Martin from many a crime scene in the past.

"Didn't expect see you out this late, sir." Murphy almost winced when he caught himself implying that the Commissioner didn't work nights. X had just been given part of his role.

"Past my bedtime, that what you're saying, Murphy?"

"No, sir. Not at all. I just thought you weren't coming by until morning."

"Ah, early birds and all that. I couldn't sleep. But don't think you won't see me in the morning, too."

"Always a pleasure, sir," Murphy said.

X watched the sergeant visibly relax without losing the posture, stamping his feet a little to keep the blood flowing. "Oh, and Murphy, keep up the good work."

The Agent knocked on the door only to be greeted by Inspector John Burks. X felt a small chill run down the back of his neck as one of the detective's eyebrows came down. He wasn't sure if it was because Burks suspected something or because, like Murphy outside, he hadn't expected Commissioner Foster until the morning. Burks was one of the reasons the Agent had gone to such extremes in applying his disguise. The detective may have been a nuisance, but ultimately he was a grim dealer in mystery. He solved crimes and he believed Secret Agent X to be a criminal.

"Yeah, I know, you weren't expecting me to be here until morning. How are we doing, Burks?" The Agent hoped not being expected truly was the case, and Burks hadn't just talked to the real commissioner on the phone. X reminded himself to maintain a relaxed composure, battling his body's natural attempt to tense in preparation. Luckily, after a lifetime of adventure his fight or flight responses were almost instantaneous. When Burks widened the door, X was comforted by something else completely. "Miss Dale, a pleasure to see you here, ma'am."

Betty Dale was a reporter for *The Herald.* To say the Agent knew her was an understatement. To say she was scooping every other reporter in town—on a story they couldn't get close to—was nothing new. Betty sometimes seemed to be one step ahead of the Agent himself in her effort to appear wherever the news was hottest. The Agent had to force himself not to smile too much upon greeting her, because more than once her cleverness and courage had aided him in his battle against crime. It didn't hurt that she was easy on the eyes, either.

"Miss Dale was just leaving, Commissioner. Weren't you, Miss Dale?" Inspector Burks said, trying to shuffle the young reporter to the door.

"Actually, I was hoping to finish speaking with the family. And, have a few words with Dr. Bledsoe before I left," Betty said, gracefully pulling her elbow beyond the inspector's grasp.

The commissioner held up a hand to stop her evacuation. "I'm afraid I'll have to apologize for Inspector Burks, Miss Dale. I left him with strict orders that no reporters were to be allowed in. I'm afraid he's just trying to cover up for his own discrepancy." The Agent almost felt guilty reprimanding Burks, but he also enjoyed it. Not only was it payback for their little altercation earlier, but it was also imperative for the Agent to maintain his authority as Commissioner Foster. "However, I will have to ask you to keep the fact that the house is under police surveillance off the record."

"Consider it done, sir." Betty pushed her copper-blonde hair away from her mouth with a pencil, revealing the interest in her blue eyes. "Do you mind if I ask why? Off the record, of course."

"Because eventually, we hope to catch a kidnapper. And while I doubt very seriously you're a spy, Miss Dale, I'm afraid that's all I can tell you without breaking too many of my own orders."

"Thank you, Commissioner, and I understand." Betty smiled. "It's just that I'd rather ask too many questions than not enough."

"All part of the job. I can't really fault Inspector Burks for letting someone as charming as yourself in. Just don't let it get around." Agent X wanted to make himself known to her. Betty Dale was one of the few people who knew of his daring work, and had ventured with him to battle the darkness of evil. In the past he had always identified himself when he chose by a series of signals with which she had grown familiar. He thought better of it and turned toward the other woman standing beyond the entry hall. "And would you be Dr. Bledsoe's wife?"

"Ann. Ann Bledsoe. Yes," the woman said. X was surprised at the youth of the woman. From the dossier of information he had collected she was supposed to be only seven years the doctor's junior. And yet even with the darkness of fatigue under her eyes, and the worry lines of weeks without sleep, she seemed twenty years younger. The Agent pondered the effects of stress and its drastic results, how sometimes a major shock can prematurely age its victim. Perhaps Dr. Bledsoe's imprisonment had been more of an emotional blow than X had realized.

"It's a pleasure to meet you, ma'am. I hope we're able to provide some sort of comfort for you in these times of need," the bogus commissioner said. "With any luck our stay here will be short, and you can soon return to a normal home life."

"Thank you for just helping to bring him back safe," Mrs. Bledsoe said. "And thank you for being here."

"May I ask where Dr. Bledsoe is now?" the Agent said.

"Oh, after a very early breakfast, he seemed eager to check on the work he left behind. So we compromised, and he's down in the basement with the kids."

The Agent already knew, having researched, that Dr. Bledsoe's basement was a home research lab. Without asking, he turned toward the door just beyond the living room. Betty Dale, eager to get her interview, was already facing it.

A blood-curdling scream pierced the walls. Everyone else in the room was still glancing at one another, confused, as Secret Agent X raced across the room and opened the door to the basement laboratory.

Before the Agent had even descended the staircase, he began to feel sick. His stomach churned. His head ached. Not with the fever of a physical illness, but with a pervading, overpowering sense of fear. No stranger to peril, X plunged heedlessly downstairs, and yet, the realization that he was afraid only added to his anxiety.

Beyond the darkness of the steps he saw why.

The figure of Dr. Bledsoe stood at the far wall of the basement, holding what looked to be some sort of projector. And yet he stood like he was holding a bazooka.

The light fired from the lens of the projector in the form of some thin, concentrated ray—a straight beam. Where it hit the opposite wall, a bright circular space of about six inches in diameter glowed, brightening the rest of the room. However, the light did not reflect back into the room in the way light physically should. Instead, it ballooned into the room—like a globule swallowing its occupants. The rounded edges of the force field went from light to instantaneously dark, writhing like some strange atmosphere not of this earth.

Dr. Bledsoe held what looked to be some sort of projector.

The children were hugging each other, cowering in the corner to the doctor's right, still screaming.

X felt weak simply entering the room, in doing so he had crossed the boundaries of the light's strange field. He surmised it to be some sort of fear ray. Dr. Bledsoe had been working with the Defense Department, after all, and a physical fear that could be fired at the enemy would make for an incredible deterrent to battle. Agent X had fought fear many times over the years. He plunged headlong through the undulating globule of blinding light, only to be confronted by a horror bordering on the dreams of the mad.

Fighting the overwhelming urge to flee, the Agent instead chose the instinct to fight. Until, the concentrated ray of light projected on the wall seemed to open into a six inch sphere of darkness, and nightmare creatures, the like of which no earthbound biologist had ever dreamed, forced themselves into the room. X saw creatures, for they could be called nothing else, battling from the other side of the wall for the chance to squeeze through into the room. A large arachnid resembling a mix of both spider and daddy longlegs, with a fanged mouth half its size had already crawled through.

The Agent had no time to console himself with the thought that perhaps his feelings of fear existed because of a trained instinct to recognize danger before it even occurred. Instead, he simply felt more fear. And then fought it.

X had seen many strange things in his adventures but nothing of this enormity. The one man agency had faced villains untold, but these villains had always been driven by the same earthly need for power. X always considered himself a hunter of criminals. It was the reason he carried only a gas gun for small arms—he was not a judge or executioner. In this case he would have been willing to change that decision.

Rather than miring himself in regret, the Agent did as always and moved on, adapting his arsenal, skill and intelligence to the situation. X fired his gas gun, once at the monstrous spider-creature on the floor, and again directly at the opening in the wall. The spider leapt at him, striking.

The Agent didn't wait for the gas to take effect instead sweeping his arm away from himself in a martial-arts defense. The palm of his extended hand cupped one of the arachnid's legs just long enough to send it spinning through the air across the lab.

And dropping at the feet of Betty Dale.

X knew the bravery it had taken to come down the stairs. The sheer strength of will it took to remain in the sickening effect of the strange light. It was no sign of weakness that Betty screamed at the fanged open mandibles of the monster she faced. The Agent hesitated for only a second.

Fixed to the wall at the bottom of the stairs was a fire extinguisher and axe encased in glass. X hurled his gas gun at the case with pinpoint accuracy. Without hesitation, Betty reached for the axe. The arachnid wailed a high pitched bleating sound as the blade came down. Still squealing, it skittered across the floor with the axe still wedged in its body.

Something else squirmed through the portal.

Agent X was already rushing the bogus Dr. Bledsoe, oblivious to the new creature. The Agent erased all doubts from his mind, forcing control of every emotion except one—his desire to complete the mission: protect the children and catch the criminal. The doctor sneered, as if enjoying the madness. He aimed the projector directly at Agent X's chest.

With the mysterious faux doctor almost in reach, a wrenching sickness struck X. The Agent felt as if his soul was being torn from his body. Through sheer strength of will he hurled himself away from the beam, and twisted beneath the lab table. The ray followed him, reflecting off the top.

"No time to treat the wounded…" X heard the voice in his head. It was an officer from the war. In the Agent's mind it was as if every moment of horror in his life had combined into one. And the endless moment was eternity. His body reacted of its own volition, shoving the lab table on its side, toward, and on top of the doctor.

This time the doctor screamed. The Agent pounded on the table in an effort to subdue the madman and then collapsed on top of it. Pushing one last time, he shoved himself in the air, off the table and towards the children. He collapsed on top of them, providing his body as a shield.

Somewhere, sometime, in the maelstrom X found himself thinking again. The children were screaming. There was glass breaking in the lab. Voices in panic upstairs. X opened his eyes. The strange hovering bubble of light no longer swallowed the room. Fire engulfed one side of the lab. X felt faint from the heat.

"Children! Listen to me!" the Agent said, picking them up by their nightshirts, he realized this was the first time he had actually seen what the children looked like. "You have to get out of here! Now!"

The boy was obviously in shock, not surprising. The girl managed to stand, whimpering. "But—but, the monster…" She pointed up the stairs.

X remembered the thing wriggling out of the wall, some sort of odd wormlike creature. He glanced around the lab at the damage done. The children acted as if they'd rather be swallowed by flame than face the horrors of Dr. Bledsoe's projections.

"That man—he was not your father." It was the only thing X could think of to say. He grabbed the children and pulled them toward the stairs.

Ann Bledsoe clenched the balustrade halfway down the staircase, her tired eyes in tears. She squealed when she saw her offspring. It was a sound of both fear and delight. The Agent put their hands in hers, and she pulled them the rest of the way up the stairs.

Agent X stumbled into the living room, coughing, still trying to mimic the commissioner. Officer Murphy was working to push the Bledsoe family out the door as gently as he could. Meanwhile, Inspector Burks fired his .45 automatic up the staircase to the second floor until the clip was empty. Burks reached into his jacket while ejecting the empty clip, inserted the next one and kept firing with no break in the rhythm.

"The monster! That worm thing?" Agent X said, nodding his head towards Burks.

Murphy nodded back. "Monster! Definitely a monster!" Murphy began a string of curse words that would have embarrassed a sailor in his effort to define the hellish anomaly, while two more policemen came in the door to back up Burks.

The Agent grabbed Murphy by the shoulder before he could follow the uniforms upstairs. "Where's Dr. Bledsoe?"

"That thing came wriggling up from the basement and all hell broke lose. The doctor came up behind it with some kind camera or something."

"Where's Betty?"

"The doctor took her with him. Somebody said he was going to treat her, prob'ly for shock. She sure got the scoop on this one. Hey commissioner what's wrong with your—"

Agent X heard the word "face" behind him as he made his way to the door. Part of his right jaw was open, a good four inches of make-up peeled away and waving in the air. He covered it with his hand as he passed the police outside.

X saw the taillights of a sedan shine in the distance to his left. The impostor still hadn't escaped the scene.

The car was in reverse, pulling out of a parallel parking space. He sprinted after it. The brake lights came on, and then the car pulled forward. X ran harder, forty yards away. The reverse lights came on again. The sedan had been squeezed into a small place. Thirty feet away. The brake lights lighted again. Ten feet. The car began to pull away.

The Secret Agent flew through the air, diving. His fingers clenched around the rear bumper as he came down, his grip the only thing keeping his face from smashing into the concrete. The car kept moving, dragging X behind it. At the corner of Fitzhugh and Palm he managed to get one ankle up. As they were moving straight once again, he was planted firmly on back of the car.

As an Agent he had been trained to always have a battle plan, but in his current condition—addled by the doctor's strange ray—he knew if he stopped to think he was finished. He had to find a way to stop the kidnappers before they reached the highway.

Coming to a stop light, X anchored his heels on the topside edge of the bumper. As the car began to speed up again, he threw himself at the bottom of the rear window frame. The tips of his fingers just caught the edge. He saw the impostor's profile in the backseat with a gun pointed at Betty's head. The impostor looked over his shoulder, turning around, and looked X directly in the eye.

"Hit the gas, we have to shake him off!" one of the goons in the front seat yelled. The tires squealed.

The sedan began swerving back and forth. X held on. The gangster on the passenger side fired a pistol through the rear window. Glass shattered over the Agent as the driver slammed on the brakes. X felt himself flung forward, but he continued to hold onto the bottom of the window frame. He let the momentum slide his feet upward over the trunk beneath him, and shoved with both feet as the car continued sliding to a halt.

The Agent landed on the hood of the car at the exact same moment the car stopped. The driver hit the gas. X rolled over and held on to the frame beneath the windshield this time. The car pulled around a lengthy curve by the shore and X began sliding over the edge of the hood. A revolver popped out of the passenger side window and into the Agents face.

X did the unthinkable. He grabbed the arm of the gunman with his left hand and let go of the windshield with his right. Rotating as he slid off the hood, the Agent wound up facing the front of the car, seeming to fly through the air as his right hand grabbed for the rearview mirror on the door's side. Hanging in the air from the right side of the car—supported by only the gunman's arm on his left and the rearview mirror to his right—he resembled a gymnast performing in the rings competition. The bottom half of his body continued to swing toward the ground. The car tires churned, waiting for the Agent to be crushed underneath.

A millisecond from doom, X continued his deadly arc—*and let his feet bounce off the ground in the fashion of a rodeo trick rider!* The sound of bone popping, the gun going off and the gangster's scream cut through the air as X let go at the optimum moment, and vaulted. Somersaulting, free fall through the air, he landed on top of the car. All this before the driver was even aware the Agent was still hanging on.

X anchored himself to the top of the sedan, spread-eagled, hands clenching above the doors. Bedlam broke out, both inside and outside the car, as it swerved back and forth in the traffic, trying to shed the Secret Agent. Gunfire sounded and bullets split the air around him as gunmen fired through the roof. Anticipating this, X was already sliding toward the back, away from the hired muscle and toward Betty Dale. The sedan veered into a tunnel, starting and stopping, until the driver went full tilt left, bouncing off the concrete embankment.

Exiting the tunnel, the car ricocheted back across the road to the right and rammed into a post dead center. The Agent bounced off the hood, rolling himself into a ball and tumbling through the grass. He came up off the ground as quickly as he could. It wasn't fast enough.

The gangster on the passenger side had been knocked out, as evidenced by the web-shaped crack in the windshield. The other thug exited the car pointing a .45 automatic at him. X rushed the gangster, veering to one side, trying to block the gun with a backhand. The night had been long and X was exhausted, too slow. The gunman pulled the trigger.

The hammer clicked. Empty.

The gun flew from the thug's hand as X struck it. He smiled as he realized it had been empty—stopped to give the gangster a disgusted scowl, almost shaking his head—and knocked the man out with a pile driver left.

He ran back to the getaway car pulling his strength from an empty reserve. The bogus doctor and Betty were gone. X looked up to see a small crowd gathering. The sound of approaching sirens cut through the traffic.

After escaping the scene through a series of alleys, X realized the morning was already passing him by. He pulled a portable make up kit from his pocket, and soon the master of disguise displayed another passably inconspicuous face.

The problem was his clothes. He had holes in the knees of his slacks. The toes of his shoes were raw leather, where they weren't torn apart from being dragged behind the car. The jacket, in tatters and filthy, wasn't enough to cover the scuffed and torn sleeves of his suit. There were two bullet holes in the lapel from near misses. He had to pull a wad of money out his pocket and literally wave the bills in the air to get a cabbie to stop for him.

The cab dropped X off at the car he had parked near Dr. Bledsoe's house the night before. After cleaning his hands and face with a solution he kept in his car for just such an occasion, he pulled a suit from a compartment in his back seat. He was grateful for the decision to tint all his windows as he donned the slacks and a clean shirt inside the car. The Agent applied an especially thick coating of his self-designed facial putty in anticipation; he would have to move fast this day, and had no idea of the identities he might be forced to assume.

Once again he removed the radio microphone from the secret compartment in the dashboard with one hand, as his other swept to his face, molding a new façade.

"Station X, Station X, come in."

"Station X acknowledging." It was Bates.

"What is the condition of our guest?"

"Still jittery as all getout, boss. I administered a small amount of sedative, but so far most of what he says doesn't make any sense. He keeps muttering about some sort of dark light. Keeps repeating that he only opened inches with something he calls the Gateway Machine. At least that's what it sounds like. Then he just keeps going on and on about how it's too late for all of us."

"Gateway Machine... Anything else?"

"He says we have no idea of the monsters he's unleashed. Crazy stuff. Make any sense?

"It's starting to. Any information regarding Marcus Davidson?"

"Not much. I bounced the name around every operative I could get a hold of and all I got back was a suspected alias: a Dr. Miles David Alhazred."

There was a moment of silence as the Agent recognized the name. "I need you to find out if 'Marcus Davidson' or Miles Alhazred currently owns or leases any property in the area.

"Already did it, boss," Bates answered. "Other than that dump we were at last night, there's currently no record of him leasing or owning anything on the continent. But, he's somehow connected to a religious organization called The Holy Order of Sothoth. Some kind of flaky religious write-off. They happen to own a warehouse near the one we rescued Dr. Bledsoe from. And an old church, just outside the city."

X got the addresses of both. "Excellent job, Bates. You've got a bonus coming. Keep asking questions, I need everything you can get. See if you can get more on what Dr. Bledsoe was working on—and anything solid you can find out about the Davidson/Alhazred connection. X out." The Agent replaced the microphone and sealed the radio compartment.

During the war, Agent X had been assigned to a fact finding mission under T.

E. Lawrence in Arabia. Posing as a motorcycle courier, he had quickly developed a rapport with the locals. While learning their customs and culture, X had also learned of many rumors and tribal superstitions.

One of the rumors had been of a local doctor. Schooled in western medicine at Oxford, the doctor had returned with a European name and was in search of an ancient book. The book was the Necronomicon—a legendary tome of evil, bound in flesh and written in human blood. Rumor had it that the man who possessed the Necronomicon would possess the power to release long forgotten gods, imprisoned in another dimension.

The local doctor's name had been Miles David Alhazred, and he was believed to be a blood relative of the mad Arab who had originally penned the legendary book of evil.

X—young, and not yet an independent Agent—had considered the Arab stories nonsense. However, in the years since the war, the archeological expeditions of Dr. Alhazred had become an established fact. And, since X had become a Special Agent he had seen some fantastic things. Unimaginable and unbelievably frightening things.

Dr. Miles David Alhazred had been searching for the hellish volume of the Necronomicon his entire life. There were newspaper photographs of him posing with strange, squid-like fossils, resembling nothing of this earth. In a newsreel once Alhazred had said, "What I'm looking for is more than just old bones. It would alter the destiny of man, god, and dimension." People in the movie theater had laughed the man seemed so insane.

X wasn't laughing. The Agent knew what he had seen back at Dr. Bledsoe's house. Those monsters had been real. And now Dr. Bledsoe was raving about having opened a "gateway" and "horrors unleashed."

What if Dr. Bledsoe's work had somehow overlapped with the knowledge Miles David Alhazred sought from the Necronomicon? What if rather than using a legendary book, Bledsoe had somehow tapped into the dimension that Alhazred's evil gods were imprisoned in?

Even if the legend of the Necronomicon wasn't true, Dr. Bledsoe's Gateway Machine was dangerous. The key to hell had been handed to a madman who wanted to open the door.

X wheeled the car into traffic before he had finished the thought.

Chapter Four
The Worm Turns

He drove quickly rather than fast, blending with the traffic, moving in and out between cars like water flowing into cracks. The Agent had to get hold of Dr. Bledsoe's original laboratory notes, hopefully, before Alhazred did.

Bledsoe's original contracts with the government had been through the laboratories of Radio Dynamics Ltd. In his guise of philanthropist Elisha Pond, the Agent had not only sent communications contracts to the company, but also served on its charitable board for the Colonial Research Foundation. He had a way to get in.

Sliding expertly between the city's moving traffic, X finished molding his face with one hand while steering with the other. Like his other recurring roles, he could do Elisha Pond almost by feel. The Agent pulled into the parking lot at Radio Dynamics and opened the wardrobe compartment hidden under the back seat. He grabbed a blue sport coat with The Foundation's crest embroidered on it to complete the disguise. X checked himself in the rear view mirror, got out of the car, and started to walk to the entrance—then stopped.

As a government Agent you begin to notice things other people don't. The alias of Elisha Pond noticed somebody was parked in Dr. Bledsoe's reserved space. X ran through the parking lot to the building entrance, stopping in front and brushing the millionaire's hair back to appear as if he was in no hurry. He pulled his ID card out of his pocket. Security waved him in without looking at it.

"Morning, Jeff," X said, looking at the man's name tag without appearing to. "How's your day?"

"Oh, you know how it is, Mr. Pond. These scientists are all too busy splittin' atoms in their head to actually remember their ID's. I'm just glad they never manage to get out of the lab before five."

"Never thought of that. Any new ones come in lately? I was supposed to meet some people regarding records."

"Matter of fact, two engineers I never seen before came in about twenty minutes ago. Funny thing, they both had their ID's."

"Then I guess they *must* be new," The Agent said. Any competent printer could counterfeit an ID. X had a portable business card press in the trunk of his car. The parking spot being occupied and two new employees could just be coincidence. But as soon as the Agent reached the seventh floor lab of Dr. Bledsoe he knew it wasn't. The door was unlocked.

Bledsoe had been kidnapped the afternoon of what X now knew to be the Gateway Machine experiment. According to *The Daily Herald*, the morning before Bledsoe went missing an "accident" had occurred at the lab. Fire and Police departments had been called. After the ransom demands Radio Dynamics had sealed the room and boarded the door. The thin plywood sheet barring the door had been pried from the wall and rested askew to look as if still attached.

The Agent unsheathed his gas gun and turned the doorknob. He pushed the door open quickly—both to keep the door from squeaking so no one in back might hear him, and to give him the element of surprise should someone be in front.

The laboratory had seen better days.

Settled dust and broken plaster coated most of the room. Cracks banded together from the dents in the walls, and from behind fallen, broken shelves. A secretary's desk stood to his left. Leaning on only two legs, it looked as if the other two had been bitten off. It was a metal desk bearing dents and scratches resembling having been beaten with a claw hammer. Or fangs.

The rest of the department resembled several college science laboratories after chemical explosions. The desk in the center, meant to link the work stations, was decimated. High ceilings with visible girders gave the large room a hangar effect. Two windowed offices sat in the far corners.

X could feel the presence in back before he heard the sounds of someone rooting through the debris. Soundlessly, he swept toward the left hand office being careful to stay away from the window and not stir any more of the scattered detritus. Something hit him on the head behind his right ear.

The Agent stumbled almost to the office doorway in an attempt to stay on his feet. He turned to see an olive-skinned man of average size in a lab coat, standing in fighting stance after landing from a flying kick. Before the Agent could raise the gas gun a spinning roundhouse of the man's left foot knocked the gun out of his hand and across the room.

"Who are you? Identify yourself," the Agent said, assuming a stance of his own. "Who are you?"

"Elisha Pond, I'm on Radio Dynamic's charitable board."

"Well, that's just too bad," the man said smiling and whirling his arms. One of them went behind his back. One hand reappeared, spinning a long rope of chain with a spiked metal ball on the end. His other hand held the rest of the chain as if it were a lariat ready to throw. The whirling ball whistled in the air, visible only as a blur. The whistle raised in pitch as the weapon spun faster.

X edged toward the gas gun, all the while trying to make it look as if he was merely repositioning his battle stance. The ball flew toward the left hand side of his head. The Agent ducked forward, still retreating in the direction of his gas gun, as the rope passed harmlessly over his head.

His assailant twisted the weapon in the air fashioning a blurred figure eight, suddenly extending the chain and hurling the spiked weight behind the Agent in an effort to snare him around the waist. X grabbed the extended links with one hand and crouched while raising his other arm. He arose with the rope spooled around both arms, a foot-and-a-half of space between them. The ball dangled harmlessly in-between. Then, in the same movement, the Agent quickly spun so as to begin reeling his assailant toward him. The assailant stood anchored, steadfast and immovable.

X adapted. Without hesitation he reeled himself toward his aggressor at lightning speed. Before the other man had a chance to pull back on the chain, X twisted in the air, landing in a handstand and pummeling his opponent with a mule kick. Landing back on his feet, the Agent bent, placed both arms together and let the chain drop to the floor—before punching the man twice with hammer blows, knocking him off his feet. X dropped to one knee to deliver the knockout. Something pounded him from behind.

The blow to the back of his head was so hard his chin bounced off his chest. The Agent began to black out, for a moment thinking his spine had been broken. Barely conscious of falling over the assailant on the floor, instincts sent X rolling across the room just in time. A gigantic booted foot missed the Agent and stomped the olive-skinned man in the sternum.

The Agent's vision fluctuated between whiteout and blackout. He hit the wall as one white spot broke into separate stars. X forced himself to his feet, using the wall for support as he regained his footing. It looked as if he might pass out. He was still swaying as his vision began to clear.

It didn't look good.

The man who had hit him from behind was at least six-foot five inches—his skin almost gray. Tall and gangly looking, his head seemed distorted and too large, tapering down to a neck with almost no chin at all. He stared at the Agent with dead, protruding, fishlike eyes as his awkward gait carried him across the room. The act of walking seemed almost foreign to him. The bizarre stranger's hands were almost the length of the Agent's forearm. And as the stranger held his right hand out to make a fist, X noticed his fingers were webbed.

The Agent still held his hand to his forehead, as if the room was spinning and he was trying to balance himself. He had to move. Now!

He dodged to the right as one massive hand slammed into the wall behind him, shattering the plaster. The giant's other hand slapped X's head back before the Agent had a chance to move. Every time X bobbed or weaved, the man's hand slapped him back to where he was, positioning him for a hard right cross and then banging into the same dent in the broken plaster as the Agent dodged again. The fish-eyed man kept crowding him, boxing him in with his long arms. The Agent had no room to move, the lack of space making him clumsy.

X weaved under the man's left and ducked under his arm, furiously slamming him to the body with piston blows. The fish-eyed man slapped him across the room with one hand. The Agent hit hard, slapping the floor as he landed to lessen the impact, judo style. He scuttled across the floor on hands and knees, churning to reach the gas gun. Stretching, scraping, his fingertips edged the grip toward his hand. Finally, he clenched the gun to his palm, his finger on the trigger.

The giant's webbed fingers closed over X's head like a net, the fish-eyed man tightening his grasp. The Agent couldn't breathe.

X fired the gas gun in the man's face. Normally, the effect was almost instantaneous, but the man kept clenching. The Agent could not draw a breath. The fish-eyed man began boxing X in the gut. The Agent fired again.

The giant hoisted X up in the air by his head and continued to pound him as if he were a punching bag. The Agent kicked the fish-eyed man in the chest, pushing himself away, hands and arms flailing in the air. The webbed hand continued to clutch X in its airtight grasp.

The Agent swung himself gymnast-like from the giant's arm, flipping over and out of his grip to finally taste sweet air. He wanted a chance to catch his breath, but had none. With no time for thought, his hands flew to his pocket clenching a handful of the pellets X had gathered back at his hideaway. Ducking the next blow, X slid inside the stranger's punch and slapped the pellets into the gray-skinned man's open jaws. The combination of gas and phosphorous ignited. Jets of smoke and sparks shot out of the giant's screaming mouth.

The fish-eyed man clasped his hand across his face like a first baseman's mitt and slapped X across the room. Anger was the first glimmer of emotion to show in the man-thing's eyes.

X bounced off the wall, next to one of the only metal shelving units still standing. He bit his lips in an effort to remain conscious as he began to throw everything on the shelf at the monster. Glass containers splattered chemicals across the warped visage of his assailant, and yet the fish-eyed man kept coming. Cornered, the Agent grabbed a small metal drum standing next to him. Too heavy too lift, he tore the lid off and began to pour it toward his aggressor, when he noticed the strange creature inside.

Nested in the bottom of the drum was a strange wormlike creature similar to the one that had escaped back at Dr. Bledsoe's home. The half-meter long milky white slug undulated along the bottom edge of the cask with a barely audible squishing sound as it began to emit a high pitched trill. It's only recognizable organ was a mouth akin to that of a lamprey with eerily bright red lips. Its flesh was blotted with greenish-black stains that seemed to shift and change shape as the creature moved. As if with eyeless sight, the thing looked up at The Agent.

Either the worm had crawled into the drum to hide after the initial experiment with the Gateway Machine, or someone cleaning up after the accident had assumed it to be some sort of lab animal and in their ignorance placed it in the container. That was all X had time to surmise. For as he threw the top of the drum at the fish-eyed man and looked inside at the creature, *it leapt at him as if jet propelled!*

The gaping circular maw of fangs snapped only inches away from the Agent's face as he managed to grab it by its doughy tail, still feeling the force of its leap. Fighting, X pulled the drooling thing away from his face. The strange creature seemed to somehow create its own momentum, as if guided by an unseen hand. Channeling all of his energy, X swung the grotesque thing away from himself, hurling it by the tail at the fish-eyed man. The wormlike anomaly wailed as it soared though the air.

The giant turned to run as if frightened by knowledge of what the creature would do next. His hands pawed at the air, in an effort to keep the wormlike thing away as it pounced and adhered itself to the side of his head. The high pitched wail was replaced by a sickening sucking sound. The grotesque doughy creature's mouth expanded to slowly cover more and more of the giant's head.

Both man and worm fell to the floor, writhing. X watched, aghast, as the fish-eyed man's eyes rolled up into his head, and the wormlike creature continued to feed. The man stopped moving while the greenish black blotches on the worm's flesh grew and continued to shift as it gorged itself. Then the worm began to spasm, jerking reflexively.

It twitched as it spit the giant's head from its mouth and began to bounce across the floor. The greenish blots grew and swelled, only to soon burst open leaking a brackish green-black fluid only a little darker than the markings on the creature's flesh. The thick liquid smoked, reeking of fetid flesh as it drained into the grate on the floor. The creature began to wail as if being eaten inside by... Acid?

That had to be it, the Agent thought. All those chemicals he had splattered on the fish-eyed man, one of them must have acted to kill the worm from the inside. Wasting no time, X gathered every liquid container remaining on the shelf and began to pour it on the twisting, wailing creature until it began to dissolve. He checked the fish-eyed man's pulse to find none as he watched the worm creature disintegrate into little more than a gelatinous mass.

Taking no chances, X swept what was left of the creature back into the drum with a piece of the shelving and resealed the container just in case. There was no telling what the regenerative powers of such a bizarre thing might be. He glanced momentarily at the hole in the fish-eyed man's head, thinking the same thing about the giant.

An autopsy would need to be performed. He'd call security later and let them know. As luck had it, they didn't seem to be bursting in the doors and he had no time to notify them anyway.

Running through the doors of the right hand office the Agent pulled open the desk drawers to find the bottom one still locked. He didn't even bother with a lock pick. Instead, he tore it open with a piece of scrap metal from the floor and rifled the files inside. Nothing.

He punched the bottom of the drawer out. While it may have looked like an act of anger, he was in reality looking for what he found. A secret compartment. And inside it, cursory notes on the Gateway Machine experiment.

The Agent's eyes shifted from left to right as he flipped through the pages, scanning and decoding passages mentally where necessary. The original intent of the weapon had been simple—shipping and supply. Storage.

Imagine an army that had to carry nothing other than their rifles. They could move unhindered, faster and over rougher terrain than any enemy in the world. Upon arrival they could use The Gateway Machine to "open their warehouse," using it to feed, clothe, and maintain the troops. All the while taking needed supplies, ammunition and weapons from the other dimension.

Dr. Bledsoe had applied the latest discoveries in the fields of electricity and sonics and applied a new field, radio spectrography, which up until last week had given him no result. Then, without even knowing it, the doctor had accidentally stumbled upon the frequency—and broken into a heretofore unknown dimension. Even in the notes Dr. Bledsoe neglected to write down the frequency because he hadn't known it!

That—and the fact that the only charts containing exact specifications of the weapon were locked in a safe at Army Headquarters—was a stroke of luck. It meant there was only one Gateway Machine and no way to recreate it. There was still a chance to defeat the mad Dr. Miles Alhazred.

Rejuvenated, X quickly retrieved his gas gun. He then removed the olive-skinned man's clothing and tied him up, studying his face as he did so. Searching for identification, he found none, but discovered a large silver dollar sized coin with the phrase "Yog-Sothoth" on one side and a strange, squid-like creature on the other. He pocketed the coin along with everything else on the man's person. His theory being that if clothes made the man, the things in the man's clothes finished the persona.

With practiced precision, the Agent's fingers molded his unique putty into the shapes and textures of the unconscious man's countenance. Pulling the portable makeup kit from the pocket of his sport coat, he mixed several colors and soon had an exact reproduction of the man's skin tone. Putting on the final touches, he repeated the one sentence he had heard the man utter. "Well, that's just too bad."

Though the impersonation was spot on, he hoped he wouldn't be required to use it for too long. Especially, since he didn't even know who he was supposed to be.

The Agent ran downstairs and past the security guard without signing out.

Once again blending with the traffic in an effort not to get pulled over but driving as fast as he could, the Agent sped back across the city. After considering both prospective addresses of Dr. Alhazred, X decided that the Church of the Holy Order of Sothoth was the one most likely to be used for the unveiling of The Gateway Machine. A fanatic like Alhazred would not only want to encourage the unquestioning loyalty of his followers by impressing them, but—if he actually believed in the Necronomicon—he would want to free the ancient gods at a temple of their own unholy order. He pulled the microphone from the secret compartment in the dashboard.

"Station X, Station X, come in. Station X, what is the status of our guest?"

"Station X, receiving." Harvey Bates had not left his station. "He finally slept some. He appears to be much more lucid. Says his kidnapper kept going on about freeing 'the old ones,' and it seems to scare the hell out of him."

"Has he eaten anything?"

"Eggs mostly, but he's getting his appetite back."

"Good," X said. "Go ahead and let him know you're with The Foundation. Elisha Pond has become involved and should be able to provide us with an excuse. Tell him everything's going to be fine. He needs to rest and should be back with his family by morning."

"And is it?"

"Is it what?"

"Everything fine?"

"I don't know," the Agent said.

Chapter Five
Black Mass

X drove the thought of sleep from his mind as he pulled in front of the old church on Bridgeport road. The sun was setting behind the unpainted, almost ancient eyesore. A chill ran down his spine. The church would have looked abandoned, if not for about a dozen other cars parked in the area, but as the last remnants of daylight cut through the oddly shaped, octagonal window in the tower, the place seemed almost otherworldly.

After checking his face in the rearview mirror and walking across the overgrown, weed covered lawn, the Agent had to be careful not to fall through the broken boards on the porch as he approached the door. Before his eyes had a chance to adjust to the candlelight inside, a hand reached out and grabbed him by the shoulder.

"Sorry, Raoul," a man the size of a small house said. "Even you I gotta ask for membership."

"No problem," replied the Agent, assuming he was Raoul. Reflexively, X readied himself for a battle, sticking both hands in his pockets to make fists. Then with his right hand he pulled out the large coin with the odd engraving on it; the strange talisman being the most likely thing in the man's pockets to be a 'membership' of some sort. The Agent held it out to the doorman, who nodded his approval.

"Hey, where's Howard? You know you're not supposed to leave those guys out on their own don'tcha?"

"We got in a fight at the lab and had to make a run for it. He's still out in the car shaking it off," X said.

"The boss is gonna be mad about that. You better get somebody inside to help you carry him in so they can throw him in the tub or somethin'. I don't know where Doc found those guys, but they should never of taken 'em away from the shoreline. Go on, beat it."

Raoul beat it.

The inside of the house appeared to be in much better shape than the outside. Not that the paint was fresh, but at least the wood wasn't rotting. Still, it was dark and smelled musty. Candles in ornate wall sconces provided the only illumination. Cobwebs festooned every corner and archway, adding shadows to the shifting light. The Agent headed directly through the entry hall and through the largest arch centered directly across from the entrance. While speaking to the doorman, he had seen two men in evening dress headed that way. While nothing in this unholy order seemed normal, the center room seemed the most likely place for the unveiling of an archaic monster god.

Parting the timeworn curtains leading into the main room, X witnessed a scene from somewhere beyond the ages of written history. Stone pillars seemingly shot out of the ground, supporting a high ceiling that directed one's view through the hall and towards the stage. Torches burned on the walls and around the outside edge of the platform, trailing smoke with a sickly sweet smell like the stagnant odor of death itself. Some thirty men in evening wear sipped from blood-red wine glasses and commiserated with at least a half-dozen more of the strange fish-eyed men, gathered around a granite fountain containing amphibians of a type the Agent had never seen before. The gray-skinned, web-fingered men spoke a guttural language to the gray-skinned, web-fingered men that X suspected to be related to ancient Sumerian, as one of the men in evening wear translated.

The Agent turned to the right, staying in the cover of shadows between two torches in back. He was not eager to have to play the role of Raoul in this coven where he did not know the language or customs. He had to find a way backstage before the ceremony began. One of the fish-eyed men gave him an odd look, perhaps of recognition, there was no way to tell. X worried that they might soon ask him about the fate of his erstwhile partner, the giant named Howard.

A balding man in a tuxedo walked through the old curtains at the entrance. Perhaps direct confrontation would provide X the diversion he needed.

"Sir! Sir, forgive me, please forgive me. The man I was working with needs help. He's passed out in front of the church." It was the closest approximation of Raoul's voice that the Agent could do; he had only heard the man's voice that one time.

The elder gentleman turned to the rest of the room. "One of the pilgrims from Innsmouth has passed out in the front yard!" he announced. "We need to get him inside! Immediately!" A half dozen of the men in dress and two of the giant ones shuffled toward the exit. The same giant that gave X the odd look before was one them. He paused and briefly stared at the Agent before heading out the door.

The balding man poked his finger into X's chest. The Agent backed away as the man followed him.

"How could you let this happen, Raoul? It's not like you. You know the pilgrims are out of their element." The man continued to prod and lecture the Agent. X continued to back away as the man pursued him into the corner. Once they were in the shadows the Agent unsheathed his gas gun.

The balding man emerged from the shadows holding his stomach and looking uncomfortable.

"I say, Lufkin, are you feeling all right?" One of the other Sons of Sothoth asked him.

"Oh fine, just a little indigestion." The Agent had more time to hear the balding man's voice, and he could use the complaint of an upset stomach to avoid conversation. "Probably just a little anxious about tonight's ceremonies," he added.

"Can't blame you. It's not easy waiting lifetimes for an event of this magnitude," the man said back. The Agent followed him toward the middle of the pews and sat down with his hand on his stomach.

Several minutes later, the group of worshippers that had gone looking for the unconscious, fish-eyed man came back empty handed. In an effort to thin the crowd, X—in his new role of Lufkin—told them that they best find Raoul, then suggested that perhaps the olive-skinned man had taken the giant upstairs. The small group exited, apparently less excited than they had been the first time. The Agent could feel the cold sweat drip down his back, as the same fish-eyed man paused in front of him again. The giant looked at X, as if somehow confused, before heading back out of the room. There was no way for the Agent to know if he had been spotted, for there was little recognizably human in the man-thing's stare.

Moments later, two more of the giants lumbered around the edges of the room dousing the lights. Several large torches were pulled to the edge of the stage. Dr. Miles David Alhrazed emerged from the darkness carrying a torch of his own.

He was wearing a dark gray, hooded robe that would have hidden him from view had it not been for a grin of wicked delight—and eyes that burned with hypnotic madness. The Agent felt almost forced to look away.

The audience sat motionless, as if mesmerized into paralysis by the modern necromancer. The doctor-turned-cult-leader lowered his torch into a stand, lighting a table on which stood the Gateway Machine. He then raised his arms to the crowd.

"Good evening gentleman. It is with great pleasure that I present to you the product of work that has taken centuries. Throughout the ages, even as the chosen ones toiled in devotion, our mission has often seemed unreachable. However, while searching in South America for the final historic records of the sacred Necronomicon, I was fortunate enough to meet a fellow seeker. This man's ties led me to a company doing research that was destined to bring us to the final success of our mission: A direct link to the old ones—who shall once again rule the earth. And we who have chosen to be their servants, will become—*the rulers of all mankind!*"

The crowd applauded.

Alhazred was so intensely engrossed in his own presentation he hadn't even noticed the smaller size of the crowd. X peered up and down the hall, trying to devise a working strategy. At first, worried about revealing his identity, the Agent had merely shifted his eyes. Then, suddenly, he couldn't help but notice the rest of the unholy assembly. They were frozen, sitting as if paralyzed, all staring ahead in a bewitched silence.

"Gentleman," Dr. Alhazred continued. "I give you—*The Gateway Machine!*"

Together as one the procession began to chant what can only be described as the present day ritual of an ancient black mass. "Yog-Sothoth! Sumerie! Eithon! Zin! That is not dead which can eternal lie. That is not dead which cannot die. Yog-Sothoth! Sumerie! Eithon! Zin!" The sheer repetition of the mantra was hypnotizing. X found he was losing himself in the crowd. He wanted to repeat the phrase along with the unhallowed order. "Yog-Sothoth! Sumerie! Eithon! Zin!"

Dr. Alhazred led the chant as he stood above the crowd, his voice cracking with maniacal glee. Almost dancing to the table beside the torch, he flipped the switch activating the frightful power of the Gateway Machine. A high pitched whine split the air, and the entire hall began to vibrate with a dissonance that underlined the horror of the eldritch mob's dreaded imperative. A beam of pencil thin light fired across the stage. A small circle in the opposite wall seemed to ignite before the doctor turned an aperture on the projector widening the beam. He had learned to work the machine. A circle of fire burned like a small sun before going completely black.

The flame sucked from the torches on the wall, as a solid globule of light emerged from the black and engulfed the entire stage. The concentrated brightness undulated in reptilian rhythm at the border of the glowing bubble, while inside, Dr. Alhazred began to scream his own warped gospel of the damned.

"Oh mighty Kadath," the madman intoned. "You who will be the first to greet your worshippers with the war hammer of the cosmos! We bring thee an offering! The blood of the untainted!"

Seeming to float on the air, Miles David Alhazred approached a shrouded platform that had been obscured by the darkness backstage only moments before. Clutching the corner of an ebony shroud, he yanked the black veil into the air with a sudden motion.

The sable sheet billowed across the stage and away from the dark cosmic mouth on the opposite wall, to reveal the unconscious form of Betty Dale.

The Agent reacted as if jolted by electricity. Shaking his head like he was recovering from a punch, X eyed the people, still chanting, on both sides of the aisle. Betty Dale had risked her life for X on more than one occasion. He had to rescue her.

He had to stop this. He was out of time.

The Agent stood up and began walking down the row of worshippers. Several of them stopped chanting and eyed him detestably. Others sat rapt, repeating the incantation as if the Agent wasn't even there. About to reach the center aisle and run toward the stage, a giant grey hand seized him from behind, and lifted X off his feet by the collar. The Agent stared into the protruding, dead fish-eyes of the pilgrim who had stopped to observe him before. This time there was no mistaking the emotion of the gray-skinned man-thing. It was rage.

X threw his hardest punch, pounding the giant's pug nose flat into its face. There was a moment of silence as the fish-eyed man stared back at X, as if noticing him for the first time. The giant spread his webbed palm and began to place it over the Agent's head, exactly like the gray-man who had almost killed him earlier that day. X held his arm off with both hands and planted a swift kick directly in the giant's crotch.

There was no change in expression, but the webbed fingers opened. X hit the ground like a cat and aimed a karate kick at the man-thing's knee cap. It was a move that would have disabled a normal man with bone-popping cruelty. But the fish-eyed man's leg merely bent the other way. The Agent stared in amazement as the pilgrim's webbed fingers formed a gigantic fist.

X ducked the punch and dove over the heads of the assembled faithful in the pews to the left. The worshippers, angry at the distraction, began kicking and clutching at him. Their hands came up empty as X rolled under the pews and toward the stage. Soon the entire strange congregation began stomping, punching, and clawing at the troublemaker, all the while continuing to chant.

Giants pushed entire pews out of the way as X took cover, dodging under the opposite side of the benches, while clutching hands slammed viselike grips at the air around him. He somersaulted, rolling on his back between the seats, only to dive over or slide under the next barrier—always getting closer to the stage. The flock became an angry mob. Someone grabbed the Agent by the legs, pulling him back under the first row. He rolled, supporting himself with his hands and twisted into a scissor-kick to the poor wretch's jaw.

Launching to his feet, X levered himself with the back of the seat and twisted over to wind up lying in the pew. Furious punches cracked the wood where he had just been. The mantra became a scream as some thirty men and monsters piled toward the Agent only to find he'd slipped from their grasp.

Meanwhile, the sphere of frighteningly hard, white light on stage pulsated at the edges. The brightness seemed to swallow the platform as Dr. Alhazred gazed possessively at the ever-widening circle of blackness opening into three dimensions on the wall. An oil covered worm the size of a bag of concrete flopped over the dark edge and wailed as it began to crawl across the floor. Something half insect, half malformed squid squirted through the barrier in an unhallowed conception. It turned its head and emitted a series of squishy sounding clicks in an effort to communicate with the doctor. Alhazred smiled and puckered his cheeks, voicing a similar series of clicks as if to answer.

The chitin armored squid lifted one of its two preying mantis arms to point at the Secret Agent as he stood at the edge of the stage smashing his elbow into the face of a man behind him. Dr. Alhazred screamed in horror.

"Stop him! Stop that man! The old ones demand the ceremony!" The doctor held his hands open in front of him apologetically, begging the dread life form's forgiveness, as other unnameable aberrations began wiggling, crawling and writhing—screaming, bleeding and oozing—into the glowing pustule of light. An undulating balloon of energy, waiting to burst open like an egg sac, exposing the horror of an unknown reality to a defenseless new feeding ground called earth.

The Agent bounded through the air, only to be blocked once again by the same broad shouldered, gray-skinned giant. Flying through the air, X kicked with both feet into the man-thing's chest. He might as well have kicked a brick wall.

The giant's webbed fist grappled the Agent by the heel and swung him like a club at the floor. X turned in the air, absorbing the blow with his shoulder. One more like that and his collarbone would shatter. Still dizzy, the Agent flopped through the air like a rag doll as the giant raised him over his head for the killer blow.

Hanging in the air upright as his momentum slowed, X prepared for the thrust that would shatter his skull on the granite floor.

Chapter Six
The End of Time

It has been said that time is the fourth dimension. People in times of crisis often talk of a single moment seeming to last forever. Survivors of tragedies—car wrecks, earthquakes, war—often recall the events in slow motion. As if. Time. Stopped…

One moment: X felt himself hanging in the air, his skull about to be smashed into a granite floor. On stage, the coagulating bubble of light writhed in spasms. Dr. Miles David Alhazred's face, open-mouthed, wide-eyed. An enormous tentacle corkscrewed through the onyx gateway, viscous ooze slapping its new atmosphere, the tendril twisting like a suction cupped python. And behind the entire scene, Betty.

Betty Dale.

The Agent stomped down with his other foot, grinding his heel into the soft spot of the giant's skull. An unstoppable force meets an immovable object. Secret Agent X was an unstoppable force.

He stepped off the skull of the fish-eyed man and onto the stage like he was walking off an escalator, as the web-fingered giant began to collapse. X forced his way into the light, bulldozing through the incompressible barrier. The smell of ozone and a high pressure field surrounded him. A wave of fear washed over. His head withstood the pressure. He knew the fear was a product of the ray. The Secret Agent had dealt with fear before.

One of the grotesque, spider creatures X had fought back at the Bledsoe residence scuttled up his leg. A round, fanged mouth snapped at his face. The Agent grabbed it by one of its legs and slung it back into hole without missing a step. The mad doctor pulled a dagger from his belt.

"You've ruined everything! You fool! A thousand years! Untold of power!" Holding the grip ice pick style, Alhazred charged. Screaming, he thrust the dagger at the Agent's heart.

X blocked the attack, slapping his left palm around the doctor's wrist. Twisting inside Alhazred's grip, the Agent thrust his right elbow into the swarthy man's nose. X reached into his coat and popped the madman with his elbow again, as he pulled his portable makeup kit from his pocket. Twirling to his left the Agent sent Alrhrazed spinning to the floor. X then opened the compact kit approximately ninety-degrees, as if he were going to set it down and look into the mirror mounted inside the lid. Flipping his wrist he sent the compact spinning onto the table in front of the Gateway Machine. The mirror stopped directly in front of the beam of light, blocking at least half of it and reflecting the rays back at the machine itself.

A slash of black bounced off the undulating edges of the glowing light sac. The field dimmed, glowed, and dimmed again as the solid edge of the field began to spasm. A high pitched wail cut through the assembly hall. Creatures clutched at their heads and bodies as if impaled. The flock of worshippers cried in gasps. The mad doctor tried to scream but couldn't. Miles David Alhazred seemed to be hyperventilating. Anxiety. He was panicking.

A hum began to vibrate from the globule of light like the whir of failing generators. Torches in the hall flared as the pressure of bending realities aimed itself back at the Gateway Machine!

X hurtled himself toward the back of the stage, tackling the vertical display that held Betty Dale, hurling the two of them through the velvet backdrop and onto the floor. X already had his lock pick set in hand. Once again the deft hands of the Agent demonstrated the tactile skill of an escape artist, sensing the slightest of pressures within the lock. The lock popped open and Betty's shackles fell to the floor. Gathering Betty in his arms X sprinted off into the darkness.

On stage, Dr. Alhazred was on his knees, arms outspread, wailing remorse and anger to the corners of the earth, as the sphere of blackness that once welcomed his gods began to shrink. Climbing to his feet, he ran toward the retreating chitinous, squid like creature he had welcomed minutes earlier. Begging forgiveness,

"You've ruined everything! You fool!"

blabbering, Alhazred dropped back to his knees. The dread ambassador from beyond shifted its head slightly to the side, an act of curiosity. It raised one of its tentacled appendages to the mad doctor's face as if momentarily caressing Alhazred's jaw. And then cut the man in half with its mantis claw.

Fire began to spread through the hall from the flaring and dislodged torches. The curtains and tapestry, dry with the rot of ages, ignited like kindling. Flames bolted up the walls. The flock of The Sons of Sothoth ran back and forth hysterically, trying to extinguish the fire, as sparks shot across the room. The gray-skinned, fish-eyed giants—the pilgrims of Innsmouth—seemed to dehydrate and collapse to the floor, as the rest of the unholy congregation searched for the exits, screaming and slapping at their smoking clothing.

The black circular mouth on the wall shrank as the gigantic corkscrewing tentacle slapped itself on the floor and gathered the remains of Dr. Alhazred—pulling them into the abyss as the hole telescoped shut.

In the back yard, X laid Betty on the overgrown lawn. Red lights flashed in arcs through the night as the fire brigade and police surrounded the building. The Agent checked Betty's pulse and smiled. He gently slapped her cheeks to revive her. Betty raised her hand to stop him and blinked. She stared accusingly at the balding, soot covered man in the tuxedo, until he reached up and pulled at both sides of his face putty, molding a cartoonish grin on his face.

Betty smiled back at the Secret Agent.

"Wait here. Don't move. I'll be right back," X said.

The police had cordoned off the street. No one was allowed in or out. Inspector Burks paced back and forth on the lawn in front of the burning house of worship, grabbing hysterical men in tuxedos and shoving them toward the uniforms to be cuffed and thrown in the paddy wagon. X had to circle through the woods to get back to his car and don the face of Elisha Pond once again. He carried clean slacks and a shirt back into the woods and shoved Lufkin's monkey suit under a pile of leaves. Several minutes later he circled back. Elisha Pond rounded the building, dodging the firemen and carrying Betty.

"Pond? What the hell are you doing here?" Burks said. "You're not a part of this freak show are you?"

"The world of finance may make strange bedfellows, Inspector, but nothing this strange. A couple of these men broke into the labs at Radio Dynamics and I followed them here. I snuck in back and found this cute little package," X said, holding up Betty. "Next thing I know the place is going up in flames and these men were running around screaming and chasing us. I'm guessing this must have something to do with the Bledsoe kidnapping?"

"You guess right, Pond," Burks said, scratching his head. "I don't know exactly what's going on, but you can bet your backside it has something to do with Secret Agent X."

"Really?"

"Yeah, the Dr. Bledsoe returned after the kidnapping turned out to be an impostor. Then tried to steal some kind of secret weapon. Only one guy I know fits that M. O."

X knew Burks would be furious when he found out The Colonial Research Foundation had been holding the real Dr. Bledsoe, but right now Elisha Pond didn't have the time to stand around talking. He had to meet up with Bates and get their story straight before debriefing the doctor and his family.

On the drive to the office the Agent reflected on his thoughts the night before. He'd learned something. It didn't matter if the villain was a pickpocket or a mobster or even a crazed madman, ushering in unspeakable monstrosities from another dimension. Acts of crime really are always driven by the need for power.

Oh, and one other thing. Betty Dale? One of these days she was going to be in on one of the biggest secrets in the world. Off the record, of course.

END

Keys in the Hands of a Madman

by B. C. Bell

When Ron Fortier first asked me to write a Secret Agent X story I was ecstatic. Seriously, I grew up reading reprints of the pulps and always felt cheated that I'd never gotten a chance to write for them. One problem, I hadn't read a Secret Agent X story in a while. I knew the character, but there's always that one little thing, some small trait that makes an individual unique, or completely redefines them for you. I needed to read up on it.

Back in the day, writers like William Gibson and Lester Dent used to write 150,000-words a month or more. So, both inspired and intimidated by the wordsmiths of old, I did what I thought they would do. I started writing. Then I got a hold of some more Secret Agent X, both new and old, and I was quite pleasantly surprised.

The original Secret Agent X stories were written mostly by two different writers: Paul Chadwick and Emile Tepperman. I was already familiar with Tepperman's ("guns blazing") work so I got a hold of some of the Chadwick stories.

Wow, the guy could write pulp.

Now, here's some insight into the creative method. Have you ever read about how Jack Kirby drew comics back in the forties? Kirby said that as he was forced to work faster in order to make deadline, it had an effect on his drawing; as a result his art became more exaggerated and powerful. For some reason that comment stuck with me, because I started to do something I've never done before. If you're familiar with method acting, I guess you'd call this method writing. I gave myself an impossible deadline and decided to write the story in the same fashion as the pulps of the 1930's.

Now mind you, when I talk about the craft of writing, I've spent years learning rules about keeping sentences simple, show don't tell, kill all the adverbs; and, of course, *if you write correctly you'll never need an exclamation point!*

But after reading Chadwick's version of the Agent, I had to write it pulp. The new rules were: write fast, use as many adjectives, adverbs and complicated sentences as you want while writing, come back and clean it up later. Also, feel free to tell, because while some readers may not be familiar with your cast, your established reader doesn't want to weed through ten pages of a character's minor tics to learn about something they already know. I did a little research as I went, and the rush of the writing style seemed to affect the creation of the story. I may have thrown in one too many exclamation points. *But I had a blast!*

After I'd written the opening kidnapping sequence, I read more, but all I had plot-wise was kidnappers, and a secret weapon in the wrong hands. What kind of secret weapon would it be? Nazi buzz bombs? Poison gas? Top secret nanotechnology of the 1930's? Researching, I discovered some of the old Secret Agent X covers and saw a few death-ray type thingamabobs. I liked that.

But what kind of ray would it be? Magnetic energy? Pre-laser, laser beam? Sleep? Coma? Zombies? I had no idea. So I was sitting around trying to think of the scariest thing a death-ray could produce, and up popped Lovecraft's Cthullu mythos. What could be scarier than an unnameable horror from another dimension? Then I recalled The Agent had once performed a mission for Lawrence of Arabia.

Enter Zoe Courtman. She's in a writer's workshop with me, and not only can she wield an array of deadly adjectives herself, but at one time she had also mentioned using a relative of Abdul Alhazred in a story she's working on. Since great minds work alike, I asked permission to steal her idea.

"Dude, Lovecraft is public domain," she said. OK, she didn't say "Dude," but I still want to thank her for giving me the idea.

Now, I had a beam that opens a dimensional gateway. I had Cthullu and his gang of unfriendly friends waiting to invade our own not-so-perfect dimension. And I had put the gateway in the hands of a madman.

At my current pace I already had screams coming from Dr. Bledsoe's basement, and I had only just then figured out who the bad guy was. Did I mention I was having a blast?

I knew the Agent would head to the factory of Radio Dynamics to retrieve Dr. Bledsoe's notes when I started the story, but I honestly had no idea that X would run into one of the Pilgrims of Innsmouth. I didn't even know I'd come up with something as cool sounding as "the Pilgrims of Innsmouth," it just kind of happened.

As did the texture of the prose when I reached the Black Mass scene. By this time, I was staying up at night to finish as fast as I could, and driving my wife crazy—we were visiting her family, and they were starting to give me funny looks, too. And no wonder—because reading back now, I can tell my barely conscious brain was channeling good ol' H. P.'s eldritch state of mind. I won't state my critique of Lovecraft's prose here, but damned if it didn't seem to work.

So I cranked this baby out, and had fun with it, but it was more than that.

I was also getting to write the adventure of a hero. You can't begin to guess how great that is. I mean, I love the characters I create. I make them as real as possible, but it comes as no surprise that my characters are usually far from morally, physically or mentally perfect. Flaws are realistic. The Agent has some flaws if you're looking for them, but let's face it, these pulp guys are BIGGER THAN LIFE. They had to be. It was a tough time and they needed heroes.

Maybe there's some karmic price to be paid for cynical realism. It's sad to think we live in an age so jaded, that we don't even have to accept it when our leaders are found to be corrupt; instead, we've come to expect it. I think that says something. You get what you ask for.

In the 1930's they not only asked for heroes, they expected them. And they got them.

So, any other lessons to be learned from the 1930's according to the 21st century? Well, maybe… Then again, I'm pretty sure we weren't as innocent back then as we like to pretend. And maybe we aren't as jaded today as we like to think we are.

We all need heroes. Hope this will help you be a better one.

B. C. Bell
8/18/08

B. C. Bell is the author/ illustrator of the now legendary mini-comic Dismental Tales. His short story "How Pappy got Five Acres Back and Calvin Stayed on the Farm" was a winner in the 2007 SFReader.com Annual Short Story Contest. He is currently re-finishing his first novel, and putting together another pulp adventure for Airship 27's Jim Anthony Super Detective Anthology. You might as well read his stuff because his wife and his dog say he won't go away. For more information visit him at www.myspace.com/noirishell.

AFTERWARD
THE MORE THINGS CHANGE

With the publication of this, our second volume of brand new *Secret Agent X* stories, we at Airship 27 Productions take a major step closer to completing our reprint phase. If you're a regular reader, you'll know that we began producing our pulp titles several years ago with a different publisher. After our partnership expired, that publisher opted to remove all our titles from his catalog. Meaning once inventory supplies at outlets like Amazon and Barnes & Nobles were depleted, these books would no longer be available to pulp fans. My partner, Rob Davis, and I thought that was unacceptable and when we hooked up with our new publisher, Cornerstone Book Publishers, one of our first queries was if we would be allowed to reprint those early books. Seeing the quality of our product, publisher Michael Poll gave us a big thumbs up to proceed accordingly.[1]

Rob and I then went about collecting the old files, dressing them up and whenever possible adding a little something extra to each book. In reprinting *Secret Agent X – Volume One,* we did this by first offering up a brand new story for the collection. Then we had the cover re-colored by New Zealand artist, Shane Evans. Now it fits in perfectly with the cover of this volume, which was colored by Chris Carney. We had no intentions of altering it in any shape or fashion. It's a gorgeous cover and our thanks go out to Chris for allowing us to reprint it. Likewise to our first three writers, who were all part of the original book; Kevin Noel Olson, Greg Gick and Sean Ellis. These stories are fantastic action adventures and if you are reading them for the first time, I envy you. You're in for a real pulp treat.

Like Volume One, we found ourselves unable to reprint one of the original four tales and so sought out a new one. The new story, by B.C. Bell is top-notch and a bit different than most *Agent X* cases, which suited us just fine. Part of our goal is to broaden the scope of this classic hero and we constantly challenge our new cadre of pulpsmiths to imagine new threats and scenarios, something not all that easy to do when you consider how long this character has been around. Yet good writers like Bell always rise to the occasion.

And on that note, I can enthusiastically repeat a theme I set out in the first postscript of this book. All of us here at Airship 27 Productions, are fanatical fans of *Secret Agent X* and want to continue bringing you new adventures of pulpdom's original super spy. As this volume goes to press, we are already into production with an all new Volume Three and Volume Four. Some of these will feature writers who have appeared before such as Andrew Salmon, Kevin Noel Olson and Brian Meredith. It seems every time one our new pulp writers sink their creative teeth

---

1   Obviously, since this was originally written things have changed. Airship 27 Productions now is its own publisher via Amazon's KDP Print-On-Demand affiliate.

into *Agent X,* once is never enough. And of course we will be debuting works by names you have never heard of before, talented new writers eager to add their names to the *X Files*.

So, dear readers, our reprints are almost finished. All we have left to re-do are the first two *Captain Hazzard* books and they are in the wings awaiting brand new covers by the amazing Mark Maddox. All our new reprint editions to date are available at the major outlets I listed earlier. Please keep in mind that those places still have a few copies of the earlier editions and are selling them alongside our new, improved reprint editions. Obviously we'd recommend you choose our newer editions when filling in your library of Airship 27 pulps. In all instances, they are honestly bigger and better books. Of course you can also buy all our titles at our own on-line store, always at a discounted rate. Simply go to airship27hangar.com.[2] As our own catalog continues to grow, you'll find some truly terrific books there.

Thanks as always for your continued support. The future for Airship 27 Productions is indeed a bright one and we've got a lot of great titles on the way. As the old adage goes, the best is yet to come!

Ron Fortier
2 Sept. 2008
Somersworth, NH.
airship27.com

---

2   This portion of the aftword has been updated to reflect Airship 27's online catalog's address created after this book was initially assembled. It includes over 300 books to date and climbing.

THE RETURN OF PULP FICTION'S GREATEST SPY!

Secret Agent X, the original super-spy, is back in these five stellar collections. Written by today's best New Pulp Writers, the Man of a Thousand Faces once again defends America from all manner of evil threats.

Arguably the most popular character at Airship 27, here are the first six exciting installments in the Anthology series. Welcome to the daring exploits of pulpdom's original super-spy as brought to you by Airship 27 Productions!

www.ingramcontent.com/pod-product-compliance
Lightning Source LLC
Chambersburg PA
CBHW070046260626
47159CB00005B/2136